BLACK
POWDER,
WHITE
SMOKE

BLACK POWDER, WHITE SMOKE

LOREN D. ESTLEMAN

A TOM DOHERTY ASSOCIATES BOOK

NEW YORK

BLACK POWDER, WHITE SMOKE

Copyright © 2002 by Loren D. Estleman

A Forge Book
Published by Tom Doherty Associates, LLC
175 Fifth Avenue
New York, NY 10010

www.tor.com

Forge® is a registered trademark of Tom Doherty Associates, LLC.

Library of Congress Cataloging-in-Publication Data

Estleman, Loren D.
    Black powder, white smoke / by Loren D. Estleman.—1st ed.
      p. cm.
    "A Tom Doherty Associates book."
    ISBN 0-765-30189-X (acid-free paper)
    1. African American men—Fiction. 2. California—
Fiction. 3. Freedmen—Fiction. 4. Outlaws—Fiction.
I. Title.

PS3555.S84 B57 2002
813'.54—dc21

                            2002069266

First Edition: September 2002

Printed in the United States of America

0 9 8 7 6 5 4 3 2 1

For Debi,
with love and lots of gunplay

Fame, if not double faced, is double mouthed,
And with contrary blast proclaims most deeds;
On both his wings, one black, the other white,
Bears greatest names in his wild airy flight.
—John Milton, *Paradise Lost*

PART ONE

—

THE DEVIL'S ACRE
AND THE PORT OF MISSING MEN

ONE

They're still talking about this one down on Gallatin Street.
Honey Boutrille was sitting in at the piano for his regular man, who was down with the drip, hitting all the wrong keys because he couldn't read a note and had no ear (although he was convinced he did), when a customer from the West End mutilated one of Honey's whores in the back room of the House of Rest for Weary Boatmen. This much was agreed upon by witnesses. What followed is still in dispute as to some details.

The House of Rest was known by the New Orleans police as the Port of Missing Men. After a dockman with a wife and six children disappeared there in '81, a flying squad of officers had swept through the establishment with axe handles, followed by city laborers with crowbars and shovels, who pulled up the floorboards and dug for the remains of twenty-odd victims rumored to be buried on the premises. No bones were found, but ten or twelve empty bloodstained wallets turned up, and the owner was jailed and the front door padlocked. Honey had then bought the House of Rest for one hundred dollars cash, with a like amount paid to the magistrate for permission to reopen. There wasn't fifty dollars' worth of good lumber in the whole construction, built as it was with timbers from old flatboats and warped cypress planks, but the location was good and half the population of the French Quarter was in the habit of going there when it tired of the more glamorous establishments on Lafayette and Basin. The new proprietor further sweetened the deal by stocking the back bar with good whiskey and cognac and assembling a string of high-yeller whores with refined features and flexible joints. He'd recovered his investment the first week and started buying his tailoring and haberdashery from a shop on Tulane Avenue.

Honey—born Honoré Philippe Toussaint-Louverture Boutrille—was as black as anthracite, and like anthracite the angular bones of his face appeared to glow with a blue flame. Apart from that, he presented a disappointment to white men whose experience of Negroes fell no closer than minstrels in greasepaint. His hooded eyes seldom showed their whites and his polished teeth remained hidden inside a mouth that only smiled when something amused him. He favored dove-gray English bowler hats lined with red silk and European-cut suits with pinched waists, rolled lapels, and one American feature: extra room under the left arm for his pistol rigout.

The revolver was not beautiful. It was a short-barreled double-action .45 British Bulldog with most of the checking worn off the grips and no blueing left on the steel. A much more attractive weapon had been presented to him by one of his whores on the occasion of her leaving the line for marriage, but he had traded the gold-plated Colt's Lightning to a riverboat pilot for a case of .45 cartridges and cash. The Bulldog had saved his life a number of times and it showed only when he used it.

He was the child of slaves, and although at age three he'd chopped cotton on a Louisiana plantation, he had no memory of it. That was the year Mr. Lincoln turned the slaves loose. Two miles away from the fields on the family's flight to freedom and the unknown, a Copperhead unloaded a LaMatte pistol into his father's face. Young Honoré was raised by his mother and two aunts in Baton Rouge until age twelve, when his mother died of a disease of the stomach everyone blamed on bad apples and his aunts told him that without his mother's income from the sugar refinery where she'd worked they couldn't afford to keep him. They packed him off with a pail full of fried chicken and steamboat passage to New Orleans, where they said a boy could find work in the plants and distilleries. He'd found work, but not of the kind they'd described, and had spent thirteen years wishing he could wipe it out as easily as he'd forgotten his time on the plantation.

On this sopping, buzzy night late in August, he was observing the twenty-fifth anniversary of his birth. He'd told no one of the occasion, from a hard-learned conviction that every little bit of information one gave up about himself counted against him and for his enemies. A second glass of cognac as he punished the piano was the extent of his celebration, and he'd waited until the day bartender went home and his replacement came on before he'd ordered it. He was reckless about nothing except which keys he hit.

When the thuds and shouting from the back disrupted one of his chords, he hesitated, then went back to the beginning of the measure and started over. He kept the order at the House of Rest, and although he was conscientious, he was not a zealot. A portion of rowdiness was permitted—his was not the Mansion House, where a certain gentility was maintained by muscular, well-dressed ushers to keep the graft manageable and the Ladies' Reform Committee at bay—and first-time customers were instructed that prompt payment of damages was enforced by the proprietor. He went on playing, ignoring the disturbance, until his concierge, a one-eyed mulatto too old and fat for the line whom New Orleans had named Madame Pantalon, came trundling up and wheezed into his ear that Mademoiselle Josephine was being murdered by the man from Texas.

Texas was not the man's home. He had spent four years there at the urging of his father, who had made his fortune a generation earlier exporting molasses to Europe and had since ingratiated himself with the gentry so far as to dread the threat of expulsion as he feared the grave. The son, Winton Claude Saint-Maarten, had crippled the husband of a young woman in a duel of honor. As the husband was connected by family with the Department of Commerce, the removal of the son from the vicinity appeared to be the best course until peace could be made. The assassination of James A. Garfield and the new administration that followed severed the injured man's ties with Washington, and Saint-Maarten was allowed to return. However, during his time in Texas he had fallen in with shabby company, and brought back with him the guerrilla ways he had learned there. It developed that in the midst of an enthusiastic session with Josephine de la Mothe, who claimed to trace her ancestry to the explorer Cadillac, Saint-Maarten's left earlobe was bitten almost through. In his pain and rage he had snatched a bronze cupid off a table near the bed and bludgeoned Mademoiselle de la Mothe into a bloody stupor, shattering her cheekbone and caving in all her teeth on one side. Madame Pantalon explained much of this in short bursts as she scurried to keep up with Honey's long strides on the way toward the back room.

The door to this room was reinforced with timber, framed likewise, and secured with a brass bolt that had been rescued from a captain's stateroom. There was no forcing it, and since cries to

Saint-Maarten to surrender himself went unanswered, and any bullets fired through the planks risked striking the victim, Honey had nothing to do but wait out the assailant.

The ensuing thirteen and one-half hours heaped another legend atop the pile that prevented New Orleans from sliding into the swamp.

The room had no window, and no exit apart from the door that led into the main saloon. Punching an egress through another wall, or tearing up the floorboards and digging, were desperate alternatives at best: The rear half of the building was constructed on a dock, beneath which the sluggish waters of the Mississippi were believed to crawl with fifteen-foot-long alligators and leeches the size of prawns. (Rumor said the 'gators had developed a taste for human flesh after the incident of the owners of the twelve bloodstained wallets.) Honey Boutrille did not delude himself that his own reputation was so fearsome as to persuade someone of Saint-Maarten's temperament to test his luck with the carniverous local fauna. The proprietor dragged a chair away from one of the tables—deserted all, in the wake of his sudden appearance in the main room with Bulldog in hand—and sat astraddle the seat facing the door with his chin resting on the back and the pistol on the floor within convenient reach of one of his long arms.

After three hours, Madame Pantalon brought food. A chamber pot was provided, and a maidservant even older and fatter than the madame took it away for emptying. Honey gnawed the flesh off a roasted chicken, washed it down with gin—he feared typhoid and avoided water except for bathing—and wiped the grease off his hands with a damp towel. His attention never strayed from the door, from behind which drifted the occasional feminine whimper, cut off by a sharp hiss and sometimes the crack of a hand. By these lights only he knew that the room was still occupied. No conversation passed through the planks.

He drank only when he ate, to restore his fluids and not to the point of inebriation. He smoked three General Thompsons, to remain alert. The blue smoke crept up toward the rafters and joined the phantom haze of a thousand other cigars, hand-rolled cigarettes, and bowlfuls of shag, eureka, and honeydew. He crushed the butts beneath the toe of an elastic-sided boot, adding to the gray ash and brown leaf that paved the floor. Now and then he unslung the nickel-plated watch from his vest pocket and looked at the time. He wasn't expected anywhere. A knowledge of the hour enabled a man to remain oriented. At the end of each half-hour, he stood and stretched his limbs and rotated his neck. Then he sat back down.

He was thinking of getting up to stretch again when the bolt grated on the other side of the door.

He rose without a sound, lifted the chair carefully to avoid scraping the floor, and set it down gently to one side. He straightened with the Bulldog in his hand and eased back the hammer. He never fired the weapon without cocking, unless there was no time; the heavy pull of the double-action mechanism interfered with his aim. He waited until the brass knob started turning, then turned his body sideways and lifted his gun arm to shoulder height, sighting down it at head level. The knob completed its revolution. Nothing happened for a long time after that. Then the door began to drift away from the frame.

The minute hand of a clock never moved slower than that door. He held the revolver loosely, allowing air to circulate between his fingers. He didn't tighten them until the door was open a third of the way.

The door stopped then, and after an interval, Mademoiselle Josephine's face appeared in the opening. Her chin was high, the way she carried it when in full cry of the Cadillac relationship, but the pose seemed more artificial than usual, and today the elegance ended there. The left side of her face was a mask of dried blood, the eye on that side purple and swollen and the corner of her mouth drawn up to expose her raw and naked gums. She was breathing rapidly and suddenly a clot broke and a fresh scarlet stream burst forth from her left nostril and streaked down to the corner of her jaw.

Half of another head appeared behind hers. Her chin jerked up another notch. She gasped, and Honey knew she was being held by her hair. Light from the Chesterfields glided the length of the blade across her throat; a Texas knife, big as a sickle.

The woman wore only a thin cotton shift, soaked through with sweat and caked with blood. Her nipples stood out like rivets.

The head behind Mademoiselle Josephine's was bald in front, with a creamy band across the top where the tan ended. Below that was a round face, shiny, its one visible eye a dollop of blood-flecked spittle quivering in the socket. Blonde stubble prickled on his cheeks, a shade lighter than the Vandyke beard he'd grown while he was away. The arm holding the knife wore a striped sleeve and he'd pushed his pilot's cap to the back of his head to keep the visor from blocking his vision. His breath came in shuddering pants. Honey could smell the sour mash at ten paces.

"Don't stir a hair!" Saint-Maarten's voice, normally a pleasant tenor that attracted women and handsome boys, was shrill. "I'll cut her head clean off!"

"Why'd you want to go and do that, boss? It's the prettiest head in the place." Honey held his position.

"This cannibal tried to bite off my ear. Don't you feed them?"

"I feature she got lost in the act. You too, boss. It's just nature."

"She's a harlot and an octoroon. If I wasn't drunk on that cottonmouth piss you pour here I'd sooner stick my phizzle in a mousehole."

"A rathole, I heard. The girls tell me you's hung like a elephant."

"You'd know, you African nigger. Let me pass."

"Where you fixed to go, boss? I heard you done got tired of Texas."

"I'll throw you her head if you won't stand aside."

"You do that I'll shoot you right out of your boots."

The eye stopped quivering. The hand holding the knife moved. A thread of blood slid down between Mademoiselle Josephine's breasts.

Honey fired. The eye disappeared. The slug took off Saint-Maarten's cap along with the back of his skull. The knife tilted. Honey stepped forward, catching the woman under the arms as her knees bent. Saint-Maarten fell away.

In less than a minute the room was filled with employees of the House of Rest for Weary Boatmen, in shifts and full street dress and artless nudity. Madame Pantalon looked down at the human wreckage and crossed herself. "They string you up for this."

"I know it." He held Mademoiselle Josephine tight. She was wailing, her cries muffled against his chest.

"Take the train."

"I'll take the river."

"No one takes the river no more."

"That's what they'll say."

"Damn dirty shame."

He disengaged himself from Mademoiselle Josephine. She sagged into Madame Pantalon's arms. He nudged Saint-Maarten's ribs with his toe. "Someone get this piece of offal out of my establishment."

TWO

Two minutes into the attempted robbery of the Southern Pacific outside Sacramento, Twice Emerson suspected the luck he'd been running on since the war had trickled out.

The plan was to fell a Ponderosa pine across the tracks on a steep downgrade, forcing the train to stop where it would not have sufficient steam to reverse directions up the grade. But the tree hung up in the telegraph line, changed directions, and landed square on top of their box man, splitting open his skull and emptying it of everything he knew about how much blasting oil was required to snap the lid off a Hall and Whitman without destroying the coins and currency inside.

After that, things went downhill, literally.

The engineer, three times a victim of previous robberies, suspected the treefall's timing and shoved the throttle forward. The sudden acceleration startled one of the bandits' horses into throwing its rider. Another took frustrated aim at the departing caboose, but managed only to shatter the red lantern that swung from the back. The yellow flame pulling away from the mantle licked out like an outthrust tongue. The whistle made a hee-hawing noise warping into the distance.

The band split up immediately. The S.P. had been hit just often enough to have acquired expert status in arranging assistance: A wire dispatched from the train's first stop would contain the bandits' location, and Wells Fargo detectives were adept at conjuring armed posses out of squirrel nests and knotholes. Billy Nogales cut out two men for a run to Mexico, the local recruits retreated to their homes in and around Sacramento, and French Tom announced his plan to make his way back up to Quebec and look up one of his wives. Twice Emerson kept him company, but only as far as San Francisco. They parted in a stand of scrub over a swig apiece from the canteen in which French Tom carried his skullbender.

"What's in Frisco?" Tom rammed in the cork.

"Place called the Devil's Acre. A man can get lost in that block and never come out until he's of a mind."

"Canada's better for that."

"I'll see you Canada, and raise you half of Alaska. It ain't a patch on the Barb'ry Coast."

"In Quebec, there's four ways to run. Run west from Frisco and you get yourself drowneded."

"Nobody runs in the Acre. Posses and Pinkertons and the whole damn Sioux Nation wouldn't follow a man in there day or night."

"What makes you safe there if they ain't?"

Emerson grinned. He polished his teeth with spruce twigs and he liked to show them off. He bragged he'd had the only complete set in Bloody Bill's hundred. "I ain't. But you surround yourself with slash-throats and renegade niggers, you don't need to waste time worrying about who you can trust."

"Good luck, brother."

"Watch them falling trees."

They parted without shaking hands. The pair had never had anything in common beyond a mutual dislike of drawing wages. When Twice Emerson read in a month-old newspaper that French Tom Minto had been blown to pieces by a Russian bartender with a Stephens ten-gauge in Yreka, the first thing he thought was, if someone was going to collect the five-hundred-dollar reward on French Tom's head anyway, he'd as soon have cracked a cap on him in the scrub outside Sacramento and put in his claim.

Emerson's birth name wasn't Twice, although he preferred it. His father, Olaf, teaching himself English from the tiny store of books available in the Michigan lumber camp where he found work, discovered he shared a last name with a writer in Boston, and declared himself an adherent. He christened his child Emerson Emerson and told friends he'd admired the Great Transcendentalist so much he'd named his son twice. One of his listeners misunderstood: The first time the boy visited the camp, he addressed him as Twice, and the name had caught. The wife whom young Emerson abandoned in Missouri told a reporter that she'd learned her husband's baptismal name only when the minister called him by it at their wedding.

Olaf Emerson was a drunk and a beater of his wife and children. This was not unusual among the men with whom he worked, but he had another wife and family in Sweden and was under a king's order for arrest on a charge of desertion if he returned. When Twice was seventeen, Olaf hacked open his own leg when his double-bitted axe bounced off a knot. A doctor cleaned and dressed the deep wound and sent him home in a wagon, with fresh dressing and alcohol and instructions for daily cleaning and rebandaging to avoid infection. Twice ignored the instructions and prevented his mother from carrying them out. When the doctor came by at the end of a week to see how his patient was getting on, he found the leg black and stinking and Olaf raving in Swedish. The younger Emerson obediently held his father down on the bed while the doctor sawed the leg off at the hip, but the rot had spread to the genitals and he was dead by morning.

The body had not yet cooled when Twice packed a tattered valise with his other shirt, socks, underwear, and a .36 Colt's Paterson revolver his father had won off a former fur trader in a tree-topping contest. It had a nine-inch barrel and a trigger designed to disappear into the handle without the requirement of a guard. It lacked ammunition—Olaf had fired away his small store of powder, balls, and percussion caps on a forgotten Independence Day—but it was the only thing of value he'd owned and his son had no intention of leaving it with his mother, a woman for whom he held no regard. Ignoring her protests and those of his squalling younger brother and sister, he found a ride on a wagon headed for town. Over the course of a week he worked his way south, trading errands for food and sleeping in barns, until he got to Detroit, where he joined the Twenty-fourth Infantry on the promise of regular pay and found.

He deserted after Gettysburg. The Twenty-fourth suffered the highest casualties of any in the battle and he had taken a Confederate saber through the fleshy part of his right forearm before he'd managed to put enough daylight between himself and his assailant to raise his Springfield rifle and blow out the man's intestines. The rebel was armed with a .36 Colt's Navy revolver. Although the weapon was worn out to the point of uselessness, the supply of caps, powder, and balls young Emerson found on his person were not. He left the Navy and took the rest with him.

The plan was to head north, in the opposite direction from the retreating rebel army and its Union pursuers. However, infection set in, and in his fever Emerson crossed into Maryland, where he broke into an unoccupied farmhouse and helped himself to food and a change of clothes. Eight miles south, he collapsed in the road. When he came to, a gap-toothed southern guerrilla was straddling him holding a red-hot bayonet. He struggled, but the scrawny fellow was stronger. When the flat of the blade touched his wound, Emerson shrieked and lost consciousness again. But the cauterization worked. His wound began to heal.

The guerrilla band had ceased to engage the enemy and had fallen to scavenging the castoff from both armies. Mistaking Emerson's .36-caliber pistol for a Confederate Navy, they assumed he was a fellow fighter for states' rights. Deep Southerners all, they attributed his Scandinavian accent to Missouri, and since they knew next to nothing about that divided state, he succeeded in telling them stories gleaned from what he'd read in secessionist newspapers he'd found in the ashcans of train stations and fluttering across the line of march, and making them sound as if they'd happened to him. Years of dissembling to avoid paternal beatings had made him an accomplished liar, and there was not a brain among his listeners that could work out a simple sum of arithmetic. Their leader, a red-faced oaf, elected by reason of his bulk and physical strength, said they were on their way to Missouri to join Captain Anderson's bushwhackers and invited Emerson to accompany them as their guide.

After managing to stumble into Missouri, Emerson slipped away from the ragtags. He surrendered himself to a camp of guerrillas who had gotten separated from Anderson, and mimicking the speech of Alabama and Mississippi he had learned over the weeks, he told the commander he was a Southern volunteer who'd been captured by Yankee spies and escaped. He could tell the commander didn't believe half his story, but he counted himself fifty percent ahead for that.

Anderson's men crossed the river and fell upon the guerrillas from Maryland, butchering them to a man. There was now no one who could link Twice Emerson with his origins. That was how he'd come to hook up with Bloody Bill Anderson, and to learn the trade that would support him, in between stretches behind bars, for the next twenty-three years. He'd helped invent daylight bank robbery in Liberty, Missouri, and had ridden off with the Jameses and Youngers until the rewards piled too high and he began to suspect the friends and neighbors who had offered them safe harbor in the Missouri hills. He took the train West without saying good-bye to his wife of three months, and when he ran out of America, he got off in San Francisco.

There on the Barbary Coast, and particularly inside the diagonal slash of block framed by Broadway, Kearny, and Montgomery streets known as the Devil's Acre, he found a burrow safer than all of backwater Missouri. It was a place where even the police refused to venture unless in great numbers, in which event the news of their approach would reach every banio, deadfall, and grubby dance hall days before the assault. Emerson had found his home.

It wasn't cozy, although after a number of months in residence he'd managed to furnish his back room in an underground saloon on the east side of Kearny with most of the comforts of a fairly unimportant Oriental potentate. The establishment had no official name—locals had called it the Slaughterhouse when first he made its acquaintance, but the proprietor had rechristened it the Morgue when he burst a bottle of beer against the skull of a drunken customer—but it was the place Emerson headed whenever his situation had become untenable outside the Acre. His companions were whores, thieves, and opium addicts. The whores advertised their merchandise naked in the windows and doorways of the street and the thieves' pockets sagged with the lead pipes and socks filled with buckshot they employed to subdue inebriates on the hardpack and relieve them of their pokes. The hoppies bedded down in the alleys and reported to the saloon, red-eyed and twitching, to perform errands for the price of a pipe. Their hands were always crusted with their own blood, spilled from their wrists at knife-point in order to inject low-grade morphine from eyedroppers when the Chinese dens were too dear. Emerson had affection for them all: He could trust them not to be trusted.

He held only two kinds of "Coasters" in low regard: freedmen and Chinese. In all his time in Michigan he had scarcely seen a Negro, but the native hatred of the race for whom states' rights had been set aside had passed to him during his time with Bloody Bill. The sight of a black dandy strutting down the hardpack meeting white men's gazes on the level was enough to make Emerson twist a hand inside his collar and hoist him by the seat of his pants and propel him toward the nearest pile of horseshit. He was a big man, fair-skinned, with the lean rangy muscles of his woodcutter father, and very few in the Acre could stand up to him in unarmed combat. (He avoided associating with those who could.) And there were entirely too many Chinese in San Francisco to his taste. Being outnumbered irritated him; two years of running from federals and twenty-one of hiding from posses had taken away all its novelty. Just thinking of the hordes of little yellow men and women spilling over the edges of Chinatown, and hordes more coming in daily, reminded him of ticks in a mattress.

He was certainly in no mood to find one of them seated in his favorite chair when he entered the Morgue after the Southern Pacific disaster. He'd been riding three days and was set on cutting the dust with his back against the bar's far corner, and so when he saw the old man huddled over his rice wine or whatever, he crossed the floor in three strides and yanked him to his feet by his white pigtail and dragged him howling and jabbering to the side door where the customers stood to piss and put his foot against his back and shoved. He got a grunt of appreciation from one or two spectators as he returned to his place and swept away the old man's cup and called for a bottle of yellowtail.

Cora Bonnet, the proprietor's mistress and so the mistress of the Morgue itself, brought it. An earlier lover had slashed her throat with a breadknife, but the wound had healed, and the high lace collars she wore to conceal the scar gave her an aristocratic air. Reporters at the *Call*, a newspaper which had been crying for an end to sordid activity on the Barbary Coast almost since Sutter's Mill, referred to her in print, derisively, as Madame Dubonnet.

"You might have to eat that one," she told Emerson. "That was Lem Sop."

"And who in hell is Lem Sop, apart from a chink with a mouth full of mud and piss?" He made a pass at her buttocks, snatching his hand away just as hers came down swinging the sap she wore strapped to her wrist. The number of shattered wrists and hands on Kearny Street had increased after she'd taken to wearing it, then fell off as word spread.

"*Boo hoo doy.*" She curled her lips around the foreign phrase.

He hesitated. Then he showed his white canines. "Horseshit. He's too old for the tong."

"His nephew ain't. He's head dog of the Suey Sings."

"What's he called?"

"Yee Hee something. The chinks that talk American call him Short Bob. Hangs his hat at Waverly Place."

"He better leave it there, and his head in it. Home's the only safe place for him."

"That's good advice."

"Go peddle your papers. The tong's just a story to scare little yellow kids to stop shitting the bed."

Everyone in the Acre knew about the antiquated ball-and-percussion revolver Twice Emerson carried stuck in his belt in front, the handle turned toward his right hand. He never talked about or showed the New Model Remington he carried in his left side pocket. It fired five .32-caliber self-contained cartridges and had a short stud trigger that never hung up in clothing. At close range it was more reliable than the Colt's Paterson and he didn't have to make his own bullets.

The following night, a young Chinese came at him with a hatchet from under a staircase while Emerson was weaving his way home from the Eureka Dance Hall. The hatchetman wore a gray slouch hat, and Emerson wasn't aware he was a celestial until the blade caught the light from a window. Clearly his intention was to lop off the former guerrilla's right hand as he reached to defend himself with the Colt's Paterson. But Emerson was ambidextrous. He pivoted outside the hatchet's arc as he fired the Remington through his pocket. When the Chinese stumbled, he lost his hat and his queue came unwound, but he recovered himself and ran away, holding his side with his free hand. Emerson snapped a shot after him but heard the slug twang off brick.

The next day, Cora Bonnet found Emerson taking a shave in the Great Eastern Barbershop on California Street. She had on the purple dress with matching gloves she wore whenever she left the Morgue, and a hat with a veil.

"There you are, right in the window with razors all about.

Why don't you just jump off the roof of the Bella Union?" She laid
a sheet of rough paper in his lap. It was covered with Chinese characters painted on with a brush.

"Am I supposed to read this?" He picked it up and turned it all
the way around.

"My laundress read it for me. She brought it in. There's dozens
just like it all over Chinatown. Short Bob's promising a thousand
dollars for proof of your death."

"Hell. The Southern Pacific's only offering five hundred."

"What you going to do about it?"

"I can't kill every chink in town. I guess I'll talk to Buckley."

At age forty, Christopher A. Buckley was the most powerful
political boss in San Francisco. He negotiated peace between rival
factions throughout Barbary and in return for handling the police
received a percentage of most of the gambling, brothel, and opium
profits. Blind from a ten-year-old bout with scarlet fever, he kept
office at a rear table in the Snug Cafe, the saloon he owned on Montgomery, smiling behind the smoked lenses of his spectacles and pro-
fessing to recognize visitors by the way they shook hands. He heard
Emerson's complaint and told him his best course was to leave town.

"I'll not be run out by a pack of yellow midgets," Emerson said.

"From what I hear, you're the only thing the Suey Sings, the
Soo Yops, and the Kwang Docks have agreed on since they set up
shop. As they see it, they owe it to their ancestors to chop you into
kindling. Put bluntly, as a man of peace I'd rather have them do
that than have them go to war like they did in '75. But if it gets out
I let them carve up a white man, I might as well deed the city over
to the Republicans."

"What if I just kill Short Bob?"

"I cannot counsel murder. In any case, another would just slip
into his robe and renew the call for your scalp."

"All this on account of an old chink took my seat."

"It is about saving face." Buckley reached inside his linen jacket and stuck out a thick fold of banknotes. "That should stake you to a ticket east and some good hotels along the way. I'd choose a line other than the Southern Pacific."

"It's different if it's you running me out." Emerson pocketed the notes.

"As you like. It may interest you to know that Short Bob wears a Chinese chainmail vest under his shirt day and night."

Returning to the Morgue, Emerson found the proprietor planing splinters off the bar. He was a former prizefighter with ears like bunched carnations.

"You still got that streetsweep?" Emerson asked.

The proprietor unhooked the cut-down Harrington & Richardson shotgun from its nail and laid it atop the bar. "Twenty dollars."

"I'm borrowing it, not buying it."

"You're a mite more than a risk to bring it back."

Emerson traded one of Buckley's notes for the shotgun.

That evening, he booked a seat in a chair car on the Southern Pacific there were no alternatives—but he used an assumed name, and since there were no likenesses of him floating about, only vague descriptions on readers, he still had possession of his five-hundred-dollar head when he changed over to the Oregon & California two days later. By then, Yee Wai, a twenty-four-year-old Chinese known in Chinatown as Short Bob, had been dead forty-eight hours, found lying in the entrance hall of his home on Waverly Place by his wife with a hole as big as a kettle blown through his chainmail vest.

PART TWO

PRINTER'S DEVIL

THREE

No one ever interviewed interviewers (once the practice began, where would it end?), but if anyone were to ask Ernest Valerian Torbert whom he considered the greatest man of the nineteenth century, he would have answered, without hesitation: "Ottmar Mergenthaler."

Once the business of proper spelling was discharged, the interviewer of the interviewer might have asked what made the accomplishments of *Herr* Mergenthaler, whatever they might be and whoever he might be, more significant than those of George Washington or Ulysses S. Grant.

"He freed more Americans than Lincoln."

And then Torbert would explain how for four centuries, thousands of forgotten individuals had inched forward the progress of printing through the mind-erasing process of assembling bits of movable type in handheld composing sticks, line by line, paragraph by paragraph, column by column, so that royalty and then the nobility and then the gentry and finally the common cobbler could read the Word of God and the racing results from Syracuse. History would never know how many of these printer's devils went mad,

committing suicide, murdering their employers, or being borne
away in constraints rather than submit to a quarter-hour more of
arranging dirty bits of lead in scooplike devices to be transferred to
chases and locked and then slathered with pungent ink.

All that was past, thanks to a native of Wurtemberg, Germany,
who abandoned the watchmaking trade to come to the United
States, where he applied his attention to detail to the invention of a
machine that would forge and compose lines of type in a fraction
of the time a printer's devil required to assemble a single word.
The Mergenthaler Linotype Company set up production in Cleveland, Ohio, in 1885, and in a scant year the narrow, towering,
intimidating machines had lock-stepped their way into the composing room of every major competing newspaper in the country.
Overnight, many scores of round-shouldered drones had climbed
down from their high stools, seated themselves before metal key-
boards, and transformed their work from grinding swink requir-
ing only first-grade literacy and two opposed digits on either hand
to the status of a skilled occupation, with customs of protocol and
the beginnings of a guild.

No one interviewed Torbert, however, and so he hugged this
information to himself, like a hand of cards or a Talmudic inscrip-
tion whose meaning he alone had uncovered.

He kept his office on the ground floor of the Biederman building in Chicago, where the Jupiter Press maintained three floors
and the basement. The office had begun life as a janitor's closet,
and he could extend both arms from his scrolltop desk and touch
both walls. This was no hardship. He needed no space beyond the
sweep of the carriage of his Sholes and Glidden typewriter and a
wire basket to dispose of the slag. He liked the room's proximity to
the basement's northeast corner. There, two yards below his feet,
he could hear the chattering of the five Linotypes as they squirted

language into matrices and sent them by conveyor, a split-second behind the operators' fingers scampering over the keys. It was the flute opening to the later, *basso* concerto of the rumbling cylinder presses stamping out pages of close print. Torbert had a tin ear, couldn't tell Beethoven from Baedecker, but the ponderous movements of a big-city publisher transforming the imaginations of a hundred hack writers into yellow-and crimson-bound capsules of entertainment for millions never failed to bring out the conductor in him. He hummed in time with the thundering of the presses and the chugging of the Linotypes and rang the Sholes and Glidden's bell at the end of each measure.

At age eighteen, Ernest Valerian Torbert had served with distinction aboard the *U.S.S. Minnesota*, helping to quell panic among the crew after the Confederate steamer *Virginia* ran her aground at Hampton Roads. He wrote a novel about the battle twelve years later while employed as a typesetter on a newspaper in Cincinnati. The critics compared him to Richard Henry Dana, but the book sold only two hundred copies. By the time it came out he'd acquired a position in the newspaper's editorial department, but kept his job in typesetting. He wrote obituaries and social items by day and set his own copy by night. Later, he told anyone who cared to listen that he'd learned economy of style with a composing stick in one hand, editing down his prose in the pressroom in order to finish by midnight. He considered his second novel, a Dickensian treatment of Cincinnati lowlife, an improvement over his first, but it was rejected by fifteen publishers and for years he'd used the manuscript to hold up one corner of the heating stove in his one-room flat in place of a missing leg.

His fortunes changed when he relocated to Chicago. There, he found work writing advertising copy for the meat-packing companies; his flair for making one firm's sides and sweetbreads sound more succulent than those of its competitors had him turning away business. He'd started by offering his services cash-free, accepting small shares of stock in compensation. Today, the monthly dividends he received from Armour alone maintained his choice quarters overlooking Lake Michigan. However, he held onto his tiny office in the Biederman Building, where he described chops and tripe in extravagant terms to meet his expenses and wrote a hundred words per day on his third novel, a spirit-stirring tale of African exploration, heavily influenced by Haggard. He'd decided to foreswear personal experience and bank on the same imagination that had convinced thousands of idiots that animal flesh was ambrosia. At forty-two, the hero of the *Minnesota* had cast adrift the last of his callow illusions. Meat would not balance his accounts forever.

Short and thickset—*absolutely corpulent* offended his preference for language that transformed ground-up pig snouts into "delectable morsels of lightly seasoned sausage"—he contained his belly in vests of broadcloth in winter and seersucker after Decoration Day and concealed his jowls beneath a rich growth of black beard. He wore gold-rimmed spectacles and avoided wearing hats, but carried them, woven straw or brushed wool felt according to the season, for when the wind blew off the lake and he missed the trolley and had to walk. Hats made unsightly ledges in his pomaded hair. Good clothes and a well-kept appearance got him into some very nice bedrooms on the Boul' Mich'. He had never been married, and among the daughters of wealthy butchers he was tagged eligible.

Typing, he paused in the middle of a paragraph to consult his copy of *King Solomon's Mines* on the spelling of the Kalukwe River. He was a lover of other writers' storytelling skills and was still engrossed some ten minutes after he'd found what he wanted when his door opened, bumping the back of his chair. Knocking being futile while the presses were running, that polite custom had been relaxed on the Jupiter Press premises. He slammed shut the book, returned it to his file drawer, and rolled down the type-writer's platen, removing the half-page he'd written from sight.

"I hope you'll pardon the interruption. I imagine it's no simple thing to find a new way to say something about meat."

The rumbling burr of his visitor's speech announced the man's identity even before Torbert turned. Argus Fleet, tall and stoop-shouldered, with a scholar's brow and white burnsides he combed straight out from his face to form an eight-inch halo when he stood against the light, had been trained by his minister father to speak from the pulpit. However, he'd lost his faith when the old boy was apprehended in a naked condition with the president of the Ladies League for Relief to Veterans of the Mexican War, and had turned to publishing instead. These facts Torbert knew about Fleet, and one other: He'd managed to rescue one of his presses from the Great Fire of '71 and printed the first history of the conflagration within three days of the event. It had sold three thousand copies in four weeks. The profits bought the equipment necessary to relaunch the Jupiter Press from the level where it had left off before the fire. In a short fifteen years, the company's sales had grown to match and in some cases surpass those of longer established firms in New York and Boston.

"Meat built this city," Torbert said, leaning back in his chair to take in all of Fleet. "You shouldn't make sport of the subject."

"Carrots and potatoes are more nutritious and they don't leave you flatulent."

"I'd hate to try to put that in terms acceptable to the reading public." Halfway through this statement, the presses and Linotypes ceased. His raised voice rang in the small room.

Fleet held a dilapidated leather portfolio under one arm. He shifted it to the other and tugged a gold watch from his pocket. "Two minutes ahead of schedule. I issued a memorandum to the press operators last week to oil the gears more often. It's had its effect. Are you busy?"

"I don't know one end of an oil can from another."

"I've men enough for that. In any case, you're too fat to get into all the places."

"If it's the rent, it's not due for two weeks."

"You've not missed a payment yet. I have a proposition for you. It involves some travel, and of course you will have to end your association with the meat companies, but the remuneration is good and it will get you out of this closet for a while."

"I'm too fat to move. You said it yourself."

"The exercise will suit you." When Torbert didn't respond, Fleet filled the silence. "It's in the manner of a literary enterprise."

"I left all that behind when I left Cincinnati."

"I suspect you did not. By the bye, I don't believe white hunters subsist on monkey during safari. Gazelle is the diet of choice, according to Stanley."

Torbert glanced at the Sholes and Glidden. The page he'd been typing was completely obscured.

"One of the advantages of owning a business is that I possess keys to all the offices," Fleet said. "If you wish to keep your activities secret, you should lock your drawers. Your landlord is a curious man by nature."

"Apparently a sneak thief as well. I think you had better look for a new tenant."

"Balderdash, Ernest. You've scaled your share of balconies. The publisher of the *Centinel* is an old friend. I wrote him asking to send some of your old tearsheets. I read your book as well. The naval one, I mean, although I read enough of your African romance to know it will never sell. There is no life in it. You should stick with what you know."

"Doing that is exactly what put me where I am. Did you think I wrote books to mark time while I waited for my great meat adventure to begin?"

"I'm offering you the chance to put that behind you. Do you follow the daily journals now that you no longer contribute to them?"

"Enough to keep up with the latest assassinations in Russia. And pork futures, of course. I have my investments to look after."

"You should pay more attention to what's been happening in our own back yard. What do you know of New Orleans?"

"Whores and Mardi Gras. That's just an impression. I've never visited."

"I'm asking you to consider it."

Torbert looked at the calendar tacked to the wall above his scrolltop; not that he wasn't already aware it was September. "Mardi Gras takes place in the spring, unless I'm mistaken. That leaves whores. No one would print what I wrote."

"I would. Jupiter would. Whores are in it, but it is not about whores." As he spoke, Fleet unbuckled the flap of his leather portfolio, withdrew a folded newspaper, and slapped it down on Torbert's desk. It was a copy of the *Tribune*, folded to one of the out-of-town columns.

FATAL SHOOTING IN NEW ORLEANS.

Torbert read the three inches of close print that followed the heading.

"A Negro killing," he said when he'd finished.

"A Negro killing of a white man," Fleet said. "And not just any white man. A son of Louisiana industry and a Texas gunman besides. There's a book in this fellow Boutrille."

"The market is crowded with Billy the Kid and Sitting Bull as it is."

"Billy the Kid is dead and Sitting Bull's in custody. Their story is told. When was the last time you thrilled to a blood-and-thunder yarn about a black mankiller?"

"Chances are he's as dead as the Kid by now. They don't waste time down in Dixie; rope, perhaps, but not time. Boutrille's already decorating some lamppost in the French Quarter."

"You read the article. The vigilantes staked themselves out at the train station, but he disappointed them. He either left afoot, or on horseback, or took the boat. My money is with the boat."

"Who'd collect? This item is two weeks old. The trail's as cold as Lincoln."

"I'll pay you a thousand and expenses to go down there and ask questions. A thousand more if you find him and conduct an interview. These sums are merely advances against royalties."

Torbert laughed. He'd heard rumors of authors receiving royalties on copies of books sold, but he'd never encountered one personally. Still, the amounts unsettled him. Such sums did not change hands without a deal of risk involved. "Are you pitching a book?"

The flap was still loose on Argus Fleet's portfolio. He took out a stiff sheet the size of a dummy for a newspaper advertisement, wrapped in tissue. He unwrapped it and stood it up against the typewriter's keyboard.

The background was scarlet, against which a caricature of a grinning Satan, black as coal, stood with one arm around a buxom white woman in a torn petticoat and his other hand gripping a huge smoking pistol. At his feet lay a white man in cowboy dress.

He was clutching his chest and his face was twisted in the agony of death. The yellow scrolling legend read *The Blacksnake of New Orleans, or The Devil of the Delta: A True Tale* Told by Ernest Valerian Torbert, author of *The Wreck of the U.S.S. Minnesota.*

"Do you not think you're getting a bit ahead of yourself?" Torbert asked.

"Artists are cheap. Are you interested?"

"Awfully decent of you to put in a pitch for my first book."

"I'm not that generous. I bought the rights from your original publisher. We'll reissue it at the same time as *The Blacksnake of New Orleans.*"

"Have I no say in the matter?"

"You can say no, in which case I'll find another writer and present you with the rights to *Minnesota.* Good luck finding a publisher. Your old one let it go cheap."

"A dime novel, Mr. Fleet?"

"Certainly not, Mr. Torbert. They sell for a nickel now."

Torbert studied the illustration. The black man's eyes were as red as hell's maw. Something trilled up his spine. Nothing about his African story caused that. Meat certainly did not.

"What are the women like in New Orleans?"

"Marketable."

"I haven't paid for it since the navy."

"Down there it's almost respectable. It becomes more so the farther you head West. Women are outnumbered eight to one and serve a necessary purpose."

"Good God, the far West. Banish that thought. My scalp is my best feature."

"You've spent too much time with my backlist. All the tribes have been subjugated. It's getting to be a tame place. Eighteen seventy-six was particularly hard on the popular press. In one ten-week period, Custer, Hickok, and the James-Younger gang came to grief. Practically everything since has been filler."

"In that case, send one of the lads from the composing room. You're not rich enough to pay me to go West."

"Who suggested anything of the sort? We're discussing New Orleans."

In the press room below, a bit of lead clinked to the slab floor. It was that quiet in the janitor's closet.

"I'd rather not use my own name," Torbert said. "I may still write my *Uncle Tom's Cabin*."

"May I take that as an acceptance?"

"It's your building. Take it as you will."

"What name would you like?"

Torbert handed him back the book cover, thinking. His gaze went to the insignia painted across the shell of the typewriter. "J. P. Glidden."

"I understand Glidden. Why J. P.?"

"Jupiter Press."

The two men shook hands.

FOUR

Louisianians who had resided along the river long enough to distinguish a sand bar from a snag by the sound of it scraping a wooden hull referred to the *Rose of Sharon* affectionately as "Grandma Rose." At ten years of age, she was the oldest stern-wheeler still in service on the lower Mississippi by two years and had been carrying freight and passengers nearly twice as long as the oldest side wheeler. Side-wheelers, faster and more elegant, snagged exactly twice as easily, and many of the pilots who operated stern-wheelers pushed them beyond their limit, hauling in excess of two hundred tons and challenging speed records in their effort to compete with the growing popularity of express coaches and railroads, and blowing their boilers. Grandma Rose had outlasted all of her sister ships launched in St. Louis in 1876, and the consensus was that no other would approach her record of longevity. River cartage would never again be what it had been in the years before the Union Pacific tracks sutured together the halves of a divided nation.

Honey Boutrille just hoped the old tub would hold together until he reached Pointe a la Hache.

After paying off Madame Pantalon and the whores of the House of Rest for Weary Boatmen and leaving money with a doctor to care for Mademoiselle Josephine and her smashed face, he'd had funds sufficient to engage a private compartment on the boiler deck. It might have been occupied previously by a Morgan or a Vanderbilt; but that would have been in better days. Now a passenger could lie on the bunk and see blue sky through fissures in the cabin roof. The boards of the deck were as uneven as boars' teeth and the proximity of the boiler steam-cooked him by day and drenched him in condensation at night. The ceiling and bulkheads actually sweated. No sooner would Honey manage to fall asleep than a drop of rusty water the size of a man's thumb detached itself from a joist and landed on his face with a loud splat. Nothing had changed since his last voyage at age twelve, except then he'd shared his quarters below the main deck with a couple of hundred tons of sorghum and cotton.

He didn't regret killing Winton Saint-Maarten, but as he lay there in his soaked underwear listening to the inhaling and exhaling of the pistons and the smack of the paddles, he wasn't sure the mademoiselle had been worth leaving the only place he had ever called home. Her airs of nobility had tried the patience of all her fellow employees, and a number of customers had complained of missing watches and banknotes after spending part of an evening with her. A light amount of harvesting the clientele was tolerated at the House of Rest, but it was the opinion of the proprietor that Josephine had abused the privilege.

Still, there was no help for it. Saint-Maarten was as dead as the Confederacy, the French Quarter only existed at the sufferance of the slain man's class, and nothing awaited Honey in New Orleans but a long rope and a short drop. He was already thinking ahead to Pointe a la Hache. His original intention had been to steam all the way down to the Gulf and book passage by sail west along the coast to Texas, but the longer he remained aboard, the greater the chances of a telegram outracing him and a reception committee convening at the bottom of the gangplank, ready to carve him up and toss the pieces to sharks. Better to disembark while they were still searching the trains up north, ferry across the river, and arrange something by land. All the Mississippi ports were closed to him, and his way of living could not sustain itself away from a constant stream of human traffic. Strike out Louisiana. He lit a General Thompson, watched the smoke slither through the cracks in the roof of his compartment, and wondered if there was work for a colored saloonkeeper in Houston.

When he finished the cigar, he put on his clothes and mackinaw and went out on the hurricane deck. A brisk wind was blowing up from the Gulf and most of his fellow passengers were still in their compartments. There weren't as many as there had been when he'd made the trip from Baton Rouge. That was getting to be a long time ago. There had been fewer trains then, and the prospect of riding on one had involved wrapping up in dusters and steamer rugs to avoid cinders and frostbite. Then the Pullman had arrived, with its parlor stoves and upholstery, and porters to see to every comfort. Spurs were built to take passengers to all the little burgs formerly accessible only by hot, dusty, bone-chattering rides in mud wagons and dog carts, and boxcars and flatcars carried the cargo that had made steamboats the lords of Memphis and points south. Robber barons had squeezed out most of the competing railroads, and now a man could board the transcontinental in New York City and ride all the way to San Francisco without having to change the carnation in his buttonhole. And all the time this was going on, Honey Boutrille had been sipping cognac and playing the piano badly and watching the stern-wheelers and side-wheelers growing

fewer and farther between, unaware that the event held any significance. It was enough to make a man ponder whether the French
Quarter was the center of the world after all.

"The railroads paid good money to ship them boilers and iron
wheels back in '69," said a voice at his elbow. "If I thought for a second where it'd all lead, I'd of pitched the first one overboard in St.
Louis."

The pilot of the *Rose of Sharon* was leaning next to him on the
rail. Honey hadn't heard him approaching. It alarmed him that a
man of such bulk, with a dead leg that he had to help along with a
stick, could come up on him without his noticing. He might have
been a flock of vigilantes. At better than six feet and two hundred
fifty pounds, with a close-cropped white beard stained yellow with
tobacco, Captain Joe Crank was the first man Honey had ever seen
who managed to smoke cigarettes without appearing effeminate.
He smoked them short enough to singe his whiskers, never touching one after he'd fed it to his face. He punctuated his statement
about railroads by spitting his stub over the rail, then dug inside his
dirty black coat for his makings and rolled a replacement. The peak
of his shapeless pilot's cap rested almost on the bridge of his nose,
which looked as if a man more powerful than himself had clamped
it between thumb and forefinger and given it a mighty twist.

Honey said, "Pitching them overboard wouldn't have stopped
the trains from coming, and you'd be out payment on delivery."

"That's true enough. Some things you do just for your own-
self."

Crank's passenger watched him slide his gray tongue along the
cigarette's seam and set fire to it with a match he'd struck on the
seat of his canvas trousers. "I thought only fancy men smoked
those."

"I had a pipe, but I kept losing it overboard. Picked up the cigarette habit in a mining camp out past Denver. They're just about all they burn out there. Cigars come dear."

"Boss, I druther go without."

"You can stow that *boss* bilge. I married a nigger oncet. She could turn it up and down like a wick. You're the fellow blowed the sawdust out of that Texican's head in New Orleans."

Honey reached for his pistol rigout. Crank's hand swept up like a cottonmouth and clamped hold of his wrist. He breathed smoke and sour mash into Honey's face. "Shut down your boiler, buck. I ain't sending you over. I never cared for Texicans, specially the ones wasn't borned there but stomp around like they held Crockett's coat at the Alamo. I got a job for you, if you've a mind to listen."

"If I haven't?" Honey kept his voice even. The man's grip made his hand numb.

"I'll just pitch you over and feed you to the wheels. Them paddles make gumbo out of 'gators."

Honey let the tension go out of his arm. Crank gave his wrist an extra squeeze—*He'd been holding back!*—and let go.

"I don't turn the wheel over to my mate without sound reason," said the pilot, in the same quiet tone he'd used when speaking about pitching boilers overboard. "I got a rooster problem and I need one of their own who can handle himself to see it don't get out of hand."

"Rooster?"

"Roustabouts. Deckhands. I'm partial to coloreds, who're used to working like mules. Some of them got *too* much mule in them, though. I got wind four of 'em are fixing to desert today."

"I didn't know we were putting into any ports today."

"We ain't. There's a bend ahead where I got to steer in close to shore or run adrift on a bar. They're fixing to jump overboard and swim."

"Why not let them? They're not slaves."

"It means being shorthanded, and having to heave to and beat the bush for replacements. I got a schedule to keep. If you're as handy with that widowmaker as I hear, you might save me the trouble and time. Just snap one over their woolly heads and they'll fall into line."

"Can't you do that?"

"I ain't exactly no sharpshooter. I might miss missing. They got peculiar ideas these days in Baton Rouge about killing niggers. They're agin it. Also they'd scatter and maybe jump overboard early. The 'gators in these parts is fat enough. But a bullet from one of their own is another order. It'll shock 'em and maybe they'll reconsider their position."

"Why do they want to desert? Are you mistreating them?"

"I show 'em my bark right enough, but every manjack knows I'm decenter with them than I am with Irishmen. You can bounce a cotter-pin off the skulls of them sons of Erin till the sun comes around and not get nothing for it but a sore elbow. Meantime I let these black gangs get away with things another pilot'd shoot them dead over, so long as I get from them what they signed on for. I won't have desertion. It spreads like shingles."

"I think I'll pass."

"I ain't asking a favor, I'm offering a bargain. You can refuse, but if you do you won't live to see the pleasures of Pointe a la Hache." He looked sly and coughed smoke. "No, it ain't me, it's them vigilantes. They know you're on this boat."

Honey's thoughts went to his neck. He turned up the mackinaw's collar. "How would you know that?"

"I heard one of the roosters hollering to a buck on the bank just past Bertrandville. They do like to share news. He was talking frog. I calculate he wasn't aware I savvy the lingo. There's a bald chance the word hasn't got downriver, but was I you I'd hate to try living on it. And there's no saying how many more of those conversations I missed."

Honey agreed, without saying it. He watched a dog's carcass drift past. "What's your bargain?"

"There's a good sand beach two miles above Pointe a la Hache when the river ain't high, which it ain't. I'll heave in there. What you do and which way you go is 'twixt you and Almighty Jesus, though I wouldn't recommend south."

"West bank?"

"Well, sure. There ain't a thing east till you reach the Sound, which you never would. They'd catch you and string you from a white ash before ever you smelt the water."

"I'll think on it."

"Buck, you're out of thinking time. We pass that beach at noon."

He wished he'd brought a cigar to drag on. He'd left them in his compartment. He reached inside his coat—no interference from Crank this time—and loosened the Bulldog in its holster. "Which one do these roosters listen to?"

"You'll find him stoking the firebox, or sitting on the woodpile, more like. Big, bald-headed buck, lazy as a cat."

"Is he armed?"

"They all got knives. Handy with 'em, too. You might want to wind a thick scarf around your throat."

"Never could abide one. I like to turn my head."

"Turn it plenty. A man's back is all the same as his front to this crew."

"Will you back me?"

Crank unbuttoned his coat. The dull black gutta-percha handle of a Schofield revolver stuck up above his belt buckle. "Like the

Bank of bloody England." He grinned around the stump of his cigarette.

Honey asked him to wait while he went to his compartment. He returned a moment later and took the stairs down to the main deck, followed by the pilot. The open staircase looked down on the firebox. There a stocky man, naked except for a pair of filthy dungarees, was busy choking chunks of wood as long as his thigh through the open hatch. His head was shaved clean and shone like black enamel. He saw Honey as he turned to reach for a fresh chunk and paused in mid-crouch, looking up at him from under a brow as thick as a plank.

Honey put his hands in his trouser pockets. Crank, still on the stairs, hooked his stick on the railing and leaned a hip against it, one hand resting on the handle of his Schofield.

"What's your name, friend?" Honey asked.

The man straightened slowly. The naked blade of a knife nearly as large as Saint-Maarten's Bowie hung from a loop on his belt. He answered in rapid French. "Ahaz is all I go by. Who calls me friend?" His voice was light for his bulk, almost a tenor.

"I answer to Honey. The rest takes too long." He replied in French and added, in a low voice, "The captain knows the language."

"If he told you that, he lied. I've heard him called names I wouldn't call a bug's arse and he just nodded back. You're that gun sharp from New Orleans."

"He said the same thing. He heard it from a deckhand, talking in French."

"We don't talk about that kind of thing. Some of the mates understand and might want to collect on the reward. Anyway, it was all over the boat before we even caught the current. News travels fast on the river."

"Get on with it," Crank called out. "That box don't feed itself."

Honey knew then the man didn't speak French. He took his right hand out of his pocket and held out the two cigars he'd fetched from his compartment. "Smoke, brother?"

"My brother's dead in Memphis." But Ahaz took one. As Honey patted his pockets for a match, the rooster turned and pulled a length of wood out of the firebox. He lit his cigar from the flaming end and offered the flame to Honey, who bit off the end of his cigar and leaned forward, feeling the heat on his face as the tobacco caught. The chunk went back into the fire and they blew smoke at each other's shoulder.

"If you two ladies want tea, I can drain some water out of the boiler," Crank said.

"I wasn't aware a reward had been posted." Honey was still speaking in French.

Ahaz gnawed the end of his cigar with an iron tooth. "There's always a reward. But any black hand who'd take money on a black man's head had better be prepared to deal with Ahaz." He leaned forward and made his voice hoarse, as if he thought he might still be overheard and understood. "That cigarette-smoking bastard's rotten cargo. What did he tell you about me?"

Honey told him. Ahaz started talking before he finished. "There's no desertion planned. Plenty bitching, but there's nothing better on the river for the wages. He just wants to make you give me reason to let out your guts because he hasn't the sand to do it himself. Then he'll roll your carcass down the gangplank in Pointe a la Hache and collect."

"You could be telling me this to set us against each other. If I kill him, you're free to jump ship. If he kills me, you and the others can overpower him and cash in on my corpse."

"That's a touch. But which one of us has proved a liar?" Ahaz looked up at Crank and made his tone sweet. "Is that not right, you rotten stinking heap of shit?"

At the phrase *tas de merde*, the pilot grunted. "Don't plead your case with me, buck. I'm just here to keep the peace."

"You see?" Ahaz said. "Now, which one's talking to you face to face, both hands empty"—he took his hand off his cigar and spread the fingers—"and which one has a pistol on your back?"

Honey was moving before he heard the hammer click. He sprang the Bulldog free and let the weight of it in his hand whirl him around and fired just as Crank's finger tightened on the Schofield's trigger. A gust fluttered the open flap of Honey's mackinaw. He fired again without thought. Crank grasped for the staircase railing and missed. He bent over it, slid down three steps, and got his feet tangled with his stick. He pitched headfirst to the deck. The shallow-drafted boat rocked a little under the impact.

As Honey inspected his side for a wound, Ahaz loped past him, drawing the big knife from his belt. He stooped over the pilot and Honey heard the big blade go in with the sound of a cleaver slicing open a melon.

There was a ragged hole in the flap of Honey's coat, as if his cigar had burned it when it dropped from his mouth. Crank's bullet had missed his ribs by the span of a hand. His head went a little hollow and he steadied himself against the woodpile. He'd never been shot at before.

Ahaz struggled with the knife, then placed a calloused bare foot against the pilot's body and jerked the blade free of bone and gristle. When he turned around, he was holding Crank's pistol in his other hand.

Honey's Bulldog dangled at his side. He was aware that a crowd had begun to gather, deckhands and passengers pausing on the stairs and forming a half-circle behind him, but they kept their distance and had nothing to do with Ahaz and Honey. He fixed his gaze on the hand holding the Schofield. He'd read about gunmen staring each other down, but that was fiction. Eyes didn't pull triggers.

Ahaz made a hoarse crackling sound in his throat and turned the revolver around clumsily until the butt pointed at Honey. He straightened his arm, bringing the handle inside Honey's reach.

"Two's better in Texas, I heared," he said in English. "I never could work the things."

FIVE

He couldn't remember ever having robbed a train belonging to the Oregon & California, but then he'd spent three months in 1883 drunk as General Grant to deaden the pain of an infected ear and wasn't lucid on what he'd done during that time. It was another sign that his luck had gone south with states' rights that the conductor remembered him.

Emerson had planned to follow Christopher Buckley's advice and stop for a few weeks in the better hotels in Salem and Portland; eat oysters and dip his phizzle in whores that didn't smell like onions for a change, then when the money ran out, tap a bank, steal a good horse, and see what was doing in Canada. French Tom had told him the Mounties were strung out thin across the western territories and American silver went a long way with the Métis half-breeds, who hated the government in Ottawa and would rather hide out a renegade from below the border than breed. A year at the most, then Emerson could return to the Devil's Acre. He calculated that was plenty of time for the tongs who still held a grudge against him to finish killing one another off. Chinese were like ants, turning over a dozen generations in a year.

The conductor changed all that. Emerson could always tell when he'd been recognized, either from a reader or personal experience, and the way the twitching white-haired fellow with the muddy brown eyes kept staring at him as he punched his ticket and handed it back told him they'd met before. The conductor hurried his way through the rest of the passengers in the car and let the door flap open behind him as he stepped into the next. Emerson didn't wait for him to come back with a detective. He got his roll and saddlebags and rifle down from the rack and went out to the rear platform.

The train was entering a bootjack. It would have to slow down to take the curve, but the cinderbed was narrow on either side and lodgepole pines came right up to the edge, waiting to stave in his ribs when he rolled. His best course was to wait for the steepest part of the grade, when the engine was laboring and before it had to speed up to make the climb. A couple of seconds either way and he might as well have stayed in San Francisco and taken his chances with the *boo hoo doy*. He measured the intervals between chugs and got ready to pitch his things and dive after them.

The door to the car pulled open. He hadn't time or a free hand to draw either the Colt's Paterson or the Remington. He swung the blanket roll with the lever-action Marlin wrapped up inside, cocking as he turned, and threw a .40-60 slug through the center of the doorway. The man who was coming through—Emerson glimpsed a gray herringbone coat and vest, a platinum watch chain, and what might have been either a pewter whiskey flask or a pistol in his right hand—fell back, and Emerson threw himself off the platform, hugging the roll to his chest as if to cushion the blow when he struck down.

He felt crisp mountain air and then the sudden sickening shock when the earth swung up and hit him. His breath tore out of his lungs. He heard himself grunting as he rolled, gravel sliding, sharp uneven claws ripping at his clothes and flesh, saw brown earth and blue sky and black trees barreling around him, and then he stopped with a crunch and a light snapped in his brain. Darkness then, black as loam and sharp as the taste of blood on his tongue.

Pain woke him. His lungs had reinflated out of old habit, grating together the shards of one of his ribs. The stab made him gasp. His eyes sprang open, and for a moment he thought he was blind. Then he saw the whorls and ridges in the black bark two inches in front of his face. He'd come that close to dishing in face and brains against a tree. Another tree had broken his momentum, and with it part of his rib cage.

A high-pitched wheeze reached him, strained thin through the trees. If that whistle belonged to the train he'd been riding, he couldn't have been out more than a couple of minutes.

He was still gripping his blanket roll. One arm was pinned under his side, but he unwound the other gingerly, waiting for the lightning pain that would tell him the arm was shattered. He felt every bruised muscle and the patch where the skin had been flayed from his elbow, but no break. He spent the next few minutes taking inventory: bending and straightening each knee, rotating his ankles, patting his top hip and thigh in search of protruding bone. The gravel of the cinderbed had torn triangles out of his coat and shirt and laid open one leg of his dungarees from pocket to hem. His exposed leg was peppered all over with rills of blood as if he'd tangled with barbed wire.

After ten minutes or so he rolled over onto his hands and pushed. His sprained right wrist bent double and he fell on his face. After that he caught hold of a tree root with his left hand and worked his joints along the trunk, pushing with his legs, until he stood upright. By the time he was done he'd formed a new respect for inchworms.

He leaned his shoulder against the trunk and looked around. Tins, utensils, a plug of tobacco in silver foil, and other items from his kit made a trail from the rails down the grade to where he'd come to rest. The Colt's Paterson lay in the grass. In a sudden panic he slapped the pocket where he kept his poke. He caught his breath when a cracked rib pinched, but he'd felt the bulk of the folded banknotes and let out his breath in careful installments. It was one thing to be battered and bleeding, quite another to be battered and bleeding and broke. He'd had it both ways and would take the former six times a week and twice on Sunday.

Hearing his own name in the familiar phrase, he smiled, cracking open a scab on his lower lip and releasing a fresh fountain of stinging blood. *Twice*, Billy Nogales had said, *you'd find sport in Old Scratch whilst he was feeding you to the oven.*

"And make him bust his old black gut," he told the silent Cascades. He checked the New Model Remington for damage and returned it to its pocket.

He gathered his necessaries, stuffed them into his saddlebags, and set off along the railroad tracks in the direction he'd been headed when he was forced to leave the train, holding his side to keep his ribs from shifting with the uneven gait of his feet on the ties. He had no idea how far he was from civilization or if he had enough provisions to get him there, or if he'd be grizzly shit long before he spotted his first chimney. Every few yards he had to step around filth from the train's toilets. For the first time in his life he had a sense of what an Indian must have felt watching the smoky clanking bastards snorting their way across the plains and through the high country, leaving behind a slimy, reeking trail like a fat snail.

But that was afoot-thinking. A man's thoughts couldn't be trusted when his feet weren't in stirrups or crossed in a coach. How big a mess you made didn't matter when you were moving away from it at top speed.

When dusk crept up the foothills he fashioned a lean-to of pine boughs, ate sardines with his fingers, drank the oil, and buried the tin along with the rest of his provisions to keep bears from picking up the scent. He built no fire in case the conductor had wired ahead of the train or behind it and the railroad had sent a gang to search for him along the tracks. He sat with his back against a tree, huddled inside his coat, filling the lean-to with his body heat, the Marlin across his lap, and slept on the edge of awakening. An owl hooting or a squirrel chugging through the brush and fallen needles couldn't stir him, but a twig snapping beneath a heel three hundred yards away would bring him into a crouch, rifle in hand. He'd spent the last two years of the war catching his rest in that manner, and the habit stayed with him even when he'd been safe in his bed on the Barbary Coast, when the tong hadn't known his name and the slash-throats were all out hunting the streets for drunken pilgrims.

A bear padded close around midnight. The vapor of its spent breath drifted in and he smelled its rank, tallowy stench, but the wind was blowing his way and the beast must have been following some other scent, because it paused only briefly, then moved off. Emerson's aches had aches and his ribs lanced him when he forgot and took a deep breath, but he drew his rest from long training. When at first light he rose and kicked apart the lean-to so that no one would know it had ever been inhabited, he hoisted his roll and resumed his journey with new strength.

On the fourth day he smelled woodsmoke. He found the smudge above the trees and left the tracks, following his nose and taking sight lines on broken branches and bald spots on trunks to keep himself from turning circles, until he heard the clink of metal on metal. It sounded only a few feet away in the clean, pine-scoured air. He adjusted his course in that direction. There was a sound behind it that he thought at first was wind in the boughs, but then he heard a gurgling and knew it was running water.

The air smelled of hot grease. It was a camp.

Instinctively, Emerson drew close to the trunk of a tall fir and peered between its limbs. He saw shimmering heat waves, then a finger of fire, and then a broad back moved into his line of vision. A figure in overalls and a slouch hat bent over the fire. Something spat and sizzled, then the figure turned away, giving Emerson a glimpse of a bearded, sunburned profile and barbed steel hooks glinting from the crown of his hat. He'd heard there were crazy fellows who hiked many miles into the high country with nothing on their minds but fish, but he'd heard of black tribes in Africa who pierced their lips and stretched them to stupendous proportions with wooden blocks as well, and had never expected to encounter any of them either.

Then he heard the long, shuddering snort of a horse and his thinking became practical.

He stepped into the clearing where the campfire was burning. One hand gripped the Remington in his coat pocket.

A stream was pouring bright as quicksilver down a rocky cut, with blackened stumps spotting the banks where the area had been cleared at least a generation earlier. Someone—a trapper or trader—had erected a cabin there, but fire or time or a combination of both had taken it down, leaving only two walls of a stone foundation built without mortar. The fisherman had chosen that spot to pitch his green canvas tent and kindled his fire in the shelter of the corner where the two walls intersected. A few yards downriver, a shaggy bay bred to carry man and packs strained at the end of its picket to graze on a low aspen. The horse looked slow but sturdy.

"Lonely up here for a man without partners," Emerson called out.

The fisherman, who'd been squatting over his skillet with his back to the newcomer, spun on one heel, holding his clotted spatula like a weapon. His eyes were mostly whites in a gaunt face that sprouted whiskers from the very tops of the cheekbones to the bib of his overalls; but it was a young face, with no more creases in it than a deck of new cards.

"My friends are fishing upriver," he said after a moment. His accent was slightly Scandinavian and reminded Emerson of his father. That was no good for the fisherman.

"They must have their tents with them. That little scrap's barely big enough for you."

The fisherman's eyes twitched right, then back to Emerson. The tent stood in the other direction. A pile of gear lay to the right, a woven creel and a willow pole on top.

"Horse throw you?" he asked.

Emerson couldn't tell if the man was naturally suspicious or if he himself gave off some kind of scent, like the bear. His clothes were torn and there were patches of skin missing from his face. He hadn't seen his reflection in days. He supposed he looked as wild as berries.

"You're burning your fish," he said.

The fisherman glanced toward the skillet. Then he did a foolish thing.

Emerson watched him dive for the pile of gear. He let him get his hand behind the creel before he took the Remington out of his pocket and shot him through the deep part of the chest. That broke his momentum and he fell on his shoulder, but as he turned over onto his back Emerson fired again, hitting him square in the middle of his bib pocket. He lay gargling blood.

Emerson waited until he'd finished, then walked over and placed his foot on the man's chest and shook him. The body moved without resisting. He looked down at the rifle lying on the ground behind the pile of gear and laughed. It was a single-shot .22, a boy's weapon, good for shooting doves and bottles off fence rails. The young man was lucky he hadn't run into a grizzly. But not lucky for long.

He rescued the fish from the skillet, using the spatula to transfer it to his folded kerchief, and cupped it to his mouth to eat. It was perch, a little burned but tasty enough for a man sick of old fish packed in stale oil. He separated the hairline bones with his tongue and spat them out.

The gear included a pack saddle and blanket. He got both onto the bay without much coaxing. Inside the tent he found a pint of whiskey with two swallows left. When it was empty he tossed it onto the rumpled blanket and filled his pockets with tins of peaches and tomatoes and half a plug of tobacco. He'd have killed the man for the peaches alone.

He untied and mounted the bay—holding his side and cursing in half-forgotten Swedish; for that he blamed the fisherman—and began picking his way down to the flat. The horse was gray about the muzzle, not enough fight left in it to care who sat on it. It would choose the best way back to the stable. Emerson calculated civilization was less than a pint of whiskey away.

SIX

"How long's it been since you saw that thing?" Mary Alice Dunwaddie asked. She was stretched out on her four-poster on Canal Street, watching Ernest Valerian Torbert peel himself out of his red flannels.

He glanced down, but all he could see was his swollen belly. "As a matter of fact, I examined it this morning in the mirror in my hotel room. I like to keep a record of its progress. It never stops growing, you know. A professor at St. Ignatius has been asking me for years to will it to the medical school there for future study. I haven't given him an answer. I'm not persuaded I won't have use for it in the hereafter."

"What size was it to start? I've sent shrimps bigger than that back to the kitchen."

He stroked his beard, appreciating her in her chemise with her slightly chubby thighs crossed. Her breasts spilled loosely over the pleated linen and her cheeks were positively fat, but rouged with restraint, and her shock of curls—*red, by the grace of agents other than God's,* was the current popular phrase—was becoming. He admired her honeyed accent, which drew the sting from most of her remarks. "I was told you courtesans were schooled in the arts of flattery. How long did you say you'd been doing this?"

"A lady doesn't. However, I am third generation. My aunt was companion to our last governor but one, and my grandmother comforted Andy Jackson for ten days after the Battle of New Orleans. I had a lithograph of her riding in the carriage he gave her, but I had to sell it when Winnie went to Texas. General Jackson captured the carriage from General Gibbs." She selected a ready-made cigarette from a mahogany casket on the night table and fitted it into an amber holder. "As for flattery, I never caught the knack. Winnie didn't seem to care one way or the other. There was only one way to bring him out of his black humors, and it wasn't with words." She struck a match and filled the room with herb-smelling smoke.

"Winnie" was Winton Claude Saint-Maarten, the man slain in the House of Rest for Weary Boatmen. It had cost Torbert the price of one cognac in a place called the Stack o' Dollars to learn the identity of the dead man's closest intimate. Armed with her address and a bunch of flowers, he'd taken himself to Mary Alice Dunwaddie's cottage, one of several charming bungalows erected in that neighborhood for the express purpose of sheltering mistresses of the wealthy; Petticoat Lane, the locals called it. He'd been humbled by the display of rare and exotic blossoms already spilling out of the box under her front window. However, she'd accepted his bouquet with a smile and a curtsy that would not have shamed a lady at the Court of St. James. Fifteen minutes later, he was naked in her boudoir.

He climbed in beside her. She was all soft flesh, seemingly without bone or muscle, and her tongue filled his mouth so thoroughly he thought for a moment his own might have to seek other quarters.

When hers at last withdrew he said, "What about your mother?"

"My mother?" Her hazel eyes went wide.

"You mentioned your aunt and your grandmother. I couldn't help but notice the omission."

"My mother is the chairman of the Orphans League. She's a disappointment to the family."

They coupled. Afterward they lay spreadeagled atop the counterpane, waiting for their perspiration to dry in the air that was barely stirring through the open window.

"Winnie was a moody fellow, was he?"

She pried herself up on one elbow and stuck out her lower lip in a pout intended for the back row of the balcony. Perhaps she'd been expecting a compliment, but there was a spark in her eye he knew well. The same people who set the dogs on him when he'd said he was with a newspaper always took down the Sunday china when he told them he was writing a book. They all wanted to be Robinson Crusoe.

"He was a shit." She whispered it in his ear, punctuating it with the tip of her tongue. "I don't suppose you can write that."

"I can if I put in dashes, but it doesn't look well on the page. Why don't I substitute 'brute'?"

"Either way he was a shit. Have a look." She sat up, licked a palm, and rubbed it briskly against the underside of her other wrist. The powder came off, exposing five purple spots on the skin, four on one side and one on the other. "He grabbed me there and twisted it behind my back. Three weeks ago, that was. I can tell you I was a gay blaze of color the first week, like Sousa's band."

"What was the reason?"

"Kiss me and I'll tell you."

He moved close, pursing his lips. Her palm stopped him. "Not there."

When he resurfaced, gasping for breath, she took his phizzle in her hand and pulled him close.

"Nothing," she whispered.

"Nothing? He gave no reason?"

"I might have spent the night with his coachman."

"You might have?"

"His coachman is colored. Most of them are. I cannot tell them apart in the sun, and as I said, it was night. I don't suppose it matters if it was his or not. They talk to each other, and New Orleans is a small town."

"I'm surprised he didn't kill you."

"I think he lost the taste after Texas. It was a duel that put him there. It's an uncivilized place, crawling with Mexicans and red Indians. He said he'd die before he let them send him back."

"When did he say that?"

"After he twisted my arm."

"Good God."

"Now that I think about it, that was the night."

"Which night?"

"The night he went to the Port of Missing Men."

"What's that?"

"The House of Rest. In *The Mascot* they call it the Port of Missing Men. The editor's been trying to shut the place down for years."

"That was the night he got drunk and battered the whore? The night Honey Boutrille shot him to death?"

She nodded. "John Barleycorn was no friend to Winnie. Two swallows and he lost his breeding." She frowned, looked down. "What's happened here? You're limp as a stocking."

"Did it never occur to you that you were responsible for what happened that night?"

"Of course not. I wouldn't be caught dead in the House of Rest. I'm a courtesan, not a whore."

"It's an important distinction."

"I should say it is."

"The whores should be happy not to have to claim you."

Her open hand stung the left side of his face and struck him deaf in that ear. She wasn't all soft flesh after all. He dressed quickly and went out, but not before a corner of the mahogany casket caught him on the back of the head, splitting his scalp.

He scrubbed the smell of Mary Alice Dunwaddie's powder and corrupt blooms off his body in the enameled tub down the hall from his hotel room, then folded the wash rag and rested the back of his head against it, letting his wound bleed out into the nappy fabric. He hadn't been in New Orleans three hours and already he was a casualty. He'd gone through the war without a scratch.

The city was one great brothel. It even smelled of houses he had visited during his naval training in Hampton Roads, the air acrawl with perfume, semen, and the harsh soap they used to scrub the stains from the sheets. But nothing on that apron of the military had approached the raw candor of Burgundy Street, where whores as young as twelve and as old as seventy sat rocking in wicker chairs on sagging porches with the whole of their torsos exposed by their unbuttoned Mother Hubbards, smoking pipes, chewing plugs, and advertising their particular specialties in voices as loud as any teamster's. A colored porter on the train had warned Torbert to remain alert, as some of these women were known to spit tobacco into the eyes of a passing stroller, blinding him, then drag him off the street, club him over the head, and hurl him, senseless and penniless, into the gutter or worse: Piles of gentlemen's half-burned garments had been discovered in the alleys behind some of these houses during the last police search. Torbert believed the story, but he had not felt any more secure in the presence of Miss Dunwaddie, whose aunt had been mistress to a governor of Louisiana. The city was ruled by women of low character. Idly, he groped inside the pocket of the robe he'd hung on the back of the chair beside the tub, took out the .32 Marston derringer he'd been carrying since the war, and inspected the load in each of the three stacked barrels. He'd packed it along to protect himself against bandits and Indians, but they didn't frighten him half so badly as the fair sex.

Back in his room he dressed for evening in a new collar and cutaway, dropped the Marston into a side pocket, and walked to the corner carrying his silk hat. There he boarded the trolley and got out at Gallatin Street, where a young man in a straw hat and yellow gaiters removed the silver toothpick from his mouth long enough to point out the sign hanging from the roof of the House of Rest for Weary Boatmen. Torbert had walked right past the building, thinking it was a pile of packing crates. The entire street seemed to have been built from scrap, of no more substance than the painted canvas walls of a theater set, and far less convincing. Opening the door to the House of Rest, he half expected to find himself looking out on a street on the other side.

New Orleans, however, continued to surprise him. The interior looked and felt absolutely ancient. The walls were hung with paintings of nude women, pink, fleshy, and sprawling, and parchment-like posters trumpeting attractions long since gone, from the evidence of the dates and the condition of the advertisements, which seemed to remain only to keep the weather out. The floorboards were stained as dark as walnut with tobacco-splatter, crushed cigar-wrappers, and possibly excrement: The place had a sour barnyard smell beneath the smoke and fermented grain. Cobwebs as thick as trampolines made a false ceiling that jiggled in the current of air stirred by the opening and closing of the door. Hurricane lamps and Chesterfields, the latter presumably brass beneath the verdigris, shed greasy orange light through blackened glass chimneys, but the illumination barely reached the floor. He'd heard of underground public-houses in the City of London that hadn't seen the sun in five hundred years; the House of Rest, from the appearance of its exterior, had managed to create the same impression in less than five.

The street was not yet dark, and at that hour the place was nearly deserted. An emaciated Negro with his braces drooping off his thin shoulders sat at the piano, not playing but supporting his head in his hands with his elbows propped on his knees, looking as if all his concentration was required to keep from sliding off the stool to the floor. Another Negro with a broad face and a brutal mouth nearly too wide for it stood behind the bar, which was a paneled hickory desk that might have been reclaimed from a hotel lobby. He was doing nothing in a way that seemed remarkable to Torbert, who was accustomed to seeing bartenders polishing glasses, mopping up spills, wiping dried foam from the taps; keeping busy after the manner of men who feared idleness as something akin to atheism. This fellow didn't stir his thick bare forearm from the bartop even when the visitor stood in front of him. Torbert felt conspicuous in his evening dress. He'd chosen it with some casual thought of awing the natives, but that had been a mistake. He put his silk hat on the bar and asked for a glass of bourbon.

"Which kind? We carry a dozen labels." The man's voice was a rumble, oddly gentle.

Torbert scanned the bottles lined up on the back bar. He saw brands he'd only heard about in Chicago, and some he had never heard of at all. At length he selected Monogram. The bartender fisted that bottle off the shelf, uncorked it, and filled a glass. The color was a warm, rich orange, not the pale yellow Torbert had come to expect from places that cut their stock with water, and not the deep red that resulted when vegetable dye was added to clear grain alcohol to fool the undiscriminating drinker. It was sweet and smoky to the taste. He laid a quarter on the bar and told the man to keep the extra dime.

"Is the proprietor on the premises?"

"He's away."

"So I'd heard. Is there someone who can tell me a bit about him?" He placed a card on the bar, one of two hundred and fifty he'd had printed, reading simply *J. P. Glidden—Journalist.*

The man glanced down at it, but his face showed no comprehension. It was plain he was illiterate.

"I'm a writer. My readers back East are eager to know more about the shooting that took place here last month. The Saint-Maarten shooting?" It had suddenly occurred to him there might have been others in the interim.

"Mam'selle Josephine!"

The man's eyes hadn't left Torbert's, and for an instant he thought the bartender was shouting at him. Then the man slumped at the piano rose and went through the back door. His bowlegged gait suggested a genital rash or worse; Torbert had seen his share of it in the navy, enough to be careful about where he spilled his seed. The man came back a moment later and resumed his erstwhile position on the stool, elbows on his knees and his head in his hands.

Another five minutes went past before Mademoiselle Josephine appeared. She was a young woman with her dark hair pinned up, striking in profile, an octoroon at most. There were darker complexions to be found along the Boul' Mich', and not a drop of Negro blood in a bucket. She wore a plain muslin dress, the toes of worn slippers poking out under the hem as she walked. Curiously, she turned left immediately and circled the entire room with her left side to the wall, stopping finally at the opposite end of the bar, where the bartender set a snifter in front of her and splashed a dollop of honey-colored liquid into it from a squat bottle.

Torbert picked up his glass and moved down to her end of the bar. One of the woman's hands, slender and without rings—much finer, he noticed, than Mary Alice Dunwaddie's, whose nails were bitten and none too clean—was resting on the bar, and clenched into a fist as he drew near, but she made no attempt to shrink away.

He waited for her to take a drink. She was watching the snifter as if waiting for the contents to settle. When it ceased rippling and she still had not moved to take the stem in her hand, he reached out slowly and touched her cheek. She started, but didn't move away. He took her chin between thumb and forefinger and turned her face toward him. Shadows cast by the lamp above his head settled into the caverns and fissures on the left side.

She was watching his face. He kept his expression even, and when he let go of her chin, she didn't turn away. He fished a five-dollar bold piece out of the fob pocket of his vest and slid it along the bar until it rested against the base of her glass.

She spoke for forty-five minutes. He had to ask her to repeat details because of slurred words, and because she couldn't read she couldn't tell him how to spell her full name and by the time he found out how far his guess had missed, his book was in its third printing. But by the end of that three quarters of an hour, he was wondering how much argument Argus Fleet would give him when he said nothing about the cover of *The Blacksnake of New Orleans* was appropriate.

PART THREE

A THOUSAND STAGES

SEVEN

Casper Box—immortalized by a fellow thespian in his first vaudeville revue as "the original Pandora's Box"—was a small man with a large head, which he sought to de-emphasize by wearing tight clothes and big hats; as a result, storming around in his strained buttons and wobbly-brimmed planter's straws, he left the impression of an animated mushroom. Those who laughed at him, however, contained their mirth until he was out of earshot. At age twenty-four he'd been Barnum's advance man during Jenny Lind's sensational U.S. tour, and it was said the World's Greatest Showman had learned more from his young associate than he had imparted. A few words from Box in the right company could birth a career; a single word could bury it beyond hope of Lazarus. He was physically dangerous as well, having served three years in the New York State Penitentiary for shooting a man to death in a duel of honor. He never traveled without his brace of matched flintlock pistols in the rosewood case he'd had designed for them.

From a distance, strangers often mistook him for a boy. Up close, the bootblack in his hair and handlebars brought out the lines in his sixty-year-old face. He had small, vicious eyes, a bulldog jaw, and (provided one did not dishonor or fail to return his probity) the biggest heart in show business. Former clients who could no longer mount a unicycle or imitate bird calls touched him regularly for generous loans and he sent expensive bouquets to each of his three former wives on their birthdays.

At the height of his career in the 1860s, he had managed half the major eastern and European talent touring North America. Ordinary people who knew nothing of the machinations behind the canvas flats knew of him as the man who had turned down an offer to represent Edwin Booth out of loyalty to Abraham Lincoln, who had fallen victim to Booth's brother, John Wilkes. (Booth at this time commanded $25,000 per month on tour.) Now Box told the reporters who gathered around him on railroad platforms and at the bottom of gangplanks that he was semi-retired, having decided to concentrate all of his waning energies exclusively upon Miss Adabelle Forrest, the Quick-Change Queen of Atlantic City.

"And who might her majesty be, and what might her subjects expect of her reign?" asked the gentleman from the *St. Louis Enquirer*.

"You can judge for yourself tomorrow night at the Mercator. You fellows of the press have been white to me—all except you, George Teal, but you have Mr. Pulitzer to answer to, and he hasn't approved of me since the tribute Mr. Billy Wydra paid to him in *The Mad Pole*, and I ain't one to suckle a grudge—so here's free passes for you all. You might want to consider bringing along a spoon to scoop your eyeballs back inside their sockets. I ain't been associated with a performer of her stamp since the Swedish Nightingale."

"You do batter one about the head with Jenny Lind. She hasn't sung a note in fifteen years." This remark was offered by George Teal of the *Post-Dispatch*; who, it was true, had not filed a favorable review of one of Casper Box's discoveries since 1880, the year Brooklyn mimic Billy "The Happy Hunky" Wydra put on milk-bottle spectacles, goat's whiskers, and an unfortunate putty nose and taunted theatergoers: "Do you not credit the authenticity of my nose, sir? Well, sir, you may *pull*-it-sir!" Quite apart from enlightening a public that had theretofore insisted upon rhyming the first syllable of his name with "mew," the oft-repeated challenge had enraged the great journalist and cost Box, by his own accounting, some seven thousand dollars in revenue in the Gateway City.

"Yes, and how many others can you still name who trod the boards under Millard Fillmore?" Box's mean little eyes twinkled. He was never happier than when demolishing hecklers and fencing with representatives of the Fourth Estate. In his own limelit days he had performed a knife-throwing act and juggled flaming javelins.

"Who in blazes is Millard Fillmore?" demanded the young man from the *Democrat*, to hoots and Bronx cheers from the others.

The *Enquirer* reporter frowned at his printed pass. "The Mercator's condemned. We led the campaign after a boy fell through the lobby floor and broke his neck."

"All the rest were booked for the season. Miss Forrest became available at the last moment. I persuaded the fire marshal to lift the order for the run of the show."

This brought a respectful hush from the men on the platform. Archie Cochran did not bribe cheaply.

George Teal broke the silence. "Will you indemnify our widows when we fall into the basement?"

"Repairs have been under way for a week. We open tomorrow night. Gentlemen, may I present Miss Adabelle Forrest?" Box swept off his big hat and held it behind him, concealing the black smudges on the inner band.

Bowlers and boaters came off as the tall slender woman approached from the other end of the platform, trailing a porter pushing a cart top-heavy with trunks and carryalls. She wore a yellow dress, daringly without a bustle and betraying a minimum of petticoats, and cut to reveal her ankles as she walked. One slender arm, white-gauntleted to the elbow, bent up to secure her picture hat to her head. The white woven brim was twice as wide as Box's and flapped like a pennant in the brisk wind.

A second woman, feet clattering to keep up with the caravan, looked like a noon shadow of the first, squashed into a short stout package in a dark wool dress and unbecoming hat designed to absorb and disguise the stains of travel. Her cheeks were flushed; not, Box noted, entirely from heat and exertion. The flimsy material of her reticule did little to conceal the outline of a flask.

"Casper," the first woman announced, "this wicked creature informs me the yellow trunk is on its way to some mythical kingdom called Little Rock. I told him that's quite impossible. All my portmanteaux go where I go, and it's abundantly clear I would never be found in a place of that name."

The porter—middle-aged, square-built, of a brown to match one of the cylindrical valises built to contain Miss Forrest's hats—braked the cart with a practiced gesture and removed his cap. "Sir, I explained to the lady her trunk must of been put aboard the wrong train in Chicago. Schedule says the six-twenty-seven to Little Rock pulled out about the same time on the next track over. We can wire Little Rock with a description and if it's there they can put it aboard the next train to St. Louis and we can deliver it to her hotel day after tomorrow."

"Casper, tell this fellow the opening is tomorrow night. I cannot go on without the contents of that trunk."

"What's in the trunk?" Box asked.

"All the changes for the French farce. Shall I perform it naked?"

At "naked," a fine dust of paper and graphite flew up from the notebooks of the reporters present. Box smiled to avoid grinding his teeth: Six weeks' worth of lessons in elocution and deportment had done little more than smooth Adabelle's outer edge. He had even heard the X when she pronounced the word "portmanteaux." He produced a thick fold of banknotes, peeled one off, and handed it to the porter. "Please see what you can do to get that trunk here by tomorrow. It's yellow, as she said, with BOX COMPANY PLAYERS stenciled on the lid. There might be an express train. I'll pay any extra, up to and including the price of a first-class compartment."

"Yes, sir. I ain't making no promises for Mr. Harriman." The porter folded the note inside the sweatband of his cap and put it back on.

"Lizzie, this was your responsibility." Box pulled his moustaches down at the stout woman.

"It wasn't my fault, sir." She was breathing heavily, and sweating gin. "All the cases was on one cart, sir. Miss Forrest was wanting me and I didn't rightly think they could miss any once they'd started. Not unless they done it deliberate."

"How many in the company?" George Teal asked. He regarded the luggage cart, whose cargo towered over the head of the tallest journalist on the scene.

"Just Miss Forrest; although I employ the term *just* advisedly. A quick-change artist must have changes." Box drew the printed inventory from a pocket and snapped it open. "Thirty-six dresses, fourteen suits of clothes, four dozen hats—forty-two ladies, five gentlemen's, one boy's peaked cap—fifty-one pairs of shoes, eighty pairs of stockings, twenty-three scarves. I'll not go into the rest out of respect for the lady's privacy." He pocketed the sheet with a flourish. He had the list memorized, but he liked the defenders of the free press to pretend they were being served fresh. He'd recited the same numbers in Hackensack, Pittsburgh, Columbus, Detroit, and Chicago. No two journals had reported them the same.

The youth from the *Democrat* looked up from his total. "Why eighty pairs of stockings? That's thirty more than she has dresses and suits of clothes."

"They wear out, young man." Miss Forrest tilted back her head and looked down the not inconsiderable length of her nose at the reporter. "Would you have me darn them between performances?"

He flushed violently and bent his head to his notes. His companions guffawed. One of them pushed his hat forward over his face.

The man from the *Globe* asked Miss Forrest what program she was presenting.

"A selection from *East Lynne*, to start, followed by the abduction scene from *Pirates of Penzance*. I shall perform Hamlet's soliloquy just before the interval, and finish up with the bed-chamber scene from *A Husband's Vengeance*, Violetta's entrance from *La Traviata*, Act Two of *The Third Spouse*, and—pending the appearance of the elusive yellow trunk—*Elle Dangereaux* in its entirety."

"And which parts will you be playing?" asked George Teal.

"All of them."

A numb silence followed, shattered by a cannonade of questions. Box held up a defending palm, took Miss Forrest's arm, and steered her toward the line of two-wheel cabs waiting outside the station. He placed another note in the porter's hand and implored him to pay attention to Lizzie's instructions regarding which trunks to send to the Mercator Theater and which to the Southern Hotel. "Mind she gets off in good condition," he added. "Without her assistance onstage, Miss Forrest will be forced to perform in a state of extreme decortication."

"Decort—" The porter stumbled over the word.

"Wearing nothing but her rings."

In the cab, Box crowded himself into a corner to avoid collision with Adabelle's hat. His own rested on his lap. "Heed an old trouper's advice and save the dramatics for the boards," he said as they jolted away from the pursuing reporters.

"But, really, Casper. The yellow trunk!"

"Yellow trunk be damned. This ain't Hackensack. If they like you in St. Louis, they'll love you in Denver. If they love you in Denver, they'll fling themselves at your feet in San Francisco. Start out throwing tantrums and by the time you get to California they'll be waiting with tar and feathers."

"And what am I to do if the trunk doesn't arrive?"

"Then you don't do the farce."

"The farce is the climax of the evening! It brought them to their feet in Detroit."

"In Chicago it brought in the police. It cost me half of our share of the receipts to line Paddy's palm. Jail's good for press but I'm too old to sleep on a cot. My rheumatism acts up in a Pullman." He took a pinch of snuff and sneezed at the horse's backside. The animal snorted and twitched its tail. "Do another turn from *Hamlet*. Them tights is as good as a peignoir any day."

She raised her chin in thought; or more likely to dissemble her wattles. She was hard on forty and her press biography had been altered recently to establish 1853 as her new date of birth. "I could do 'Alas, poor Yorick.' Oh, but where shall we get a skull? I cannot fathom the incompetence of the Union Pacific."

"While you're clawing around for someone to blame, look to Lizzie. It ain't as if her responsibilities offstage are too much to bear."

"Lizzie's a treasure. I don't know how I'd manage without her."

"You'd just double up on chambermaids, though I don't know where you'd find the time. You're lucky none of those girls has had mothers so far. You'd have more press than I could arrange for the Russian ballet."

"I don't know what you're talking about." She watched a little girl selling candles on a corner.

"All I'm saying is exercise a little control."

She patted his hand. "We cannot all be Pope Casper the First."

"If you're bound on calling me names, make it Pandora's Box. I never liked it but I like it better than that."

"Pope Casper the First," she repeated.

The trunk had not arrived by curtain time the following night. Box, employing the baritone he had plumbed and polished on a thousand stages, announced that in place of *Elle Dangereaux*, Miss Forrest would perform a medley of popular songs. She had no vibrato and her voice cracked when she ventured beyond half an octave, but she could manage such fare as "Carry Me Back to Old Virginny" and "Shake That Wooden Leg, Dolly Oh," and the lyrics were familiar enough that the audience would probably chime in and go home flushed and satisfied.

Musical skills aside, Adabelle Forrest was a distinct talent. Her energetic reading overcame the heavy melodrama of *East Lynne*, a Victorian staple, and Box held the opinion that neither Gilbert nor Sullivan would find serious fault with her truncated *Pirates*. She had a slender, athletic figure, most comely in Hamlet's doublet and tights; mingling among the crowd in the Mercator's smoke-laden lobby during the fifteen-minute interval, the wily old manager overheard considerable praise for her form if not her projection, which he would repeat to her with judicious editing lest her elephantine ego get the better of them both and she commenced to think she could survive without Casper Box. He'd lost Fay Templeton in just that fashion, and the fact that her assumption had proven true remained a delicate point with him. If he could squeeze two complete seasons out of Adabelle, he could retire.

However, it was neither her figure nor her life force that had impelled her into Box's orbit. Her felicity with costume changes, performed instantaneously onstage with the aid of a painted screen and the presence of an experienced dresser, was the very novelty the theatrical veteran had been searching for in the aftermath of the Templeton desertion. Verdi and the Bard alone were no longer sufficient to divert American audiences grown accustomed to medicine shows, hell-fire preachers, and the lectures of Oscar Wilde; they must have spectacle. The legerdemain of a split-second transformation from runny-nosed waif to Patagonian princess (accomplished through the prosaic means of one-piece garments open in the back and secured with a minimum of hooks), coupled with the tantalizing possibility of a falling screen and a glimpse of partial female nudity, had packed the house in jaded Atlantic City. The frontier beckoned. It had cost Box his nest egg to purchase her contract, but the sensations of Philadelphia and Detroit (and for all its sacrifice in bribery to keep Box's company out of jail, the word-of mouth following a miscue on Lizzie's part in Chicago, a hook gone unnoticed, and the unplanned public unveiling of a nipple) had convinced him his investment was sound. While there was indeed only one Swedish Nightingale to a century, it was just as clear that there was but one Quick-Change Queen to a lifetime. Getting the most out of the situation was just a matter of keeping the lady's vanity in check and her hands off everything in skirts.

When the program continued, the creditable local orchestra got her through the mawkish claptrap of *A Husband's Vengeance* and helped keep her head above water in *La Traviata*; but when she assayed *The Third Spouse*, portraying all three corners of a love triangle and making even Box accept, for a distracted moment, that there were three thespians onstage, she absolutely brought down the house. She was fully costumed for the musical medley and forced to wait several minutes for the cheers and applause to fade before she was able to sing a note.

The next morning, the yellow trunk was standing in the hotel lobby when Box bustled in bearing the morning newspapers. It was a most positive sign on top of the *Globe* review, which he'd skimmed on the way, nearly stepping into the path of a brewer's dray while reading the phrase "luminescent and puckish." He burst into Adabelle's room, then had to step back into the hall, pinching snuff and cursing, while Lizzie scrambled out of his headliner's bed and into her dress. When he went back inside, the maid was busy laying out Adabelle's street clothes while her mistress sat up in a brocaded bed-jacket, sipping tea.

"Honestly, Casper, it was your mother's responsibility to teach you to knock at doors, not mine."

"My mother ran off with a groom when I was six." He threw himself into an armchair and began snapping open newspapers. "Well, the man from the *Globe* would marry you in a minute. The *Enquirer* says you 'defy the laws of nature with the charm of one who is ignorant of them,' and that *Democrat* pup thinks you're a witch."

"Not, one hopes, a typographical error?" She smiled over her cup.

"You seduced the fellow, more fool he. Speaking of farces, your long-lost trunk is downstairs."

"Splendid. You're avoiding the *Post-Dispatch*."

"No, it ain't so bad. 'Miss Forrest's wardrobe wizardry very nearly manages to distract one from her woeful inability to carry a tune three feet without collapsing.'"

"Bastard."

"Teal has his position to consider. You can't do better than Mr. Pull-it-sir for the money."

"I should have thought we could do better than the Mercator. I've never performed in a theater before where the sets were more substantial than the stage. I was positively in fear for my life."

"Everything else was booked. It was either that or bypass St. Louis. I remind you that it was you who couldn't decide until the last minute whether to go on tour or sail to Paris with some duke that already had a duchess in Holland."

"It was Hanover, and the duke was a baron. Barons with baronesses are the best kind. They never oblige one to turn down a proposal of marriage. In any event the affair had a tragic end. I came West to forget, and here you are forcing me to remember my sorrow."

"The tragedy being that the baron was a pauper, and Paris turned out to be Jersey City." He turned the page. "Here's a fellow in San Francisco who's run afoul of the tongs. An old guerrilla, and a train robber into the bargain. I wonder that Cody hasn't snapped him up for his damn Wild West exhibition."

Lizzie said, "We should of hung all them secessionists in '65. A body needs a Colt's Dragoon just to ride the train in peace."

"Or failing that, a flask," Box said. "The authorities have traced him to Portland. He shot a railroad dick near there and jumped the train. Twice Emerson, they call him. I can see that on a playbill."

Adabelle saucered her cup with a click. "Don't talk rot, Casper. Murder isn't an exploitable talent."

"You could say the same thing about changing clothes. It's all in how the thing's done."

That evening, with the yellow trunk lashed to the fender of a four-wheeler, they set out for the theater. Six blocks short of their destination, a uniformed policeman flagged them down. He told the driver curtly that he was re-routing traffic because of a fire. A brass-boilered fire wagon clangored past.

"What's burning?" Box called out.

"A theater, sir. The Mercator. It's a goner for certain."

"Oh, Casper, my costumes!" Adabelle's nails sank into Box's upper arm.

"Travelers' luck." He patted her hand. "Let's hope they like *Elle Dangereaux* in Denver."

EIGHT

One hundred bales of cotton and one fugitive from New
Orleans reached the foot of the Brazos in the middle of a
September rainstorm. Honey Boutrille had barely alighted from
the flatboat when the foreman of a group of local volunteers seized
him by the shoulder and told him to get to work filling sandbags; a
hurricane was coming, he shouted, and there was nothing standing between it and Houston but Galveston Island. The foreman
never knew how close he came to eternity.

The Bulldog was in Honey's hand and cocked before the man
spoke. He didn't see it in the driving rain, and exhaustion combined with high fever slowed Honey's reflexes. He put away the
pistol and turned to join the volunteers.

Moments later, he plunged into the sun. His body was aflame.
Sweat coated him, turning to steam the instant it was exposed to
the blazing air. His head expanded to make room for the people
and things that filled it. He saw faces he hadn't seen in years, the
greasy stubbled visages of the only men who would take in a boy on
his own in New Orleans; felt the bite of the buckles at the ends of
their belts, saw himself kneeling at their command. He saw the

punched-in hole that had been Winton Saint-Maarten's right eye, Captain Joe Crank sliding down the stairway railing aboard the *Rose of Sharon*, the boards on the deck of the flatboat from Houston, scrubbed as white and smooth as fresh ivory, obscured by the dirty gray water of yet another swabbing, felt the sting of blisters forming on his hands where he gripped the handle of the mop.

They string you up for this.

I'll just pitch you over and feed you to the wheels. Them paddles make gumbo out of 'gators.

No use hiding, boy. Your Uncle Floyd's got something for you.

I'll cut her head clean off!

Rinse that deck, buck. That soap's slicker'n snot.

A boy can make his way in New Orleans. Stop your blubbering and do your auntie proud.

On your knees, you little picaninny, and hold still. I can't thread no moving needle.

Now, which one's talking to you face to face, both hands empty, and which one has a pistol on your back?

Gunfire slammed inside his head, ringing off the sides like rocks chucked at a bucket. . . .

"Well, the fever's done broke. If it's on time depends on if he wakes up."

"Can't we just shake him?"

"He's got this far on his own. I never seen a man's temperature get to a hunnert and six without killing him. I gots to put my faith in nature."

"Or God."

"God done went on holiday before Fort Sumter. I don't see where he never come back."

"He ought to be fed. It's been three days, and I don't know when he ate before that. He's skin and bone."

"You can try broth, but strain it. A piece of chicken just might shock him to death."

The second speaker, a woman, made a sound in her throat. "Me, too. It's fish, and we done boiled away everything but the bones day before yesterday."

"Mind them bones. Be a crying shame if he choked now."

Honey opened his eyes. A broad brown face with great black muttonchops drifted his way through layers of paste. The meaty lips broke into a kind of snarling frown, which his first words told Honey was a smile.

"Good day to you, son. I thought you'd quit this earth. I'd hang out my shingle if folks wouldn't powder my behind with buckshot for getting above my station."

"You're a doctor?" His voice sounded like two sticks rubbing together.

"No, I'm too dark for that by half. But I patched more holes and poulticed more fevers orderlyin' with the Thirty-Sixth U.S. Colored Infantry than I reckon any ten white doctors seen since Old Man Hippocrates was a pup. You're the worst I ever come across didn't end up shaking Massah Bonc-Facc's hand, though. Johnson Six is the name."

"Johnson Six?"

"There was five other Johnsons serving in my company. There was a Johnson Seven for a while, but a twelve-pounder done taken his head off at Petersburg. I reckon you could say I owed my promotion to Robert E. Lee. Anyways, folks done got out of the habit of calling me Otis, and I done got out of the habit of answering to it. You come in by schooner or flatboat?"

Honey took a second to catch up with the change of subject. "Flatboat. There wasn't any work for me in Houston, so I took a job on a cotton-hauler." His eyes grated when he moved them. A lantern hanging from a nail doled out wobbly light on plank walls that reminded him of the House of Rest for Weary Boatmen. A sheet gone almost transparent from washing hung from a length of rope strung from wall to wall, separating the bed from the rest of the building. Someone was moving around on the other side, clanking a pot against a stove. "I remember I was filling bags with sand. I thought at first the hurricane hit."

"It blowed itself out off Mexico. That's old news even to Mexicans. You been here a spell. They almost stacked you up with the sandbags, corpses being better ballast, but somebody noticed you wasn't through breathing yet, so they hauled you here."

"Where would that be?"

"The Whordle and Grace Cotton Company warehouse." The snarl-smile returned as Honey looked around again. "Well, the house behind it. Mrs. Natalie Proudfoot's the caretaker. That means she sweeps up and sets out the rat traps. It's her hospitality got you this far. This here's the lady now."

A hand swept aside the sheet and a square-built colored woman in a butcher's apron came through, carrying a steaming china bowl with a long-handled spoon in it. A pair of large tired-looking eyes regarded him without emotion from a round, unseamed face, as ageless as polished stone. She wore her hair tied in a bandanna from which all color and pattern had been scrubbed long ago. "Hold his head up," she told Johnson Six.

Honey tried to prop himself up, but his head, which had seemed so empty a moment before, was suddenly as heavy as a cotton bale. The former orderly's big hand cupped the back of his head and lifted it while the woman arranged herself on a three-legged stool beside the bed and thrust a faded checked cloth under his chin. She shipped liquid in the bowl of the spoon, blew on it, and slid it between Honey's lips.

When the broth made contact with his tongue, he realized he was hungrier than he'd ever been. It was odorless, but the grease coated the inside of his mouth like a second skin and the aftertaste was rich with fish and some kind of herb. He drank half the contents of the bowl and would have continued if she hadn't withdrawn it at Johnson Six's insistence.

"A full belly's no good for a starving man," he told Honey. "You ain't used to it. You needs what strength you got to get better. Throwing up's a fool waste of it, and soup besides. There's more for later. When it starts to taste as bad as it smells, you'll be well enough to walk out."

"I can't smell anything."

"That's the catarrh. You got pneumonia in both barrels, worst I seen since the war. They must of worked your insides out on the Brazos."

"How'd you know to ask if I came in on a schooner or flatboat?"

"Them blisters on your hands. All the colored folk hereabouts got calluses on their calluses. Whatever you done to get along before didn't involve no mopping nor lifting, and there's no work for a colored man around here that don't. That means you come in from someplace else. It wasn't in no first-class cabin or you wouldn't of had them blisters to begin with." The orderly turned away. When he turned back, he was holding Honey's mackinaw folded in his hands. He partially unfolded it, exposing the Bulldog pistol in its holster. "You had on nice clothes for a laborer. I had you figured for a fancy man until I seen this."

The pistol made him think of Captain Crank's Schofield and

where he'd put it. "I had a valise." He couldn't remember when he'd lost sight of it.

"It didn't come here with you. Galveston's got more thieves than cotton."

Most of his money was in the valise. He wondered what had become of the banknotes he'd had on him. His brain was clouding over. Johnson Six's face was losing definition.

"You want to keep that broth warm," Johnson Six told Mrs. Proudfoot. She got up and carried the bowl out. She hadn't spoken except to tell the man to lift Honey's head.

The edge of the curtaining sheet had caught on the stool. Johnson Six freed it so that it fell between them and the woman. He had on a shabby frock coat with worn velvet facing on the lapels. He reached inside it, brought out a leaf of paper folded into quarters, and opened it before Honey's eyes. Honey had to squint to read the bold print.

$500   REWARD $500

FOR DELIVERY OF THE FUGITIVE NEGRO

HONORÉ "HONEY" BOUTRILLE

TO ANY DEPUTIZED AUTHORITY

FOR THE

MURDER

OF WINTON CLAUDE SAINT-MAARTEN

IN NEW ORLEANS, LOUISIANA,

AUGUST 20, 1886.

A description in smaller print appeared below. The letters ran together into a black smear. Honey felt himself falling away. Johnson Six's face shrank into a closing hole at the end of a tunnel. The man's deep voice came to him through rising water. "Get on your feet quick, you renegade bastard. Coloreds got it bad enough in Galveston without you giving white folks a reason to come in and rip open the district. I'd put in for the five hunnert myself if I thought they wouldn't pay me off by sinking me in the harbor and claim it for theirselves. . . ."

There was more, but Honey was too far under to hear it.

When he opened his eyes again, it was dark. He could see the outline of the threadbare blanket that covered him, and a stain of light on the hanging sheet from a lantern or lamp burning on the other side. He heard crickets and the broken plaint of a steam whistle floating across water. The harbor was busier than the Mississippi.

He'd been listening for some time before he realized it wasn't a steam whistle. The sound rose and fell in a cooing rhythm, seeming now close, now far away. Someone was humming a lullaby, or rather a hymn, and it was one he remembered from long before New Orleans.

> *My days are gliding swiftly by,*
> *And I, a pilgrim stranger,*
> *Would not detain them as they fly?*
> *These hours of toil and danger.*

He peeled aside his blanket and then the sheet beneath, then had to rest before he tried to rise. He had on a man's cotton nightshirt, soft as feathers from many launderings. A very long time passed, during which he had to think about moving each limb before he could will himself to move it. The humming continued throughout, as rhythmic and as separate from thought as wind passing through a downspout. Finally he stood at the foot of his bed, feeling the cool, uneven planks beneath his bare feet, swaying with one hand supporting himself on the bedframe, and eased the curtain aside.

Another bed stood at a right angle to his, with less than three inches between them. The sheet alone had divided them.

Mrs. Natalie Proudfoot, wearing the butcher's apron she'd had on before, sat on the very edge of the thin mattress, humming and holding the hand of the man who lay beneath the covers. She'd removed the bandanna from her head; Honey was surprised to learn it had hidden a handsome growth of chestnut curls. The man in the bed seemed to be stretched out to an impossible length, but after staring at him for some time Honey decided that was an illusion created by the man's extreme emaciation. The bones of his skull appeared to be in the act of wearing through the dark skin stretched across them. It was a face of great age, yet it was topped by a cap of hair as black as a skillet. The man was no older than Mrs. Proudfoot, and possibly younger. The skin itself had an eerie bluish cast in the light of the lamp hissing on a nearby table. Honey had never seen it before, but he'd heard his aunts speak of such things when his mother lay dying and he had not been allowed near the bed. It was the glow of a human soul preparing to depart the body.

> *For O we stand on Jordan's strand,*
> *And soon we'll all pass over,*
> *And just before, the shining shore,*
> *We may almost discover.*

Honey replaced the curtain and crept back into bed. At the last second his strength gave out and he fell back against the ticking. The slats creaked. For a time after that he lay without breathing, listening for a noise that would tell him he'd betrayed himself to his hostess. No one approached the curtain. He let out his breath. He was sharply aware of the sensation that he'd trodden upon something private and sacred.

NINE

They had a reader out on him in Portland, with the new reward posted, but the description was old and general and hadn't resembled him closely when it was new, so Emerson ignored it. The liveryman who paid him two dollars for the tired old bay didn't look at him a second time; it was a logging town, filled with raw-boned Norwegians and Swedes. His was just one more fair face in the throng.

It was a rare bit of good luck, and he failed to turn it into a streak.

The town started out well. On the recommendation of a stranger who asked him for a match on a street corner, he pushed through a door in an unpromising city block of ramshackle construction into a room roughly the size of the entire Devil's Acre, with some seven hundred feet of glistening mahogany bar describing a square in the middle of the floor. Hundreds of stemmed glasses—brandy snifters, champagne flutes, and delicately etched cordials—suspended upside-down in racks twinkled above the heads of an army of bartenders, behind whom a bevy of fat naked women awaited the bidding in a Roman slave market on a canvas as big as a boxcar; the pink appeared to have been applied with a roller. There was a stage, a grand pipe organ worth thousands, and dozens of gaming tables covered in green baize. At that early hour there were perhaps a hundred customers present, drinking at the bar and clicking ivory balls around the billiards tables, but the immensity of the room made the place seem deserted.

A bartender in handlebars and a starched collar materialized before him the instant he hooked a heel on the brass rail. "Welcome to Erickson's. What's your poison, friend?"

"Whiskey."

"House brand O.K.? I could read you the inventory, but you'd die of thirst before I finished."

"Bar whiskey's just coal-oil and water."

"Not here, friend. August Erickson don't put his face on nothing but the best."

"Pour it out."

"Twenty-five cents."

"I never paid more than fifteen for a drink of whiskey in my life."

"You never been to Erickson's. Lunch is included." He waved a hand toward a counter by the wall. Trays of sausages, sliced bread, and smoked cheese shared the marble top with crocks stenciled KIDNEYS and MUSTARD.

Emerson smacked a quarter down on the bar. "If there's a trout swimming in my glass I'll blow a hole in your brainpan."

It turned out to be good sipping whiskey, poured from a bottle with a squarehead on the label in pince-nez and imperials. When Emerson signaled for a refill, the bartender beamed. "I do something with Jamaica rum and a lemon peel you'll want to write home about."

"What kind of place is this?"

"A workingman's club, Mr. Erickson calls it. He says there's no reason a man should top trees all day and then spend his wages drinking swill with the roaches. You see them booths up on the mezzanine?" He pointed at a row of velvet curtains near the pressed tin ceiling, with an oaken railing running past all the way around the room. "Finest girls in the Pacific Northwest. Not a crab in a carload, and Mr. Erickson won't take a cent from any of 'em. That's the kind of man he is, and the kind of place you're in."

"I reckon he must take in a thousand a week."

The bartender remained jovial, but his eyes were wise. "I wouldn't entertain any notions, friend. Hey, Jumbo!" He bent an arm in a beckoning gesture.

Something creaked near the door Emerson had entered through and a piece of the room's architecture separated itself from a splintback chair and trundled up to the bar. The man wore a yellow jersey with horizontal black stripes, stuffed into charcoal twill trousers, brogans on his huge feet. He stooped a little, probably from a lifetime of avoiding low ceilings, but even with his bullet head tilted forward he towered over Emerson by six inches. Leaning his great hard belly against the bar, he resembled nothing so much as a three-hundred-pound bumblebee.

"This here's Jumbo Reilly," the bartender said. "Jumbo, shake hands with our newest customer."

The hand that wrapped itself around his reminded Emerson of a giant manta ray he'd seen leap out of San Francisco Bay. The big man was careful not to exert pressure, but all the same Emerson would have had to plant a boot against the man's belly and pull to free himself.

"Jumbo keeps the peace in Erickson's."

"Pleased to make your acquaintance," Emerson said.

Jumbo rumbled something in response and let go. He returned

to his chair and sat with his big hands resting on his thighs.

"I never saw anything that big didn't sleep standing up," Emerson said.

"We've not had so much as a broken glass since he came on the job."

"Where can a fellow get in on a poker game?"

"You can have your pick after dark. Today's payday at the camps. Them treetoppers can't get rid of their folding fast enough to suit them."

Sunset was hours away. "There a hotel around here that don't come with ticks?"

"Cascade's just up the street. Service to every room and a bath on every floor. Care to take a bottle with you? Two dollars."

"Not before poker."

He hadn't bathed since leaving San Francisco. This was no great hardship—he'd passed the entire war without laying eyes on a bathtub—but if the odds went his way at the table he would want to celebrate with one of the girls on the mezzanine, and such women tended to charge more when a man smelled high. He soaked and scrubbed off six hundred miles of California and Oregon topsoil in scalding water, shaved his cheeks and chin and after thinking about it his moustache, to foil the readers, and wiped himself dry with heated towels brought by a plump pink attendant. He gave the man a cartwheel dollar for his trouble and snatched his first four hours of uninterrupted sleep in two weeks between sheets as white and crisp as powder snow. As much as he'd done it, he never had made his peace with sleeping out in the open; sharp rocks had a way of migrating back to where he'd laid out his bedroll after he'd removed them, and he had a terror of rattlesnakes.

He'd sent his things off with the attendant for laundering.

When they came back he gave the fellow another cartwheel and put on clean underwear, his good shirt, and the pair of striped trousers that had brought him a heart flush in the Devil's Acre against three diamonds and a king high straight. He cleaned the Colt's Paterson and Remington, checked the cartridges for mold and tarnish, and reloaded the cap-and-ball with fresh powder and wadding. He put on his hip-length canvas coat to conceal the ordnance. He had a strong feeling his luck was about to change for the better.

Evening shadows had just reached Erickson's Third Street entrance, but already the place had a couple of hundred customers. Loggers in their woolen shirts and canvas trousers stacked the bar three deep, elbowed one another at the free lunch counter, and crowded around the gaming tables, jabbering away in their various languages and gouging fresh holes in the hardwood floor with their calked boots. Obviously there was no dress code, which suited Emerson down to the ground: The tinhorns were easy to spot in their bowlers and high hats, making them easier to avoid. He never played his best when more than two of them were in a game, because he was too busy watching them for sleeve cards and accomplices among the spectators to concentrate on who had played what card. He'd collapsed one lung of the wrong tinhorn in Placerville on account of such confusion, and spoiled a fine run of luck for the trouble.

He got a different bartender this time, had him draw a beer—choosing a local brand for a nickel over imported German for a dime—and walked around with it, sipping only occasionally and scouting out the tables. At length he settled upon one where only one tinhorn was at work, a lavender-smelling gent who kept his bowler on the table and ran an ivory comb through his glistening curls between deals, and waited for a vacant chair. Whenever it came his turn to deal, the gent used the top half of the deck, and he wasn't sweating any more than seemed appropriate to a crowded room on a balmy September evening.

When a wild-haired logger went bust on a full house against another treetopper's four sixes, Emerson slid into his chair and bought fifty dollars in chips from the bank. He took two of the first three hands, lost the next four, twice to the logger who'd busted the full house, once to the tinhorn, and once to another logger, who cashed in and left, to be replaced by another gent in a printed vest and a silk hat. The presence of two tinhorns broke Emerson's concentration: He lost two more hands, cut his losses with a successful bluff on the third deal, then settled into the same pattern that had been dogging him since the train outside Sacramento. By midnight he'd lost the entire amount Christopher Buckley had staked him, minus what he'd spent on train fare and his room at the Cascade Hotel. He threw in his hand, scattering the chips on the table, damned the tinhorns as partner-playing, bottom-dealing, sleeve-carding sons of whores, and reached in his pocket for the New Model Remington. The curly-haired gent scooped a four-barreled Sharps pistol out of his bowler and thumbed back the hammer.

"It so happens my mother *was* a whore," he said, "so I'll let you have that deal. For the rest, take your hand out of your pocket and leave this establishment."

Emerson smiled, his best dumb-Swede grin, and laid his hand on the table empty. His other slid beneath the table toward the handle of the Colt's Paterson in his belt.

A shadow fell over him and a hand the size of a manta ray closed on his shoulder, crushing it. His entire arm went dead. He couldn't will his fingers to move. He couldn't even tell if they'd reached the weapon. A voice rumbled in his ear and he felt himself rising, as if some kind of pulley operation were lifting him from his chair. Jumbo Reilly maintained his grip on Emerson's shoulder, laying a loglike arm across both, and walked him gently toward the exit. The crowd parted to let them through and closed in behind them, following and calling out words of encouragement to the huge man. Most of them had not witnessed the altercation, but none seemed inclined to question the bouncer's judgment. He was as popular as Erickson's saloon.

Emerson's toes caught on the threshold. Reilly employed leverage and hurled him sprawling onto the boardwalk. The impact knocked out his wind and the rough planks scraped skin off the end of his nose. He remembered his injured ribs.

"Come back when you want to be decent," rumbled the big man. "This is Erickson's."

Emerson found another saloon on Second Street, much smaller and less hospitable than the palace he'd been thrown out of, with a surly bartender, unspeaking customers who gave him sullen looks, and fifteen-cent shots of whiskey that tasted like coal oil cut with river water. He drank up what change he had in his pockets and returned to Erickson's, this time entering from Burnside Street.

There was no sign of Jumbo Reilly, and Emerson didn't lose time trying to locate him. *When you decide to do a thing, best do it fast*, Bloody Bill had said. He positioned himself at the corner of the bar, with a view of all the entrances nearby, and drew the Paterson and the Remington simultaneously, covering the bartenders with the cartridge pistol and the customers with the cap-and-ball. He hadn't the faith in his left hand he had in his right, but no one present knew that, and it looked well.

"Hands up!" he bellowed. "I'm here for the money!"

The bartender he'd spoken to on his first visit didn't raise his hands. He was holding a shot glass in one hand and a bottle with August Erickson's face on the label in the other. He said, "You can't stick up this place. This is Erickson's!"

Emerson fired the Remington. The bottle flew apart and whiskey stained the man's white apron, with something darker spreading from behind. He dropped the glass and grabbed for the bar.

"This here's Emerson." Emerson swung the Remington on a bartender standing a few feet away with his hands as high as his shoulders. "Get the cash box."

The man stepped gingerly around his wounded workmate and bent to retrieve something from under the bar. Emerson cocked the Remington, but all the man came up with was a tin box with a skeleton lock.

Emerson heard a roar then: The sound of a mad buffalo or a locomotive charging out of a tunnel. Jumbo Reilly plowed a path through customers, sending them headlong to the floor and staggering for balance. Emerson waited until he had an unobstructed shot, then put two slugs into the yellow-and-black jersey, low and toward the middle. They smacked the big belly with a noise like a pickaxe biting into rock-hard earth. The big man retreated two steps, then resumed his charge, arms spread like a grizzly's. Emerson raised the pistol and fired at the great lowered head. A white part appeared in the close-cropped black hair. The head turned in the direction of the bullet. The top half of Jumbo's body turned just behind it and then one ankle crossed in front of the other and he fell his entire length. Emerson felt the wind. When the body struck the floor, a dozen glasses jumped out of the rack above the bar and fell with a shivery crash.

The crowd of customers surged forward for a better look at Jumbo defeated. Emerson fired the Paterson. The ball sped close to the remaining crystal, making it hum, and buried itself in the slave market painting, well above the nearest head. But the crowd shrank back. He lunged, snatched the tin box from the bartender's hands, and backed toward the door with the box under one arm, smoke uncoiling from the muzzles of both pistols. When his heel touched the threshold, he turned and pushed out through the flap door.

A number of horses were tied up at the rail in front of the building. He selected a saddled black, belted the Paterson, jerked loose the reins, and mounted, hugging the box to his sore ribs. Although the street was nearly empty of pedestrians, he juggled the box under his other arm, let loose a couple of shots wide to clear the way, and took off at the gallop.

He became lost the minute he hit the deep woods, but when he broke into a clearing he found the north star in time to keep the black from circling back toward town. When he'd put enough distance between himself and Portland, he stepped down and battered open the lock with a rock. The box was nearly filled with banknotes, more than enough to compensate him for the gear he'd left in the hotel. He stuffed them into all his pockets, mounted up, and kicked the black into a canter. It had taken that old whore Luck a long time to figure out who she belonged with, but he welcomed her back just the same.

TEN

I thought we'd civilized the frontier," said the fellow in the seat facing Torbert's. "When they completed the Trans-Continental, I believed it. When the Comanches surrendered, I was certain of it. When they shot Jesse James and arrested his brother, I knew it beyond doubt. Then I went out for a stroll in Denver and a brigand struck me over the head and relieved me of my watch and wallet."

The man had introduced himself as the chief western sales representative of the Aeromotor Windmill Company of Chicago. He was fatter even than Torbert and a bit younger, and wore a straw boater with a red silk band that matched his bow tie and the lining of his Norfolk jacket, which had a sporty belt in back. His wooden sample case stood on the floral carpet between their seats. It contained a working miniature windmill less than two feet high; he'd demonstrated it by opening the back and rotating the vanes with his fingers to turn the pulleys and belts. He'd said Torbert could tell where the salesman had been by keeping track of the windmills that dotted the plains between St. Louis and the Great Salt Lake. "Those Mormons are close with a dollar," he'd confided.

His discourse on civilization's dark state had followed the cry of a newsboy working the platform in Liberty, Texas, where the train had stopped to take on passengers and water before embarking upon the last leg of its journey to Houston. Jaundiced and gaunt, the boy's oversize cap and the canvas bag he was dragging appeared to be devouring him from either end.

"Murder and dismemberment on Prairie Street!" he called out. "Grisly details of wife-slaying and concealment! Only in the *Telegraph!*"

Torbert considered the newsboy's cry and his companion's comments on civilization.

"On the contrary, I consider it a good sign," Torbert told him. "In Chicago, a story like that wouldn't make the first column."

He pushed down his window and whistled. The boy hoisted his bag and hastened over to the coach, drawing a rolled newspaper and thrusting it up like a fencer's foil. Torbert grasped it and flipped a nickel at him. "No change back."

The gesture brought scant satisfaction. The boy caught the coin, squinted at it, and dropped it into a pocket already sagging with change. He let go of the newspaper. "Yes, sir. Thank you, sir." He drew another paper and ran off behind a passenger carrying a satchel, shouting of murder and dismemberment. "Only in the *Telegraph!*"

The lead item, headed GRUESOME DISCOVERY ON PRAIRIE STREET, was a dreary thing running half the column, beginning with a domestic argument involving household expenses and ending with a hatchet, a hacksaw, and a meek surrender to the authorities; change the names and it could have happened in any one of a dozen cities back East. It did nothing to lift Torbert's spirits. In New Orleans, he'd become excited when the story of a shooting aboard the steamboat *Rose of Sharon* made its way upriver, and had felt something of the old journalistic thrill when eyewitness descriptions of the Negro who had shot and killed a pilot named Crank matched those Torbert had obtained from acquaintances of Honey Boutrille, but despair had come soon after. The trail was cold, his quarry gone a week, and the locals' best guess was Boutrille had fled into Texas. The moment Torbert had wired Argus Fleet with this information, he'd known what the answering telegram would contain: train fare courtesy of the Jupiter Press and instructions to proceed immediately to the cotton capital of Houston.

He'd nearly thrown over the entire business there and then. A man could spend a season in New Orleans—quite a pleasant one, considering the surprising variety of diversions the seedy place had in stock—and convince himself he was still in the States, but the Sabine River was nothing if not the Rubicon. Green though southeast Texas was, hilly and fair, the leaves turning bright as Virginia and the women swishing down the aisle of the dining car in skirts and bonnets fresh from the better stores in Memphis, it was Texas all the same. The men in the smoker bellowed pleasantries at one another as if they were all hard of hearing and made no attempt to conceal the weapons they wore on their belts when they reached for their damn chewing tobacco. At the depot in Beaumont, he'd seen a wind-burned fellow in a pinch hat and handlebars with a star pinned to his vest sitting on a bench with one spurred boot resting on his knee. If the stench of horseshit and firewater wasn't precisely in the air, it was imminent. The windmill bore's remarks about the uncivilized frontier put paid to the thing. Ernest Valerian Torbert had come west.

He'd nearly thrown over the entire business, and he would have if he hadn't conceived a sudden picture of his janitor's closet in the Biederman Building, and his fingers on the keys of the Sholes and Glidden, smacking out descriptions of meat. He hadn't thought about his novel of African adventure since leaving Chicago, and wouldn't again. Fleet had been right about that. The only experiences worth setting down on paper were the ones you'd gone out and gotten yourself. If Texas was where they were, that's where you went. And the women in the dining cars *were* comely, by and large.

The rest of the local items in the *Telegraph* held even less promise than the parricide. He turned to the wire column, wondering if some news of Boutrille might have migrated with him to Texas. He was not surprised to find it hadn't. A Negro gunman was just a Negro, after all. The very fact that any mention of him had drifted as far east as the *Chicago Tribune* was evidence, if any were needed, that the wilderness was taming. When the Sioux and Cheyenne were still haring around and Billy the Kid's depredations were frightening pilgrims away from New Mexico Territory, someone like Boutrille would have had to mount an attempt on the president's life in order to make the five o'clock edition.

His eyes went to two paragraphs headed ROBBERY AND MURDER IN PORTLAND.

The *Portland Oregonian* reports the death of Anson "Art" Cowslip, bartender at Erickson's Cafe and Concert Hall, and serious injury of Patrick "Jumbo" Reilly, bouncer, during an armed robbery in that establishment on Sept. 22. Shots were fired by a man identified as "Twice" Emerson, the notorious Missouri guerrilla, sought for the attempted robbery of the Southern Pacific Railroad near Sacramento, Calif., on Aug. 30, killing

Cowslip and severely wounding Reilly. The amount of money stolen is unknown at this time.

August Erickson, proprietor of the cafe and concert hall, has posted a reward of $1,500 for the death or capture of Erickson, bringing the amount offered by authorities and citizens to $2,500.

Torbert used his pocket knife to slice out the article and placed the cutting in his wallet. A desperado worth two and a half thousand was hardly Cole Younger, but you never knew where a thing like that might lead; although God help the journalist who had to travel all the way to the end of the continent to write the story. He hoped Boutrille would commit some atrocity in Texas that would prod the officials into raising the ante on his head. Negro mankillers were just cheaper cuts and that was all there was to it.

He took a room in the Capitol, a stately, pecan tree–shaded building that had housed the Republic of Texas offices until the capital moved to Austin in 1839. The cottonwood structure was wonderfully ventilated, spacious and cool, but its creaks and groans reported every activity that took place beneath its roof to every creature that snared its shelter. When Torbert stretched out on the bed and closed his eyes, he thought he could sense Sam Houston's restless spirit pacing the halls and climbing and descending the stairs. The place suffered, too, from a distinct odor of mildew, an affliction of the city, where sunshine and rain succeeded each other so closely that one seemed always to be walking through steam.

He admitted a chambermaid to his room to turn down the bed. She was young and colored, small and very pretty, her skin a pleasing milk-chocolate against the white of her mobcap. He asked her where a Negro might stay while spending time in Houston.

"The bayou, sir," she said without hesitation. "Thass where the colored folks and the white lowlifes hang about."

"How does one get there?"

"Take the trolley out LaBranch till she stops. Then get out and walk. Was I you, sir, I wouldn't never do it. They's yellow fever there, cutthroat killers and worse."

"What's worse than killers and yellow fever?"

She spent some time popping the top sheet and smoothing out the creases. Then she straightened and turned his way. Looking down, she reached up a hand and turned up the edge of her cap. She had no ear on that side, only a comma-shaped hole in her head and blisters of scar-tissue all around.

Torbert's stomach did a slow turn. "Who did that?"

"My husband, sir. Well, we never took no vows, but I kept his house and done my wifely duties for two years. It was the third straight night of boiled chicken necks for supper that set him off. He said if I weren't going to listen when he said he was done sick of eating boiled chicken necks, there weren't no point in my having ears at all. He cut it off with a barlow knife and he was fixing to cut off the other as well, but he done passed out."

"From the blood?"

"No, sir. It was that bobtail he drunk. That man never could hold his liquor. Two shots and he was out like the cat."

"Was he colored?"

"Yes, sir, though he was high yeller and liked to pass. He picked the pockets of them that come in on the cotton boats, but he never give me none of it but what I could afford to buy chicken necks was all. That's why I ain't shamed I done what I done."

"You ran out on him?"

"No, sir. Well, I did, but before I done that I opened that man's trousers and cut off his phizzle with that barlow knife and threw 'em both in the bayou. He was dead to the world and never felt a thing."

"Lord Jesus."

"Yes, sir. The Lord Jesus done got me through six months in the women's workhouse. That's where I learned to make hospital corners." She jerked an elbow shyly in the direction of the bed she had just made.

"What happened to your husband?"

"Oh, they gaffed him out of the bayou while I was in the workhouse. I suppose he done picked the wrong pocket finally."

"Perhaps he took his own life. Under the circumstances, a man of his stamp might have thought he had little enough to live for."

"Ump. I never thought of it like that." She grinned suddenly, displaying a row of Homerically uneven teeth. "I reckon I got my own back and then some. I can still hear."

Torbert gave her a silver dollar. After she left, he extracted the Marston's loads and recharged all three barrels. He didn't trust the powder to maintain its integrity in that sultry climate. Then he went out.

H. BOUTRILLE—NEG. M., MIDDLE 20S, MED. HT., BUILD, HEAVY LIDS, CLEAN SHAVEN, GOOD TEETH. MAY BE WEAR-ING MADE-TO-ORDER SUIT, GRAY BOWLER. ARMED PISTOL, UNKNOWN CALIBER, MANUFACTURE. LAST SEEN S.S. ROSE OF SHARON, MISS. R., 8/21. BELIEVED GONE TEX.

Aboard the rocking trolley, he'd frowned over the notes in his pocket memorandum book, then licked the tip of his stumpy pencil and drawn a line through the part about the suit and bowler. The man wasn't fool enough to indulge his sartorial preferences on the outlaw trail, and there was no use drawing a picture in a potential source's mind that he couldn't match to a memory. It was an old axiom of his, unchallenged so far, that a man lost half his native intelligence the moment he became a witness.

The rows—no, clusters—nests?—of rooming houses, drinking establishments, and brothels bordering the pestiferous marshland appeared to have assembled themselves. Torbert could picture black, gaseous bubbles pushing up scrap lumber cast off from construction projects nearer the city's center, then subsiding, leaving behind blisters made of broken planks and curled tarpaper, into which Houston's forgotten citizens had crawled to escape clouds of mosquitoes and the stench of decomposing vegetation. But that wasn't the worst of it. As he approached a young Negro in overalls and a cloth cap slouched against a porch post—man and post leaning at opposite angles to describe an inverted V—the wind shifted, and he became aware that the bayou was also a repository of raw sewage. Outhouses built onto rude docks behind the structures evidently dumped straight into the standing pools of black water and quivering, yellow-green algae. The journalist, who had a horror of typhoid, pressed his handkerchief against his nose and mouth and drew out his memorandum book to read Boutrille's description aloud. The stink had wiped out the phrases he had assembled into a question.

Before he could finish, the insolent fellow pushed himself away from the post, snapped his cigarette stub into the rutted street, and snatched the book from Torbert's hand. Torbert could tell by the way he squinted at the writing that he was only pretending to read. He looked up with a sly expression in his nut-brown eyes.

"What he done?"

"I'm not a lawman. I just want to talk to him."

All trace of sentience vanished from the young face. It might have been a blank circle drawn atop a stick figure.

Torbert groped in a pocket and produced a silver dollar. When the man reached for it, he closed his hand into a fist.

The Negro turned and walked through the open door behind him, carrying the memorandum book, still open to the page bearing Boutrille's description.

Torbert waited. The book contained all the notes he'd made since leaving Chicago. He was about to go inside, one hand in his pocket gripping the Marston, when the man came out, followed by a companion.

The old Negro was the oldest man the journalist had ever seen, black or white. His wild shock of dirty white hair appeared never to have been cut or combed and the lower half of his face had collapsed upon itself. His ribs stuck out like the framework of a wrecked ship. He wore nothing but a pair of filthy trousers held up by a piece of rope. His eyes glittered at Torbert from far back in his skull.

"Lutie says try the Mill," the young man said.

"The mill?"

"The Cotton Mill, boss. How long you been in town?"

"I got in today. Is it a factory or a place to drink?"

The old man's mouth opened wide, revealing a wealth of pink gums, and a sound came out that Torbert could only describe as the smoke from the ashes of a laugh.

The young man snickered. "Since when ain't a factory a place to drink?"

Torbert took out the silver dollar, tossed it from one hand to the other, then back.

"It's a crib, boss," the young man said. "Fifteen minutes for fifty cents. Mother Jack keeps the time."

"Where is it?"

"Keep walking the way you come. You see Mother Jack sitting out front, big as Texas."

He held out the dollar. "Here's half an hour."

The young man took it. Before Torbert could retract his hand, a set of strong fingers grasped his wrist. "What about Lutie?"

He nodded. The man let go, fisting the dollar. Torbert found another silver in his pocket and thrust it toward the old man. The young man scooped it up.

"Half a hour would just about kill Lutie." He snickered again.

Torbert turned away.

"Boss."

The young Negro's tone was harsh. Torbert turned back, fingering the Marston in his pocket. The man was holding up his memorandum book. He took it and stepped down from the porch.

The Cotton Mill was a flatboat perched crossways on logs with a hand-painted sign hanging from the roof. A very large colored woman with skin faded almost white sat wedged between the arms of a rocking chair square in front of the door. She wore an old-fashioned powdered wig. With a white handkerchief sticking out of the bosom of her much-washed print dress, she bore a marked resemblance to George Washington.

Torbert mounted the deck and removed his hat. "Mother Jack?"

"I'm Jasmine Modine." She sat without rocking and looked at him without blinking. "Gentlemans dressed like you don't call me nothing else."

He apologized. "I'm looking for a colored man named Boutrille.

His friends call him Honey, but he might be traveling under a different name. He's in flight from New Orleans. I don't mean him any harm. I'm looking for conversation." He felt among the coins and paper in his pocket, made a quick assessment, and came up with a five-dollar note.

"That there'll buy you two and a half hours."

"I just want to talk."

"Price is the same. I don't axe what goes on back there. I just keeps the time." She tugged out the handkerchief and unwrapped a heavy steel watch from its folds. "I gots five ladieses on the premises. You want your pick?"

He rubbed the note between his fingers, listening to the rustle. "Can I have all five?"

ELEVEN

The *Denver Post*, Monday, September 27, 1886:

A CHARMING PRESTIDIGITATOR.

Patrons of the Alcazar Theatre were witness Saturday evening to a bravura performance of comedy and costume magic, courtesy of Miss Adabelle Forrest, the Quick-Change Queen of Atlantic City, and more lately the Phoenix of St. Louis. Unbowed by a conflagration in the St. Louis theatre earlier this month, which consumed the greater part of her dramatic wardrobe and properties, the statuesque trouper displayed the wide range of her talents in a French farcical offering entitled *Elle Dangereaux*. Chattering, sashaying, and bursting into bright chirrups of song, Miss Forrest quite deceived her hardened audience of miners, cattlemen, and entrepreneurs into believing she was not one, nor two, but *three* characters in a dizzying apologue of mistaken identity, outrageous prevarication, and comic acrobatics set against the backdrop of wicked Paris. She managed the latter by means of rapid changes of costume, many of them accomplished within the space of two or three seconds (using a screen, false columns, and odd items of furniture to mask her transformations), and some of them while singing and declaiming her lines of dialogue—although *monologue* would be a more grammatically appropriate term, since she performed quite alone. Not since Eugene Robert-Houdin bedazzled European audiences a generation ago with his feats of magic has a room filled with mature, sane citizens gazed upon so deft a demonstration of the art of prestidigitation, and we daresay Denver shall not again see its like until Mr. Casper Box's bombastic revue mounts a return engagement.

"What's pres—presti—" Lizzie's round face contorted, while her hands stood still. She could not sew and pronounce a word of more than three syllables simultaneously. One of the costumes for the French farce draped her knees, with a split seam. Adabelle had put on a pound or two since the start of the tour.

"Conjuring, child. Like a man producing a pigeon from his pocket. It's a compliment." Casper Box directed his attention to the theatrical advertisements. Eddie Foy was playing the Denver Hall. Forewarned was forearmed: Box owed him money.

Lizzie said, "I'd not half mind if they'd give *me* one while they're about it. I almost broke a finger getting her into that groom's kit."

"If they knew that, they'd know the trick. Be stoic, my girl: The better we do our work in the shadows, the darker they get." He lowered the newspaper and raised his voice. "Do you want to hear any of the others? The correspondent from the *Times* was equally enchanted, but he's an inferior poet. The *Rocky Mountain News* is reserved, and the *Commonwealth* wouldn't have you run out of town on a rail; but that's just the early edition."

"The swines. How many newspapers does Denver have?" Miss Adabelle Forrest's voice floated over the top of a dressmaker's screen with scenes from Chinese paganism embroidered on the panels. The theatrical manager and Miss Forrest's maid were seated in a pair of walnut chairs provided by the proprietor of the shop, a buxom old dragon even taller than the actress, with black-rimmed pince-nez and a French accent that Box suspected was as genuine as a wooden lightning rod. He could hear the two of them making noises of encouragement and exasperation behind the screen, struggling with hooks and buttons. Horses were shod with less fuss. He'd given up wondering many months ago why a woman who could metamorphose herself from a beggar to a queen in under five seconds required an hour to put on a single dress.

"I counted fifteen separate mastheads at the train station, including the *Pike's Peak Cattle Breeder*. I didn't buy a copy of that one. I ain't sure it was because I thought you wouldn't be in it or because I was afraid you would."

"You're a snake, Casper, and no kind of a gentleman. You ought to apply for a position with—what was the name of the filthy rag, the *Commoner*?"

"The *Commonwealth*, as if you didn't know. We'll get 'em with the full show, never fear. As to presenting myself for a job, not on your tintype. They'd never let me quit. The warden at the New York state pen said I did such a good job editing the prisoners' newspaper he considered holding on to me another year. He called me the Charles Anderson Dana of C Block. That's a damn sight better than your Robert-Houdin."

"For heaven's sake, keep your low past to yourself. It's bad enough you told me; though I noticed you waited until after I'd signed with you. The whole territory of Colorado doesn't have to know it as well."

"Colorado's a state, dear heart. Ten years now."

"I suppose that explains the cuspidor in my dressing room."

"You're lucky to have either. In Albany in '49 I had a nail."

"Last time you told that story it was a coat closet. Next time you'll say you had to change in the alley." Silk rustled; Box convinced himself it was linen. Replenishing his client's wardrobe already promised to cost him his first-class compartment on the train to San Francisco when they'd finished with the prairie. "Is there anything in any of those newspapers about your man Hawthorne?" Adabelle asked.

"Emerson. I've found nothing in a week. It's as if the Big Woods swallowed him up."

"How disappointing. No more savagery for you to paste in your scrapbook. Honestly, Casper. You're like a little boy playing at pirates."

"It beats anything I'm doing. The circuit's gotten stale. Even Shakespeare won't hold 'em today. The rubes have all seen Booth and Wilde and Jack Langrishe and by-God Sitting Bull. I couldn't compete with that one if I went out and dug up Ned Teach."

"And who is Ned Teach?"

"He was before even your time." He turned to the telegraph column. They'd dedicated the Statue of Liberty in New York Harbor. "I read yesterday where they're looking for a nigger gunsharp down in New Orleans. What do you think of that?"

"I'm sure I don't think anything of it. I haven't glanced at a front page since they shot Mr. Garfield."

"What was the point of that? He died anyway."

"Oh, damn! I mean, bother! I've run my hose. Lizzie?"

"I'll fix it, mum."

"You've missed some fun," Box said. "These days the criminal columns are a lot more entertaining than the theatrical advertisements. I'd heaps rather exhibit one of these desperadoes than Barnum's elephant, but even there they got the march on me. I hear the Chautauqua people are talking to Jesse James's brother Frank. I didn't even know he was out."

"Why not two desperadoes?" Adabelle said.

Lizzie laughed, a short bark ending in a squeal of pain. She'd stuck herself with the needle. "Bloody hell!"

"I think the word you want is *bother*," Box said. "Why not two quick-change artists? I'd run the same risk one way or the other. Incidentally, I signed us to another week at the Alcazar on our way back East. I told you they'd love you in Denver."

Adabelle swore again, this time in French. Her accent was superior to the dress shop proprietor's.

"Careful, dear. Our hostess might understand you."

"The Alcazar's a saloon! It took a bottle of Cashmere Bouquet to wash the cigar stink out of my hair."

"I wondered what kept you in the tub two hours. I thought you'd slit your wrists."

"Pray don't give me ideas. The stage is warped. All that spilled liquor."

"It didn't stop Lizzie from scooping up the coins they threw. That wouldn't happen at the Boston." He looked at his watch. "What's the time of arrival on this new get-up? You got a show in four hours." He was confident the delay had nothing to do with attraction between the two women on the other side of the screen. Adabelle worshipped youth, and the dragon had appeared more interested in Lizzie.

His featured performer stepped from behind the screen. She

was corseted into an elongated figure-eight, with yards of white material wound around her from mid-bosom to the floor and forming a pool around her feet. Yards more hung from her arms in a drapery effect and a gold chain encircled her negligible waist. She appeared to be emerging from a shimmering white fog.

"Do you adore it?" she said. "Christine Nilsson wore the exact thing in *Lohengrin*."

Box said, "She didn't stretch it out much."

The dress shop owner presented herself. Her large, mannish hands were folded under her mounded breasts. "It takes your breath away!"

"I don't doubt it for a second. She's got on more whalebone than Jonah."

"It was hardly necessary. The mademoiselle has the figure of a dryad."

Lizzie took her pricked finger out of her mouth. "Where'd she put it all?"

"It's Lyons silk," Adabelle said. "From a bolt originally set aside for the Empress Eugenie."

Box said, "Second hand, eh? What's the damage?"

"Forty dollars," said the proprietor. "It's a one-of-a-kind copy."

"It's also half what I budgeted for the first act. Not to mention it don't go with any of the characters she plays. And if it did, she couldn't get into it and back out during the whole fifteen-minute interval. She's the Quick-Change Queen, not the Slow-Shuck Kid."

Adabelle shook her head, laughing the Chinese-bell titter she'd developed for *The Third Spouse*. Casper Box suffered from the small man's sensitivity regarding laughter at his expense. He felt his face growing as black as the shellac in his hair.

"It isn't for the *stage*, you foolish man!" she said. "It's for my first reception in San Francisco."

"Your first reception?"

"There are bound to be others. Madame LaFrond has agreed to provide me with an ensemble for each one."

He folded his newspaper and stood. His voice was his most impressive feature and he tightened the clamps in respect for the plaster. Even so, it made the old dragon jump.

"You ain't in San Francisco. You got twelve more performances to do in Denver and a trunkful of material you can't use till you got costumes. I didn't pay for them songs and sketches to leave them laying around in mothballs like my grandpappy's red flannels. Lizzie, you go back there with Miss Forrest and help her out of that contraption. Use a pry bar if that's what it takes. By God, I bet Cody never had this trouble with Sitting Bull."

Adabelle Forrest, who avoided the sun and prided herself upon her white complexion, paled to the point of transparency. She turned and fled behind the screen, followed closely by the maid, still carrying the *Elle Dangereaux* dress and her sewing basket. From the other side came the furious rustle of fabric and a fluent string of Gallic blasphemies. Box figured she must have studied at the feet of a master-sergeant in Napoleon's infantry.

Madame LaFrond took a deep breath. He turned on her and she retreated into a back room.

Alone in the front of the shop, Casper Box felt himself growing calmer by the minute. He took a pinch of snuff and blew his nose into his handkerchief. That cleared his head, and with the clarity came a small smile.

"Why *not* two desperadoes?" he said aloud.

"*Comment?*" Adabelle sounded as calm as he. Among the rare things the actress and her manager had in common were a short fuse and a shallow blast. "You said something?"

"I said take your time, dear. You're still my only asset."

PART FOUR

PILGRIM STRANGERS

TWELVE

My days are gliding swiftly by,
And I, a pilgrim stranger,
Would not detain them as they fly?
These hours of toil . . .

The low voice trailed off. Silence then, or as much as ever existed in a place of crickets and river traffic and green timbers shrinking and settling with half-human groans. Honey lay for several more minutes, waiting for the song to continue. When he was sure it would not, he rose again.

He was steadier now. The fever was behind him and he'd drawn strength from the broth he'd been fed. He coughed, an alarming rattling sound, lung-hollow, and placed his fist against his mouth to deaden the noise. The cold floor chilled the soles of his feet and a draft found its way up under his nightshirt. He pulled aside the sheet that curtained his cot from the rest of the shack.

It was just that: a shack built, like the ones he'd known in New Orleans and seen in Houston, from scraps and sections of boats no longer capable of floating; needles of moonlight shone through spaces in the siding. However, some attempt had been made to turn it into a home, and it was more successful than in many of the hovels where he'd spent the nightmare of his adolescence. Lithographs of Versailles, the English countryside, and the holy City of Rome, razored out of illustrated newspapers and mounted in cheap plaster frames, hung on the walls at measured intervals, a painted vase containing a spray of wildflowers stood beside the lamp burning on a table worn smooth and white from many scrubbings, a braided rug with much of its pattern worn away lay on the plank floor. There was a stove with a warming oven, above which hung copper-bottomed pots and pans from an iron felloe suspended from the roof by chains like a chandelier. Chopped wood and kindling filled a Pears' Soap crate, and a pop from inside the stove told him it was used to warm the room as well as cook. A number of blue china plates lined a shelf, serving as decoration between meals.

The wasted figure still lay on the cot that elled off from the foot of Honey's, his face skull-like in the lamplight, aglow with a spirit undecided whether to desert the shelter of its body. Natalie Proudfoot had left her perch on the edge of the mattress for a Morris chair with one broken leg propped on a brick. She lay half-reclined in her butcher's apron, her chestnut curls tied up again in the faded bandanna and her arms resting on the arms of the chair. She snored softly.

A fresh draft brightened the flame in the lamp, chilling Honey. He coughed again into his fist, then went over and laid a tentative hand on the side of the stove. It felt warm, not hot. He found the lifter and removed a lid. The interior contained nothing more than a length of glowing ash in the shape of a chunk of wood. He added two fresh chunks from the crate, unhooked a poker from the felloe, and used it to stir the ashes into a flame. When he was sure the wood had caught, he replaced the lid. It clanked.

"If you're fixing to kill me in my sleep, I'd take it a kindness if you'd do Clyde next. He gots nobody to look after him but me."

Honey turned. The woman's eyes were open, but other than that she hadn't moved, even to turn her head his way. But he knew she could see him through the corner of her eye. She'd startled him, and he realized suddenly he was holding the poker as if it were a weapon. He hung it back up.

"I don't want to kill anybody," he said. "I was feeding the stove."

"It comes to the same thing. I can't leave Clyde alone long enough to go chop wood. The batch he done chopped before he took sick's about out, and winter's on its way. I'd as lief you hit us both with that poker as freeze to death in our sleep."

"Is Clyde your husband?"

"As good as. We didn't take no vows. He wanted to, but that didn't work out so good for me last time, so I said let's wait and see. That there was fifteen years ago come spring. He won't see spring, so I'm calling it fifteen and who's to stop me. I didn't give you that long when they brung you here. I reckon that was Johnson Six's Old Bone-Face giving us all the horse laugh." She spoke in the same tone she sang in, without inflection.

"What's wrong with him?"

"He's all bust up inside. He taken him a fall off the warehouse stairs, I don't rightly know from how far up. I found him all jumbled up at the bottom."

"Did he work there?"

"He was the night watchman. Mr. Whordle done hired him and me along with him, to keep the place orderly. One wage, two jobs. Keeps down the price of cotton."

"That ain't fair." More and more he found himself speaking at the level of most of his own kind. They'd make him a proper nigger before this was over. *Over* meaning when he'd paid for Saint-Maarten with his neck.

"It's fair as fair, I reckon. We don't pay rent. Though I expect to be on the street soon enough. I seen a seagull roosting on the roof yesterday."

"That's just superstition."

She said nothing.

"Still, I guess Mr. Whordle's better than some," Honey said, to fill the silence. "Some white folks'd turn you both out when Clyde stopped working."

"It be three weeks come tomorrow, and he ain't found out yet. Nobody goes to the warehouse after dark, and as long as I sweeps up and checks the traps, nobody gots to notice Clyde ain't been around. Nobody steals cotton in Galveston. Be like stealing tobaccy in Kaintuck. All's Clyde ever done was walk the floor and club rats."

"Someone's bound to take notice sometime."

"They will when I buries Clyde. I been putting aside a nickel a week. Reverend Bottles'll read over him for a dollar and Johnson Six says he'll build him a box for nothing. It don't cost to bury him in potter's. I don't care there's no marker, but I wants God in on the deal. Clyde ain't no heathen."

"You've got enough on your mind without having a stranger to look after."

"It's 'cause of Clyde you're here. If he could talk, he'd tell me to do what I done. He ain't spoke nor opened his eyes since the fall."

"I can pay."

She laughed quietly, and he wished she hadn't. The sound was more mournful than her song.

"Mister, I done been through your pockets. Pockets is all you got. If you done had a dime in any of 'em, somebody else done got it now."

He nodded. He'd expected no less since learning his valise had been stolen. "I wonder they left me my Bulldog."

"I reckon they didn't want to take the trouble to bust your fingers. You had a hold on it like Jacob's ladder." Her stomach rumbled; he thought at first a flatboat had run into a piling. "There's broth on the stove yet. It ought to be hot soon. I thank you kindly for feeding the stove."

"I'll dish you up a bowl."

"I'll dish you. You best get back in bed. I'll not pay Bottles to read over you. I don't care what Clyde might say. I ain't the Christian he is and that's all there is to that."

He started to argue, but he was getting hollow-headed again. He started coughing and couldn't stop. His hand filled with fluid. Dimly he was aware that she'd left the chair and had her arm around him. He leaned against her and that was all he remembered until he woke up with her hand behind his head and the taste of fish and herbs on his tongue.

Honey paused in the midst of sawing through a stunted cottonwood to fill his lungs. Although he was growing stronger by the day, he was still short of breath, and sat on the stump of a tree he'd cut down that morning to gather his strength. His palms stung less and less; he was fascinated by, and a little proud of, the hard, shiny tissue that had begun to form on the heels and in the creases of his fingers. He had always been vain of his hands. The piano-playing in the House of Rest for Weary Boatmen had mainly been an excuse to admire his manicure. Now the nails were thick and uneven and there was black dirt in the furrowed skin of his knuckles that Natalie Proudfoot's tallow soap could not reach.

He was wearing a pair of overalls and an old flannel shirt that belonged to Clyde Proudfoot. Clyde was taller by several inches and he wore the sleeves rolled and the cuffs turned up. He felt a proper plantation slave.

"Cut off any fingers yet? I ain't certain you city coloreds know when to stop sawing."

He looked up at Johnson Six's approach. The former medical orderly was a big man, and had probably been chosen for the work for his ability to heave two hundred inert pounds onto a table and hold them down while the surgeon sawed through muscle and bone. He wore a dirty linen duster over an old suit, its ragged hem snapping about his heels, and carried a scuffed Gladstone bag with a hunk of rope tied in place of its missing handle. The bag contained medical instruments, half worn-out and probably rescued from trash heaps, bottles of patent medicine, and a battered U.S. Army canteen filled with fusel oil, which he insisted upon describing as gin. Honey had been obliged to partake of it as part of his recovery. It was his theory that the American temperance movement had begun at Johnson Six's canteen.

"I wasn't born wearing a monocle," Honey said. "You're a black snob."

"Well, that's one name I never been called." He placed a foot against the tree Honey had been cutting and pushed. It crackled and heeled over. "This here cottonwood's holier'n Saint Paul. It burns fast. Take a month with no Sundays to chop enough to last the winter, and then you need the Whordle and Grace warehouse to store it."

"There's scrub oak down by the harbor, but I don't know who owns it. I don't want to get shot over kindling."

"Folks been shot for less."

That was bait, and Honey didn't take it. They looked out at the harbor a while, at the cobalt water and the ships moored at the long pier. The gray box of the cotton warehouse stood at their backs, with the Proudfoot shack crouched in its shadow.

"This ain't the peak," Johnson Six said. "Come October, you won't hardly see the water for the ships, and you can count them foreign flags till you clean run out of numbers."

"I'm looking forward to it. I like to see money being made."

"You best see it someplace else."

Honey reached down, scooped up a handful of dirt, and rubbed it between his palms. It took the burning out of his hands and seasoned the calluses. "I'll leave when I've paid my debt."

"You can pay it by hopping aboard one of them steamers and shipping out with the boll weevils. Galveston finds out Mrs. Proudfoot's harboring a nigger killed a white man, they'll burn down the shack around her and Clyde and dangle you from one of them topmasts. I don't care about you, though it's a waste of some damn fine doctoring, but I cares about Natalie and what's left of Clyde. They're my oldest friends on the island. Breaking in new ones takes time I ain't got."

"No one needs to know I'm here."

"They does if somebody tells 'em." Johnson Six opened his bag and took out Honey's Bulldog.

"I wondered what became of that."

"I gots it figured finally. Rewards ain't paid till the goods is delivered, and being colored, I'd just get cheated or strung up right along with you. That don't mean I can't sell you to a white man for a hunnert. Cash and carry, we makes the trade, he turns you in for a profit. A hunnert would bury Clyde, marker and all, and get Natalie started somewheres else."

Honey studied the muzzle. It looked bigger when it was pointed at him. "What did Natalie say?"

"I ain't told her. She's a Christian woman, believes in the blood of the lamb. I done washed my hands in blood more times than I can recollect. Soap's better. Now, you gets down on your stomach. I gots me a roll of bandages in this bag and I'm going to use it to tie you up."

Honey started to rise.

"Down, I said! Knees first!" Johnson Six thrust the pistol closer. Honey threw his handful of dirt in the big man's face. Johnson Six sputtered and reached a hand up to clear his eyes. Honey grasped the Bulldog's barrel and twisted it out of his grip. At the same time he hooked an ankle behind one of the former orderly's legs and pulled it out from under him. He fell into a sitting position. When he blinked the dirt out of his eyes, the first thing he saw was the pistol pointed at his face.

"They were right not to put a gun in your hand at Petersburg," Honey said.

Johnson Six laid his hands in his lap. "Go ahead and do 'er. I done fired my round."

"You didn't. You should have. They might not pay as much for me dead, but they'd pay something. A pistol's for killing, not for dandling people around on a string."

"I ain't no killer. You was right about why they made me a orderly. I couldn't even do a proper job with a bayonet on a straw dummy, not even was I to think it was that devil's whelp of a slaver sold my Ginnie down the river. You just go ahead and do what you gots to." He closed his eyes.

"I ought to. You wanted to sell me to a white man. In my eyes you're just another slaver."

Johnson Six opened his eyes. "Don't you kill me on that lie. What I was fixing to do I was fixing to do for Natalie."

"You don't want to hide behind a woman's skirts with me. I've got a history in that regard."

"Mr. Tim Grace, he's coming down from Austin soon. His

partner Whordle, he lives right here in Galveston and he never goes to the warehouse, but Grace is an inspecting son of a bitch. When he finds out Clyde ain't been on the job since August, he'll dump him out of that cot into the street and Natalie with him."

"That's too thin." But he lowered the hammer.

"It's thin. It ain't as thin as her chances without that reward."

"Get up."

"What for? I just got farther to fall."

"Stand up, damn you."

Johnson Six got to his feet. His eyes never left Honey. When he was upright, Honey stuck the Bulldog under his belt and returned to his stump. He was feeling hollow-headed again. His strength came and went. "What sort of man is Grace?"

"What kind of question's that? He's white."

"There's white and white. What sort of white is he?"

"I can't rightly say. I never laid eyes on him."

"You said he's an inspecting son of a bitch. How many times has he been to Galveston?"

"That's just what I heard. He's got him partnerships all over Texas: Cotton's just one. There's cattle and sugar beets and I don't know what-all. I can't rightly say when's the last time he was here. Never, maybe."

Honey watched a wagonload of cotton being towed by a four-horse team toward the pier. The bales looked like big square pillows with down spilling out each end.

"Do you mean to tell me he's never even *seen* Clyde Proudfoot?" he asked.

THIRTEEN

H e'd had his fill of conductors and their long memories, and so
when the black bottomed out north of Salem, he hiked to the
U.P. tracks and caught a freight on a climbing curve. When a load of
stoves shifted and almost pushed him off the flatcar on a trestle
overlooking a two-hundred-foot gorge, he decamped to a boxcar,
was spotted by a brakeman, and spent the rest of the way into Burns
dodging a railroad dick with a rage against tramps.

In Burns he rounded a corner and came face to face with himself on the wall of the depot.

Emerson had never seen the photograph before and had
nearly forgotten the occasion of its manufacture. It was in Mexico,
Missouri, in September 1864. A bunch of the boys had stopped
there to cut the bear loose after the good doings in Centralia,
where they'd stopped a Union troop train and made good Yankees
out of about twenty passengers and then scattered a superior force
of federal cavalry by swinging around and charging their pursuers.
Coming upon a photographer's studio on their way between
saloons, eight guerrillas, Emerson included, decided to go in and
commemorate the event by having their likenesses struck. The lit-

tle Jayhawker who squeezed the bulb could barely hold up his hod full of powder without shaking most of it off, and when it went up with a white flare and a cloud of smoke, he'd squealed and ducked behind a chair to avoid the pistols that came out in startled response.

A month later, Bloody Bill was dead, shot full of holes by federals and beheaded, the guerrillas split up, and Emerson never heard if anyone went back to claim the photograph. *Someone* had, however; and it had made its way by a route Emerson could not guess at onto a stiff sheet of white posterboard along with his name and description and $2,500 REWARD in ink so black and bold it smudged when you gave it a hard look.

There they were, boys forever, with scarcely the years to raise a decent set of whiskers between them, but old in the eyes, gaunt as grass-fed ponies, wearing their kepis and campaign hats and frilly guerrilla shirts and showing off their ordnance; three of them sitting in ordinary parlor chairs, the rest standing, leaning on their rifles or with their hands resting on the backs of the chairs. The background was a painting of Greek ruins, which Thrailkill had chosen from a selection of canvas sheets that pulled down from rollers like windowshades, because it reminded him of Lawrence, Kansas, after the raid. Four were dead, Emerson knew, killed at Sugar Creek and Wakefield's barn and one or two other places he hadn't stopped long enough to note the name, because by then the whole shebang was falling apart and they'd all abandoned states' rights to fight for their own skins, and he couldn't swear but that the continued border fighting after the war hadn't done for the rest. He was the only one he knew about for sure, and there he was, standing second from the left next to Johnny McIlvaine, skinny enough to vanish from the frame if he'd just turned sideways when the shutter tripped, with his hair to his shoulders and a billy goat beard. Some helpful soul had drawn a white circle around his head, to assist the bounty killers in their hunt.

He'd filled out considerable since then, chopped off the long locks and scraped his chin, but apart from that and twenty years of living and everything that came with it, he supposed someone could identify him from the photograph, if it was fresh in his mind and he looked Emerson in the eyes. He swore softly. He'd intended stopping a while, taking a room with clean sheets every day and a fresh whore every night. Now he turned around and went to the window and bought a ticket on the 4:15 to Boise. He pulled his hat low and kept his chin down, but the clerk never looked up from under his green eyeshade. That meant he'd die a clerk, but probably not before his season.

Emerson was a stranger, at least, to this conductor, who gave him no more than a passing glance when he punched his ticket. His hand of good luck was holding, but he didn't try to draw to it. Throughout the day-long ride he stayed aboard, not alighting at any of the stops to stretch his legs, and he limited his trips to the toilet, just in case he might encounter someone in the aisle who had seen the poster and couldn't get the young hellion's face off his mind. He dozed part of the time and spent the rest looking out at farm country, flatter than a steer's phizzle.

The regular train stops were closed to him as far as finding a place to pull off his boots. The Pinkertons who distributed posters and leaflets would have plastered them all with Emerson's features, nailing them up in stations and telegraph offices and leaving stacks behind for sheriffs and town marshals to memorize and hand out. Fortunately, the detectives were lazy sons of bitches. They seldom ventured farther than a trolley ride from the hotels where they charged their rooms and meals and bottles of whiskey (recorded in the ledger books as "informers' fees") to the agency in Chicago, leaving those towns inaccessible except by horse and foot ignorant of the badmen in their orbit. A fugitive wanting to enjoy the same luxuries had only to show more initiative.

Caldwell was the last stop before Boise. The lantern hanging under the depot roof was the only one burning within sight of the train. No one got on or off, and the train paused only five minutes before lurching into motion. Emerson climbed out of his seat, opened the door, and hopped off before it reached five miles per hour. In the shadows on the platform he faced the train and waited, one hand in the pocket containing the Remington, to see if anyone hastened to follow. The locomotive picked up speed and the caboose shot off into darkness, leaving him alone in sleeping Caldwell.

The ticket window was shut. A chalkboard mounted beside it listed the times and destinations of tomorrow's trains and, at the bottom, the noon departure of the stage to Idaho City.

Some ambitious traveler had left a creased copy of the *Denver Times* on the slat bench facing the tracks. He sat down and attempted to read it, but the lantern's wick needed trimming and he could only make out the advertisements for augers, nose drops, racing saddles, and touring entertainment. Denver looked livesome, and was probably outside the range of Pinkertons from California and Oregon. When he tried to interest himself in the densely printed columns, however, the print ran together. He tossed the newspaper aside and went to sleep stretched out on the bench, with his canvas coat bunched up under his head and one hand beneath it gripping the Remington.

He shared the stagecoach with a pale, pock-marked woman who never opened her mouth and a bearded young prospector who never shut his. The woman was traveling alone and trying to make herself small in her corner, and the prospector had failed to bully a favorable report from the Caldwell assayer he'd gone to see to contradict the one he'd visited in Idaho City. He was angrier at himself, he claimed, for not going on to Boise and getting a third opinion, but he didn't trust his partner enough to leave him alone for more than two days. He didn't trust Emerson either, judging by the way he kept the worn satchel containing his samples pinned tightly between his hip and the side of the coach with his arm resting on top of it. Emerson couldn't disagree with that decision—he hadn't washed or shaved since Portland, and his socks made grating sounds against the inside of his boots when he wriggled his toes—but he'd awakened on the bench with a stiff neck and the fellow's black mood was contagious. When he told him to shut the hell up or he'd open his gut and stop up the hole with his samples, the man turned gray under his sunburn and the woman squeaked and tried to curl up into the side-panel.

Idaho City was bigger than expected, a gold town still going flat-out twenty years after first yellow. All the buildings were sided and whitewashed and the place had a Catholic church and a Masonic hall and forty saloons if it had one, all lined up side by side like whores' drawers on washday, with four breweries to wet the wait between whiskeys. There were hotels, theaters, and the territorial jail. This last was built solidly of logs inside a formidable-looking stockade and had various outbuildings, one of them containing a gallows, if the sizeable cemetery on the adjoining lot was any indication. Emerson had spent enough time behind bars to have formed emphatic opinions about such places. They held no terror: Anything one man can build, another can break, was his philosophy. He'd paroled himself that way three times, if the last one counted; that had been a case of bribery.

Towns with hair on them like Idaho City were always hot on strong jails and cold on paying good men to keep them. The more money they invested in walls and cages, the less it cost to pay someone to open the door. Yes, sir, he liked a place with a wide choice of saloons and a good stout jail.

The coach stopped in front of the Wells Fargo office, another substantial piece of construction with bars in the windows and a reinforced-iron door with a porthole to fire out of in time of siege. He liked the look of that, too. You didn't design them that way to protect a little trickle of dust on a good day. The driver and shotgun guard swung down the strongbox and carried it inside while the passengers were waiting for their bags to be unloaded. Idaho City kept getting better and better.

The clerk behind the desk at the Bannock Hotel—pink, fleshy, and stunk up with lavender water and hair slickum—pursed his lips at Emerson's appearance, then smoothed them out when he stripped the India rubber band off a stack of banknotes and laid enough of them on the marble top to pay for a week in a room on a floor with a bath. On the way there from the Wells Fargo office he'd bought some things at the best-stocked emporium he'd seen since San Francisco, and after he'd soaked off the crust of travel, he untied the string on the bundle and dressed from the skin out in scratchy new flannels, striped trousers, a calico shirt, a hip-length corduroy coat, and fresh socks. His old boots looked even more scuffed and rundown against the finery, but they'd have to do until he could have a new pair made. He'd had his life's portion of corns and blisters during the war, thanks to ready-mades and footwear reclaimed from dead Yankees, and insisted on proper fittings.

He transferred his money to his new clothes and left his old things in a sodden pile on the floor to be disposed of by the attendant, who took his hat away for brushing, promising to return it to him at the Capitol Barbershop, which he recommended as the best in town. Emerson gave him an extra cartwheel for the information and presented himself there for his first haircut in three months and his first professional shave since before the tree fell the wrong way at Sacramento. It was a toney place with a striped pole, painted glass windows, and five thronelike Union Metallic chairs surrounded by an acre of white porcelain, with recent numbers of *The Idaho Statesman* and *Frank Leslie's Illustrated Newspaper* piled on a table to occupy the time of those awaiting a vacancy. There was no waiting, and just to show his streak was holding, he drew a nontalker of a barber who let him doze while he applied his hot towel and glided a path through the stubble and re-established the shape of his head with shears and a pair of clippers. The fellow was just applying bay rum when the hotel attendant arrived with Emerson's hat, brushed and blocked and reeking of naptha where the grime had been removed from the leather sweatband. The barber had trimmed his moustache and waxed the tips, and as Emerson stood in front of the mirror trying a new angle with the hat to keep it from sliding down to his ears, he grinned at the respectable-looking gent in the glass. No one would mistake him for the rowdy in the twenty-two-year-old picture on the shinplaster, even if one managed to make its way there from Caldwell or Boise.

He bought a five-dollar whore at a parlor place across the street from the shop, a pretty little Chinese girl who let him smack her around for an extra dollar, but it wasn't the same as killing a tong, so he stopped after splitting her lip and raising a welt on one cheek. Even so the proprietor raised hell when he saw her and Emerson had to kick the fat son of a bitch in the cojones when he demanded twenty dollars as compensation while the girl went off the line to heal. The altercation and its satisfying conclusion raised Emerson's spirits and he went off to find a game.

After rejecting a number of saloons for various reasons—too many tinhorns in one, too many exits in another, which reminded him of Erickson's in Portland and his bad luck at its table, a bouncer poised on a high stool at a third with a shotgun cradled ostentatiously in his lap—he selected one on a corner whose liveliest table provided a view of both exits. It had a moose head the size of a tinder mounted on one wall with a group of bulletholes centered square between its glass eyes and a skinny mick sawing away at a fiddle on a square platform rigged by pulleys and lanyards to the ceiling, where he could haul himself up out of harm's way in case the customers got tired of shooting at the moose and switched targets. There were no tinhorns in evidence, just a group of sober-faced miners betting sacks of dust, but Emerson's good streak had not yet extended itself to cards; he lost twenty dollars on a bluff he should have seen through like a corn crib, reclaimed all but four on the next two hands, then dropped fifty trying to bluff without even a pair. He gave up his seat to another miner and called the bartender a lazy nigger for delivering his whiskey by way of the Overland. The bartender, bald, with old scars on his scalp and a Scots brogue as thick as turd stew, poured his shot and told him in a friendly voice that if he knew Emerson's mother was white he'd never have climbed between her legs. Emerson met his gaze, saw another old guerrilla looking back at him, and paid for the drink without another word.

"You don't want to mix it up with Teague," said the man standing next to him. "He's got him a Colt's Thunderer under his apron and belly guns in both pockets and a shotgun cane when he goes off shift. If he was to fall into the Snake, he'd drown like a cat."

Emerson looked at the fellow: a lunger for certain, hollow-chested with broken splints for limbs, in a mothy town coat and a

Mormon hat with matches stuck in the band. He plucked out one, struck a flame off his thumbnail, and relit the shortest cheroot Emerson had ever seen between the lips of a man with a bush moustache. A distinct stench of scorched hair joined the noxious smoke when he got it going. His face was mealy from what must have been a nearly fatal encounter with pox. His eyes were set deep in his skull like an old man's, and they themselves were aged; yet he guessed the man to be not much more than thirty. He was no guerrilla, but that was more the fault of his date of birth than inclination. The ability to recognize one of his own was one of the reasons Emerson was still above ground.

"I'd thank you for the information if I'd only asked you for it, you nosy son of a bitch," Emerson said.

Amber teeth showed behind the man's moustache. "Just making conversation, friend. Also I'm concerned for Teague's immortal soul. One more notch in his belt and he'll burn till Judgment."

"Preaching man, are you? I'm clean out of coppers."

"I know. I seen you play." The man blew smoke, along with a spark from his moustache. "My old dad tried cracking my skull to get some Bible inside it. Come my last collection day I started at the front of the meeting house and went right on out the back with the plate. I don't feature to sit on the right hand of the Lamb myself, but, Teague, he can be saved."

"Then save him and be damned." He scowled at his reflection in the advertising mirror behind the bar. His respectable looks mocked him now. He still had most of his money, but he felt as if he'd squandered his luck.

"Teddy White's the name. My old dad liked to call himself the Right Reverend White, to prove he was sober. I'm thinking your name's Emerson."

Emerson made himself lift his glass and drink. He didn't look at the man or even his reflection. White was standing at his left, where he would see if Emerson reached for the Remington. He eased his other hand under his coat, feeling for the Paterson's handle.

"Don't you think if I know what Teague's got under his apron I'd know about that ball-and-percussion pistol in your belt? Look here."

He looked, despite himself. The squat barrel of what appeared to be a Colt's Cloverleaf poked out of White's fist under the lip of the bar. It was pointed at Emerson's belly. He exhaled and laid his right hand on the bar.

"Mister, you got me tangled with someone else. My name's Gideon."

"You read that off a label back of the bar. You ought to be better prepared, with your picture tacked up all over the Boise Basin. I'm not a bounty man, if that's what you're thinking. I couldn't risk it. There's paper out on me, too."

"If you're looking to stick someone up, you should of picked the hardrock son of a bitch that busted my bluff ten minutes ago."

White laughed, then coughed, showering sparks from his cheroot and smoldering moustache. The stub fell from his mouth at the end of a long thread of spittle. His eyes lost focus and he pressed the back of his free hand against his lips until the spasm passed. Meanwhile the pistol never moved.

A glass stood in front of him, half-filled with beer. He swept it up, drained it in a long draught, and set it down noiselessly. He had steady hands, slim and pale, without blemishes. They didn't seem to belong to the owner of the ravaged face.

"Swallowed smoke," he said. "I don't stick up *people*. Why

don't you dig into that hole money from Portland and buy us a bottle? There's a room in back with curtains where we can palaver."

"What about?"

"About sticking up a stagecoach. That's where the money is in this territory. I ought to know. I'm Teddy White, and I stuck up so many I drove Wells Fargo out of business here for six months."

FOURTEEN

H oney hated the smell of cotton.
        He supposed the aversion went back to when he'd helped
chop it, although he'd been too little to remember. In any case, he'd
been living with it almost constantly since he was forced to leave
New Orleans, sleeping downwind of it aboard the *Rose of Sharon*,
loading it onto the flatboat in Houston, and if it didn't precisely
remind him of slavery, he sure did associate it with flight, and with
his sudden descent from Man About Town to Just Another Nigger.
And here he was, spending the second of no one knew how many
nights breathing in a whole warehouseful of the starchy seedy stuff.

Not knowing how long he would be performing Clyde Proudfoot's duties as night watchman was the source of his depression.
Johnson Six had had no idea when Tim Grace, the "inspecting son
of a bitch," would be coming to Galveston, or even if he was indeed
planning on making the trip. The cotton industry was small, for all
its profits, and the town was so intimately connected with it that
the grayest rumors starting at the top made their way down the
river with telegraphic speed. The thing about rumors, apart from
the question of reliability, was that they always lacked particulars.

Grace might in fact be coming; whether it would be tomorrow or in the spring was the point to ponder.

Waiting itself was no chore. His vigil outside Mademoiselle Josephine's door would have tried the nerves of a great fighting general. But he could estimate how long it would take, and knew that it would end with a death—his, Saint-Maarten's, or both— and had resigned himself to the result. And there had been no cotton involved.

The building had been constructed for maximum storage space. Whordle and Grace would not begrudge even such room as might be required for a staircase, and so access to the three upper floors was limited to flights of narrow wooden stairs zigzagging up an outside wall, with doors on the landings. The railing was minimal, weathered and wobbling. It was from this staircase that Clyde had fallen, and Honey, who had not much use for any kind of height, limited his vertical patrol to two times per night. He considered once sufficient, for that matter, and made the second trip only to alleviate boredom. Natalie Proudfoot had provided him with a Bible to wile away the hours on his wooden chair in a corner of the cavernous ground floor, but he had not found it diverting, and in any case the light coming from the bullseye lantern on the packing crate that served for a table was hardly bright enough for him to make out the fine print. He'd borrowed a deck of blurred and dog-eared cards from Johnson Six, for the purpose of playing Patience; however, without conscious thought he'd memorized the stains and wear patterns on their faded backs the first night and knew which card would show before he turned it up. As far as entertainment was concerned, it was as useful as tickling himself.

Clyde, he decided, had not fallen off the stairs. He'd jumped rather than consign himself to another night trying to read *Leviticus.*

Tonight, Honey amused himself for a time unloading and

cleaning his faithful Bulldog revolver. He twisted a corner of one of Clyde's old bandanna handkerchiefs and threaded it through the barrel and each of the chambers, wiped off the rest, and polished each of the cartridges. Although he was thorough, not neglecting the hammer or the loading gate or the space behind the trigger, he finished all too quickly, and after blowing the lint off each cartridge and reloading, he still had six hours until dawn.

There was nothing to be gained from the business beyond the satisfaction of repaying Natalie for his board and shelter, and he was counting heavily on Johnson Six's belief that Tim Grace had never met Clyde and would accept the man he found standing guard over the inventory as the man he'd been paying for years. Natalie had not been so certain; all rich white men looked the same to her, she had reported without irony, and she knew there had been some contact with representatives of the firm besides Andrew Whordle. If the impostiture did not hold, Honey risked not only the Proudfoots' eviction, but his own exposure as a Negro on the run from killing a white man. He had not seen a newspaper since Houston—Natalie did not read, the Bible belonged to Clyde, and Johnson Six, who was also illiterate, refused to buy a copy of *The Galveston News* and raise questions—but he thought it likely the reward for his capture had risen in proportion to the time he had spent unapprehended. He was trusting a great deal to chance, and all for a man he did not know, and likely would not have spent time with even when he was in good health.

Galveston's town clock struck one, awakening him from a doze and a recurring nightmare of lynching. His left leg was numb. He stood to stamp circulation tingling into it, and as long as he was up he decided to check the upper floors. He stuck the Bulldog in the pocket of his overalls and took the lantern with him.

He paused on the fourth floor just long enough to shine the

light down the first aisle. The stacks of cotton bales rose ten feet high on either side, arranged in steps to enable laborers to climb to the top and tip bales to the floor, to be carried by others out the wide doors and passed, bucket brigade fashion, down the outside stairs into the waiting wagons. Shadows crawled up the bulging sides in the wobbly light. No one stole cotton. The individual bales did not bring enough on the market to justify the effort, and wholesale removal involved an operation too big not to attract unwelcome notice. Hiring a night guard was just something the company did to reassure investors. Honey turned back toward the door.

Something clattered at the room's far end. He stopped, then turned again and crept that direction, drawing the Bulldog from his pocket. He was about to shoot his first rat.

At each aisle he raised the lantern, high enough to penetrate the darkness at the opposite end and catch the intruder in mid-scurry. The moon was two days off the full, and he was aided by its skim-milk glow coming through the eight-paned windows near the ceiling. Nothing stirred.

Nearing the last aisle, he smelled coal oil. He stopped and ran his hand over the lantern's metal base, testing for leaks. It came away dry.

Honey listened. He heard his own breathing and the croaks and moans of a building settling into its foundation like an old man turning over in bed. Apart from that the room was unnaturally still. He'd been vaguely aware that a solitary cricket had selected the top floor to entertain itself with its ratcheting call, but now it, too, was silent.

He made a decision. As if to announce it, he turned and walked back toward the door, scuffing his heels and whistling some crackbrain tune he'd tried to play in the House of Rest. He opened the door squeakily, still whistling, set the lantern outside on the landing without a noise, and banged the door shut. He stopped whistling abruptly.

He waited again, and this time—it may have been his imagination, but that didn't make it any less possible—he thought he heard someone else breathing in unison with himself. He measured his air in shallow breaths and stood absolutely still.

The building did some more settling in the silence. Nothing else moved except his lungs, his and those of whoever was standing as quietly as he on the opposite end of the room. The room felt close for all its vastness. The air was dry, in spite of the fact that the harbor was a three-minute walk from the bottom of the stairs; the great bales of thirsty cotton leeched it of its moisture so that the atmosphere itself seemed to crackle like old butcher wrap.

For one panicky moment, the dryness clawed at his windpipe and he felt he must cough or choke to death. He swallowed, and kept his throat closed until the spasm passed. With it went the last of his fears. This was the kind of waiting he was best at. It throbbed with promise.

It lasted three minutes, he calculated later—a lifetime, for someone of another temperament. Then a floorboard squeaked, followed by an oddly familiar sound, heard faintly aboard the *Rose of Sharon* as he'd lain in his compartment, and near the stern of the flatboat from Houston, when he'd taken a break and shared the last of his General Thompsons with a fellow colored laborer: the sound of water slapping against wood. Only it wasn't water this time. He smelled coal oil.

The odor was thick and sharp and stronger than before, and gripping the Bulldog he moved across the ends of the aisles in long strides, landing on the balls of his feet while the smell grew tactile, enveloping him, scraping at his nostrils and burning his tear ducts. His eyes had grown accustomed to the light glimmering through the windows and he saw his way as clearly as at noon.

As he reached the last aisle, he almost bumped into the man.

Bent nearly double, the man was so intent on emptying the spouted can of its contents, slinging the volatile stuff across the wooden floor and up the sides of the stacked bales on either side, that he didn't notice who or what he was backing into until Honey swung the Bulldog's barrel at his head.

At the last instant, he had chosen not to pull the trigger and risk igniting the fumes with the flare from the muzzle. In that instant the man with the can spotted the shadow of his upswung arm and ducked, swinging the can around by its bail. The barrel glanced off his shoulder and the can struck Honey in the hip, cracking against his pelvis and throwing him sideways. The man let go of the can and ran for the door. Honey glimpsed the tail of a tattered coat and a great pile of unshorn hair above the collar.

He spread his feet, crossed his left arm in front of his chest, and extended his other arm across it to steady his aim. He settled the front sight into the groove near the hammer, drawing a bead on a point halfway between the fleeing man's shoulder blades, and thumbed back the hammer to ease the pull.

Just then he noticed his feet were wet. Looking down, he breathed coal oil from a puddle that had spread around his shoes, and withdrew his finger from the trigger. When he looked up again, the door was open, tipping a diamond-shaped patch of moonlight onto the floor at the far end of the room. At the same moment he heard glass breaking.

He took off running. His soles were slick with oil and he slipped once, but caught himself with a hand against a cotton bale and hurled his body forward to regain momentum. By the time he got to the door, the light coming through it had a yellow tinge.

Honey stepped out onto a landing flickering with flame. The fleeing man had kicked over the lantern, shattering the glass and spilling burning oil. But it was a small blaze, far from the fumes inside. He ignored it and stepped to the edge of the landing. The entire staircase shivered beneath him. He could feel each of the man's pounding footfalls as he fled down the steps.

A shaft of moonlight leaned against the stairs like a collapsed beam. He peered over the shaky railing and saw the ragged corner of a coat flapping beyond the edge of the middle flight. It was no kind of target, but when he leaned out farther, the whole of the second-floor landing lay exposed, white as justice in the cold light. He tried resting his gun arm on the railing, but the wood had rotted around the heads of the nails that held it in place; it was less stable than the empty air. He sank into a half crouch and steadied his arm by gripping the wrist with his other hand. He centered the sight on the middle of the landing.

Footsteps thundered. The staircase swayed and started at its nails. The man's shoes needed repair; Honey could hear a loose sole slapping the boards. He thrust away the distracting thought and concentrated on his aim.

The man rounded the bottom of the second flight and hit the landing heading for the stairs that led to the ground. The split tails of his coat spread behind him like the wings of a flightless bird. At the instant the top of his shaggy head moved into Honey's sights, the man twisted his neck around to look up at the top of the stairs. Their eyes met just as Honey squeezed the trigger.

The name of the man interrupted in the act of setting fire to the Whordle and Grace Cotton Company warehouse was never discovered, although the city marshal identified what was left of his face as belonging to a wharf rat who'd been arrested several times for petty theft and offering himself to mariners for a price. The coroner's jury ruled that death was caused by a gunshot fired by Clyde Proudfoot in his responsibility as night watchman. The bullet, a three hundred-grain slug, entered the skull through the bridge of the nose, pierced the pallate, and exited through the neck between the second and third cervical vertebrae. It was not in the coroner's jurisdiction to determine whether the deceased was acting upon a personal grudge or on behalf of one of the cotton company's many competitors, although a bottle of Hermitage, rather a pricey brand of whiskey for a man in his circumstances, was found in the pocket of his coat along with a box of kitchen matches. This information (with the exception of the charge of soliciting mariners) appeared in the *Galveston News,* along with an item announcing Andrew Whordle's decision to reward Proudfoot (currently recovering from an injury thought to be related to the foiled arson) with a generous bonus and the attention of a private nurse.

The incident remained in the columns for three days, then disappeared. Black Galveston, however, went on discussing it for months, without ever dignifying the Clyde Proudfoot part by mentioning his name.

Honey Boutrille never saw the newspaper and never heard the story as it was told in the colored community. After stamping out the fire on the fourth-floor landing, he stowed away aboard a British steamer bound for Corpus Christi on the last leg of its American voyage.

FIFTEEN

———

"We need more men," Teddy White said. "Chester Tibbett's in town."

Twice Emerson scowled at the apparition standing in the doorway of his room at the Bannock. The consumptive son of a bitch looked even seedier in the morning than he did late in the day: tobacco ash dusting his shirt and coat, a fresh hole burned in the right lapel, hair plastered to his forehead beneath the brim of his jammed-on Mormon hat. His moustache was singed more than usual, and bright red spots the size of cartwheel dollars stained his sallow cheeks. He was the living embodiment of the hangover in Emerson's head.

"Good morning to you, too, you ugly bastard. Who in hell's Chester Tibbetts and what's his claim on us?"

"Tibbett. He's just about the toughest shotgun messenger Wells Fargo ever had. He shot up Tom Bell's gang in California in '56. Took out five good men with a Stephens ten-gauge and a Colt's pistol."

"My old granddad raised him some hell in Sweden in 1809, but he's busy growing moss now. Your man Tibbett must be a hunnert."

"He's fifty, which means he's thirty years tougher than he was in California. The company ships him wherever the road agents grow thickest. I seen this coming the minute they decided to open back up in Idaho City. I had this job figured for two, but we'll need eight, and there's not six men in the Boise Basin can face a man like Tibbett. I know a man in Seattle I can wire, and two in Denver, or they was last I heard. Where's your outfit?"

"Spread all over California and old Mexico. You'd best come in before you catch fire."

White stepped past him and sat down on a parlor chair, but was on his feet again before Emerson got the door closed. Emerson, in his flannels and trousers with galluses hanging, scratched his head. It sounded like sandpaper in his ears. He poured the rest of the contents of his bottle into a hotel glass and drank it down. The liquor lay atop his stomach in a motionless pool. "How'd you find out about Tibbett?"

"I seen him, eating a whole chicken bold as brass in Delmonico's. He can eat three times a day in the best restaurant in town on what Wells Fargo pays him."

"He do that?"

"Do what?"

"Eat three times a day in Delmonico's."

"Can't say. I only just now seen him. What's that got to do with us needing more men?"

Emerson shook his head. Listening to White half the time, he'd suspect him to be too dumb to stick up his own thumbs, let alone a stagecoach, except he'd seen a reader on Teddy White in the Capitol Barbershop and the description fit him as tight as it fit anyone. Emerson stretched out on the bed with his hands behind his head. "Why don't you go down there around suppertime and see if he's in there then?"

"Now, why would I want to do that? You don't need to see Tibbett but once to know he's no good for what ails you."

"Let's stop talking about Tibbett. I never heard of him ten minutes ago and now I'm sick of the name. When do they ship out the gold?"

"Monday, after the miners finish handing over a week's hard work Friday night and all day Saturday."

"What day's today?"

"Thursday."

"That's four days. You could of let me sleep."

"You can sleep for a week, only we got to line up more men. There's no time for it betwixt now and Monday."

"Quit your bellyaching and come back and tell me if he's eating in Delmonico's tonight." Emerson took one hand from behind his head and laid his arm across his eyes. He was almost asleep when the door banged shut behind White.

Chester Tibbett didn't look like such of a much from the outside, Emerson thought, if you read dime novels and figured all the men who fought road agents stood seven feet and wore a fresh shirt every day. He was built two feet closer to the ground, unless his legs were so long his knees bumped the table, and unless his aim with a shotgun was better than with a knife and fork, he couldn't hit Idaho with both barrels. He ate his peas off his knife and they bounced all over like hailstones. He was a skinny jasper to boot, all wrists and Adam's apple and ears that stuck out under the flat crown of his hat. Sitting at a corner table amidst gleaming silver and stiff white linen and waiters with towels folded over their arms, napkin stuck under his chin, he might have been some stove-in hired hand the proprietor had invited out of charity, except for his eyes. They were as hard as a long drought and never stopped moving. No one came in or went out the door without his notice, and Emerson, watching with Teddy White from a table near the kitchen, was pretty sure Tibbett was aware of them both, though he'd scarcely glanced their way when they'd sat down.

"I heard he carries around a scarf belonged to a friend killed in a bandit raid," White whispered, although the din of voices and rattling crockery drowned out everything within two feet. "Ties a fresh knot in it every time he burns down a bad man. Them that's seen it says there's twenty-seven knots in that there scarf."

"I heard the same thing about Bloody Bill and Yankees, and it wasn't any truer of him. A man carried around a scarf that long'd trip over it and bust open his head."

"I reckon you think I'm a liar."

"It stands to reason. Otherwise you'd be in jail the first time somebody asked you what line you was in. But you're right about the rest. Bet you a double eagle to a penny spike he looks us both up the minute he gets back to Wells Fargo. They keep a book."

"He's never laid eyes on either one of us. I only know he's who he is on account of I heard someone call him by name."

Emerson blew on his soup and grinned. "I spotted him for what he is. A good way for a dog to get dead is to start thinking the dog in the other yard's dumber'n him."

"You only spotted him because I told you all about him."

"Pipe down and eat your soup."

A skin had formed on White's bowl. He sucked a piece of it off his moustache. "That straight about him looking us both up?"

"I wouldn't let it spook me none. He ain't a lawman. He's got no claim on us till we stop his stage."

"There's rewards out on us both."

"He can't collect on you. He works for the company."

"He can collect on you. You're not wanted for robbing stage-coaches."

"I don't figure to lose my appetite over it. You about through? A man could chill a bottle of beer in that chicken broth."

"I never did like soup." White pushed his bowl away.

They left the restaurant, White circling wide to avoid the shot-gun messenger. Emerson took the direct route, straight past Tib-bett's table. The man appeared to be absorbed with a steaming heap of biscuits smothered in milk gravy, much of which already decorated his shirt despite the napkin. It was a wonderment how much a scrawny runt could put away in the course of one meal. Well, he hoped Tibbett was enjoying it.

Outside, night was sliding down the peak of Silver Mountain, well capped on a balmy day in early autumn. White drew in a lung-ful of air and coughed. He drew the sleeve of his old town coat across his lips, smearing it pink. "Right now I wouldn't say no to a drink if you gave it to me in a chamber pot. How's the Golden Slipper sound?"

"You go on ahead. I think I'll take me a smoke and walk off this hangover."

"I never did come down with one. I been drunk since I could see over the bar." The road agent left him, lighting up one of his short cheroots and coughing sparks.

Emerson had a packet of ready-mades in his pocket, but he left them there. He watched night grow and decided Chester Tib-bett was the kind of man who would top off supper with two slices of apple pie covered with heavy cream.

There was a gunsmith's shop across the alley from the restau-rant. The interior smelled of solvent, walnut oil, and metal shav-ings. He rested his hands on the oak counter, looking over the long guns in the rack behind it while the proprietor finished filing the trigger spur off a knocked-down pistol he had clamped in his vise. There were rows of revolvers as well, hung on pegs, and hardware drawers with different calibers neatly lettered on the labels. Cardboard advertisements for Winchester and Colt and Lefever decorated the walls. A smitty did good business in a town like Idaho City. Emerson missed his Marlin.

"Sorry to keep you waiting." The smith, a stubby Irishman with a freckled bald head and red buggerlug whiskers, mopped his hands with a stained blue rag. "Fellow told me to ruin that there Merwin and Hulbert's in a hurry. Fancies himself a slick hand. Blow his balls off by the end of the week."

"I'd see he pays up first. What's your price on that streetsweep on the end?"

"The Remington? That's forty-five."

"What's it shoot, nuggets?"

"It's brand new from the factory, never been fired except on the test range in New York. Twelve-gauge, walnut stock, checkered grip and fore end, decarbonized steel barrels—"

"What else you got?"

"I got a secondhand Harrington and Richardson I can let you have for thirty-five. It sold for fifty bucks new."

"Not to me it didn't. Let me see that ten-gauge."

The smith took the cutdown shotgun from the rack and handed it across the counter. Someone had gone over the barrels with steel wool, but some pits remained, and there was a long scratch on the stock that fresh stain couldn't conceal. Emerson broke it, then slammed it shut. The action was loose. It rattled when he shook it. "This thing even fire?"

"It fires fine. I can't answer for long-range accuracy. But how close do you have to be?"

He hoisted it to his shoulder and swung around, drawing a bead on a crate stenciled EXPLOSIVES—HANDLE WITH CARE. It was heavy for a sawed-off; he figured it would have weighed about nine pounds at full length. He thumbed back both hammers and tripped the triggers. The firing ends struck down with a satisfying snap.

"It don't do a gun no good to dry-fire it like that," said the smith.

Emerson lowered the gun and turned to face him. "Give you fifteen for it."

"Price is twenty-five."

"Fifteen, and throw in a box of shells."

"That ain't the way to trade. You're supposed to go up."

They haggled for a while, but Emerson always found the Irish easy in matters of money. He gave him a twenty-dollar banknote for the gun and the shells and took back two cartwheel dollars in change, laying the gun on the counter to make the swap. The smith tore a length of paper wrap off a roller mounted under the racks of weapons. Emerson told him not to bother with that, but he shook his head and wrapped up the shotgun.

"We got an ordinance against carrying firearms in this town. You can't lug it around out in the open."

Emerson chose not to argue. When the ends of the paper were neatly tucked under and tied with string, he pocketed the ammunition and picked up the package.

"That Stevens is a fine weapon at a bargain price," the smith said. "Wells Fargo won't issue nothing else to their messengers."

"That's what I heard." He almost added, *That's the best thing about it*, but he held his tongue and left the shop. Shotguns were bought and sold every day and no one thought twice about it, but you never knew what folks might remember.

The benign face of fall in Idaho had turned away from him during the time he had spent in the gunsmith's shop. He never missed San Francisco more than in the alley next to Delmonico's. He liked the foggy damp cool from the bay, never felt it in his bones the way the cold crackling air of mountain night lay against his spine and stuck needles into his joints, reminding him that the twenty-six-year-old guerrilla of Centralia had died there with the bluebellies. He wanted to light a cigarette, just to feel the warm smoke drifting into his face, but he couldn't risk someone spotting the orange glow and haring in to investigate. He worked the stiffness out of his fingers tearing the wrapping away from the Stevens and avoided touching the metal parts as much as possible while he poked a shell into each barrel. He transferred another handful of shells to a pocket just in case and threw away the box containing the rest. He'd only bullied the Irishman into giving up a whole box because demanding just two shells would have attracted too much attention.

Anyway, it wasn't a long wait. He'd been in the shadows ten minutes at most when the front door of the restaurant opened and Chester Tibbett came out, picking his teeth and belching milk gravy. Emerson had hoped he'd turn in the direction of the alley toward the Wells Fargo office, but if he'd entertained any suspicions about the two men who had been dining near him, he'd decided to put off looking them up and swung toward the hotels and rooming houses at the other end of the street. Emerson had no choice but to close his coat over the shotgun, the barrels sticking two feet past the hem, and follow him.

It was Thursday night. Most of the miners were snoring in their tents, but there were some people out, and he thought Tibbett might turn into the door of a house or a hotel before Emerson had a chance to make his move. But Wells Fargo's best shotgun messenger was a pennypinch, had taken a room in one of the cheapjack joints beyond the central business district; that, or he had an itch for one of the whorehouses farther down. After five minutes of walking, Tibbett with his chin in his chest and his breath smoking in the dry cold air, Emerson pretending he had a stiff knee to mask the Stevens' barrels, the pair ran out of people to pass. They crossed through a patch of light in front of the saloon where Emerson had made the acquaintance of Teddy White, then entered a long stretch of darkness where a livery stable shared a block with a bank, closed since three o'clock. Emerson closed the distance.

Tibbett had the ears of a jack rabbit. He turned at some noise Emerson didn't even think he made, at the same time reaching inside a pocket of his whipcord coat, just as Emerson swung up the ten-gauge and blew a big black space between his hat and his collar.

The murder of Chester P. Tibbett, a thirty-three-year man with Wells Fargo and Company, was never solved, although the headquarters in San Francisco offered a thousand dollars for information leading to the arrest and conviction of his assassin. Idaho City had more to talk about four days later, when two men wearing bandanna masks stopped the westbound stage on the north fork of the Snake, blasting Tibbett's twenty-year-old replacement off the top with a shotgun and making away with seven thousand in gold dust. One of the road agents, described as emaciated and dressed in shabby town clothes, was quickly identified as Teddy White, the desperado whose operations had shut down the gold run temporarily in 1883, but the name of his partner remained a source of lively speculation long after a sheriff's posse caught up with White in Horseshoe Bend and hanged him from a blackjack pine.

SIXTEEN

Torbert paused in the middle of writing to haul out his handkerchief and mop his red, streaming face. The linen was soaked through, almost transparent. It was the third handkerchief he'd put to use since rising, and the Galveston town clock was just striking noon. He pondered the probity of including his laundry bills on his list of expenses for Argus Fleet.

In Chicago, the leaves on the trees planted in boxes on the sidewalks would be turning. The wind planing off the lake would be balmy or bracing, depending upon whether it was blowing from Michigan or Ontario, and he would have to stick his head out the window before he decided whether to put on wool or gabardine. There would be a snap in the air and the smoke from incinerating leaves would be tying up traffic on Michigan Avenue. But here on the Gulf there was no fall except when a hurricane was tossing ships and dead bodies onto the shore. If anything the air was hotter and heavier than in New Orleans.

When he finished, he returned the pen to the socket it was chained to and read what he'd written on the yellow flimsy:

ARGUS FLEET

JUPITER PRESS

BIEDERMAN BUILDING

CHICAGO

TRACED BOUTRILLE TO GALVESTON BUT BIRD HAS

FLOWN STOP CORPUS CHRISTI POSSIBLE DESTINATION

BUT ALSO EUROPE STOP WHAT PRICE PROJECT IF MUST

CIRCLE THE GLOBE STOP WIRE INSTRUCTIONS CARE

WESTERN UNION GALVESTON TEXAS

TORBERT

He handed the flimsy to the clerk, paid, and went out to walk along the harbor, where a little breeze was blowing, aswirl as always with cotton fibers. A near gale had been in progress the day he'd arrived, positively white with the chaff or whatever they called it, and he'd thought South Texas was having a blizzard. Then he'd breathed in a great mouthful and nearly choked to death.

It had cost him some money and a dose of the clap to determine that Honey Boutrille had left Houston. None of Mother Jack's whores had had direct contact, but one of them had a friend whose brother had pitched pennies with a well-spoken Negro who'd asked about work that would take him out of town. The friend worked at a similar establishment, but she was sleeping, and Torbert had had to bribe the houseman to wake her up in order to accept a bribe to tell him where he could find her brother. The brother, it turned out, had been arrested the night before on a charge of procuring. Upon inquiring at the jail, Torbert was told he was in a quarantine cell for a month for fighting with a turnkey. "It'll take him that long anyways to heal up," growled the man at the admissions desk, a bull-necked German who looked as if his face had been stepped on in a tussle with some other prisoner.

No matter. The journalist had taken the train south from there on the theory his quarry had found work on a steamer or a flatboat carrying cotton to the port city. That was the prevailing traffic, and since Boutrille had chosen a water route out of New Orleans it seemed as likely as anything.

Torbert had half hoped his hunch was wrong. Texas was loud and hot and wore its rough side out. He'd lost weight on the journey, although he would never fulfill anyone's idea of svelte; the food was either surprisingly sophisticated or would gag a dog—often swinging from one extreme to the other between luncheon and supper at the same establishment, as if the chef had run off and been replaced with an army mess sergeant who thought vinegar and plenty of salt could reclaim the rottenest sidemeat—and painful constipation was frequently his only respite from diarrhea. Now he had a drip in his pants to contend with as well. He fortified himself with whiskey, whose quality varied nearly as widely as his meals, and had acquired a hammered-silver flask to see him through the hundred yards or so that might separate one saloon from the next. Fortunately, the distance was rarely so great. He'd formed the conclusion that the rip-roaring West offered enormous volumes of alcohol as compensation for mind-warping boredom.

The man Boutrille (with the exception of the blackguard exguerrilla Torbert had been reading about who confined his depredations to the Pacific Northwest) provided the sole scarlet thread in the gray tapestry of the American frontier. The journalist had found the Negroes of Galveston an even closer-mouthed lot than their brothers in civilization, but he'd read of a remarkable feat performed by the colored night watchman in a cotton warehouse, shooting straight down with a revolver from the top of an unstable staircase attached to an outside wall and drilling a fleeing would-be arsonist square between the eyes at a distance of forty feet. He'd suspected the details, and his attempts to interview the man credited with the shot, forestalled by the man's wife at the door of their shack, had convinced him that the fellow, who was some sort of invalid, was not the same man whose exploits had been written about in the papers. It had cost Torbert twenty dollars of Argus Fleet's money in the places that sold liquor to colored customers that a man answering Boutrille's description had been seen loitering on the docks near an ocean-going freighter, and had not been spotted since. The name of the vessel and its destination he had been unable to obtain, but most of the ships that tied up at the island either went on from there to Corpus Christi or returned to their ports of origin in the Old World.

"J.P. Glidden," the flag under which Torbert sailed as the ambitious journalist in quest of stories of swashbuckle and blood for the Jupiter Press, hoped it was Corpus. Ernest V. Torbert, hot and dyspeptic and beginning to yearn for the predictability of his desk in a janitor's closet in Chicago, preferred the image of the Blacksnake of New Orleans steaming toward the dungeons and imbroglios of London and Vienna.

He returned to the telegraph office to see if there was a reply to his telegram. The operator had just finished scribbling it.

E. V. TORBERT

C/O WESTERN UNION

GALVESTON, TEXAS

REQUEST FOLLOW UP CORPUS CHRISTI POSSIBILITY
STOP WILL WIRE ADDITIONAL EXPENSES WESTERN
UNION THERE

FLEET

He crumpled the telegram, tossed it into the basket under the writing ledge, and went back down to the harbor.

Part Five

ALL ROADS LEAD TO DENVER

SEVENTEEN

"M ay I propose a toast—with apologies for this disappointing vintage—to the beauty and talents of Miss Adabelle Forrest?"

Good-humoredly, and without inquiring of Christopher A. Buckley as to what source a blind man depended upon for his standards of beauty, Casper Box rose behind his host, lifted his glass, and drank. A whiskey man himself during his own drinking days, Box could not tell the difference between champagne and bad cider and thought the batch as good as any he'd tasted. His stiff collar scratched his Adam's apple when he swallowed. He detested formal dress, but one saw nothing else in the better eateries and drinking establishments in San Francisco after six o'clock postmeridian.

Buckley was turned out in a mohair dinner jacket and trousers, with a starched collar and white bow he must have tied with gloves on. He wore his thick chestnut-colored hair long at the collar, brushed so carefully Box could count the grooves made by the bristles, and the gold frames of his smoked glasses glittered in the gaslit dining room of the Eldorado Hotel. Garnet studs glistened like drops of blood on his shirtboard; an appropriate emblem for a man who had built his political power on profits from some of the worst gambling hells and whorehouses in the country, frequented by murderers and extortion rings and no small number of wanted fugitives. Adabelle, who could smell money under a manure pile, hid her blushes—or rather her lack of them—behind a painted Chinese fan and when Buckley resumed his seat leaned over and kissed his cheek, making sure to brush his arm with one of her half-exposed breasts. The political boss actually did blush, Box gave him that, and to cover his disquiet attacked his bloody prime rib with democratic fervor. His escort, a small woman of Greek extraction with sharp, rodentlike teeth and bracelets that tinkled, glared.

They occupied a table near a balustrade overlooking a sea of white linen and sparkling silver, with waiters in tailcoats bobbing about supporting trays the size of wagon wheels, piled high with meats and long-necked bottles and fruits unknown to the East Coast. Their waiter, a Swiss with fierce white imperials, had been refilling their glasses and replenishing their table with course after course of roast meats, steamed vegetables, whole fish, and heaped oysters for the better part of four hours. Box's buttocks had gone numb and his belly was filled to bursting. Californians, or in any event *rich* Californians, consumed more flesh and butter than all of western Europe, cleansed their pallates with French champagne, and clogged Frisco Bay with the extruded contents of their bowels. Meanwhile, the sons and daughters of less fortunate Forty-niners prowled the waterfront, clubbing inebriates for their watches and peddling their bodies for pennies. Box, who in his youth had slept on the streets of New York City and in his middle years had ridden with President Grant in a private Pullman, cracking open lobster shells and watching tramps picking through the trash piles along the right-of-way, never entered the Golden Gate without a sense of dismay and profound gratitude. Had a certain offended party in 1846 not lost his nerve and fired before the count of ten, or his young vanquisher not been thrown into a cell with an elderly convict who knew how to juggle, Box might have shared the fate of such human offal. The theater was the last refuge for imposters, cheats, and whores. It was no wonder they insisted with such heat upon referring to it as *legitimate*.

"One hears such terrible stories about the Barbary Coast," Adabelle said. "I find it delightfully civilized. It's almost like coming back East."

Buckley sent away the champagne (Box calculated there was forty dollars' worth left in the magnum) and ordered a '63 Bordeaux to replace it. "The location has its amenities," he agreed. "That wasn't the case only thirty years ago, when fires and brigands took their turns at its throat. Even now, a lady such as yourself should avoid venturing as far as Pacific Street unescorted; and I would advise the escort to avoid the street altogether. This city's younger than any of us—of course I exclude you, Miss Forrest, and you, Leda—and I suppose you could say it's passing through a restless adolescence. There is a popular saying that more money has gone into a particular lean-to establishment in Chinatown than into the Bella Union, and never come out."

Box couldn't resist. "Aren't you talking about your constituents?"

"Without risking a census, I'm prepared to concede that twenty percent of the local Democratic voters have at one time or another committed a criminal act. With the exception of the tongs, most of whose members are not citizens and are therefore disenfranchised, the one thing all these hounds and cutpurses agree upon is who shall speak for them in city hall. Without me to maintain the peace, Nob Hill and the vigilantes would have burned them all out years ago."

"So you're in the way of a policeman," Box said.

Buckley smiled; and the theatrical manager had the curious notion that this wardheeler could see him, if not with his eyes than with something else, and much more thoroughly than through ordinary sight. "I suppose you are right. Thank you for suggesting the theme of my next campaign."

Box retreated, but only to approach him from the flank. "What's the situation with the tongs?"

"Peaceful at present. There hasn't been a war among them in eleven years."

"Not among them, no. I understand they've started going after white men."

Buckley's smile faded. Adabelle looked at Box with fire. Just then the wine came, and the diners were silent while the waiter filled their glasses. When he withdrew, Adabelle lifted hers. "To the hospitality of our gracious host."

Everyone drank without comment. Buckley replaced his glass precisely in the vermillion ring it had made on the tablecloth. "You're referring to the incident of last August," he said. "That's been dealt with. The foolish fellow insulted a tong leader, and was persuaded to leave San Francisco for good."

"Persuaded by who?" Box asked.

"I had that chore. I'd ask no one to perform it in my place."

"Did you stake him?"

"Money is a bloodless weapon. It's a mystery to me why it's maligned so often, usually by people who haven't any."

"Not quite bloodless. I understand the fellow used some of it to buy a shotgun and blasted the gang boss into Buddha's right hand."

"Casper!" Adabelle's face paled to translucence.

"That was speculation." Forgetting the females present, Buckley cracked his knuckles. They were swollen and scarred, likely souvenirs of his past as a bartender and bouncer. "In any case, Emerson left and took the trouble away with him."

"First to Oregon, then Idaho Territory. By my account he's made off with four murders and two robberies just since he left San Francisco."

"I read of two murders and one robbery."

"You missed the telegraph column in today's *Call.* A hotel clerk in Idaho City picked him out of an old picture as the man he rented a room to week before last. Later that week, someone killed a Wells Fargo shotgun messenger on a public street and four days after that a stage got robbed ten miles from town and another shotgun man killed. You might have noticed that things start happening whenever Twice Emerson stops in town."

"Assuming your conclusions are right, it's rather a feather in my cap I shivvied him out of town when I did. Wouldn't you agree?"

"You can shivvy me out of town anytime you like, if you stake me first," Box said. "Emerson was a bad hat long before he set eyes on Frisco. He's been wanted for one thing or the other ever since Gettysburg, the one thing being armed robbery and the other being murder."

Buckley sipped from his glass. His tranquility had returned, but it was a dead calm, flat and without resonance. "You don't understand San Francisco politics. On any given night in the Devil's Acre, a bounty man with sufficient courage and good fortune could catch his limit and then some. It's unofficial, but it's in the manner of an unwritten rule that desperadoes may take shelter in that district so long as they settle their affairs in cash and commit no crimes inside the city limits. This fellow certainly violated that rule in spirit, if not precisely in letter, when he stirred up bad feelings among the tongs. He became unwelcome then and it became my responsibility to cast him out. The death of Short Bob was unfortunate, and almost certainly bore Emerson's hand. At that point he became *persona non grata* for life."

"Meaning he's under a death sentence if he comes back."

"A fair way to put it." Buckley sat back and laid a hand atop one of Leda's. "It has the ring of a judge and jury, and it carries no appeal except to almighty God. Or Buddha."

Box popped open his snuff box and took a pinch. "I was just curious. You can't beat skullduggery for theater. I bet Frank James outpulls Dickens."

"Casper's got it in his head to place this Emerson ogre at the top of the bill." Adabelle's fairy laugh died in the vacuum.

"The logistical complications are vast," said Buckley. "For example, you would be forced to arrange your tour to exclude those states and territories where Emerson has broken the law. His career started in Missouri, don't forget. One can avoid Portland and Boise without serious effect, but St. Louis and San Francisco are indispensable."

"There's always the East, and Denver. We did just fine in Denver, didn't we, dear?" Box squeezed Adabelle's hand, mocking Buckley. He'd developed a serious dislike for the blind hypocrite, with his Greek whore on his arm and murderers' money in his pocket. It was rare company that impressed him with his own virtue.

"*I* did fine in Denver. You can't put a mad wolf onstage and teach it poodle tricks."

"I'd sign Geronimo if he'd sit still long enough for me to stick a pen in his hand."

"Here's dessert," Buckley announced, as the waiter approached, carrying a tray laden with ice creams and pastries and wedges of cake the size of chimney stones. "And, Karl, the '71 Napoleon. An excellent brandy tonight to assure a successful opening tomorrow."

In the lobby, the politico shook Box's hand and kissed Adabelle's. The women leaned in from the waist, pecked at the air near the cheek each presented, and the company parted, Buckley and Leda for their carriage out front, Box and Adabelle for the stairs.

Inside her suite, Adabelle unclasped the necklace Box had given her on the occasion of the Atlantic City opening, a delicate thing of beryls set in hand-worked silver, and flung it at him. He ducked and it struck the door with a rattle like chainmail. Lizzie, entering from the bedroom in her maid's uniform, reversed directions and pushed the door almost shut, leaving a crack.

"I'm glad I didn't teach you to throw knives," Box said. "I ain't that small a target."

"Idiot! You could have waited to pick a fight with him until after the notices came out. Christopher owns the *Bulletin* and the *Enterprise*."

"He don't own the *Call*. It's been trying to put him and the Barbary Coast out of business for years."

"Most of the time I think you're the best manager I ever had, and then you go and do something so bull-headed and foolish I'd swear you were working with Anna Held to bring me down. Why did you do it?"

"You was getting in with him too tight. He's just a skull-cracker in a boiled shirt. I seen his kind in the yard, strutting about like John Jacob Astor and snapping at sewer rats to run fetch him things. I'd not let you soil your hands."

"I appreciate your confidence. With all my heart I do. Not everyone has had your advantages. Most of us have never seen the inside of a prison." She lifted her skirts and wheeled toward the bedroom. Lizzie's scurrying footsteps on the other side of the door spared them both a collision.

"I never said the system was perfect," said Box, to an empty room.

The next night at the American Theater, the bilious face of George Washington painted on the curtain rose ("Unfortunately," sniffed the next morning's review in *The San Francisco Call*; that journal's righteous editor having come to lump in all public amusements with the despised Barbary) upon Miss Adabelle Forrest's one-woman program, presented in its entirety for the first time since the Mercator burned down in St. Louis. The costumes for the selections from *East Lynne, Pirates of Penzance, Hamlet,* and the rest had been purchased from Madame LaFrond's shop in Denver and the alterations completed by Lizzie aboard the train west; all except Violetta's elaborate dressing gown for *La Traviata*, the finishing thread upon which she had bitten through three minutes before the second curtain, with Adabelle shrieking at her in English and French throughout the final stitchery. Observing without interfering, Box made a note to pay the maid an additional half-dollar per week beginning with their swing back East.

Despite her jitters, or perhaps because of them, Adabelle was in rare form. Box, who knew every line, pause, and bit of business in *A Husband's Vengeance* by heart, found himself so caught up in her impersonation of an enraged cuckold—complete with false whiskers and a burning cigar—that he nearly jumped out of his boots when someone touched his shoulder backstage. It was Rheingold, the manager of the American Theater, informing him that Mr. Christopher Buckley wished to speak with him in the manager's office.

He found the man of the people seated behind Rheingold's desk, resting his hands on the gold knob of his stick. Tonight, Buckley wore a silver-gray Prince Albert over a silk waistcoat embroidered with birds of paradise. A garnet stickpin transfixed his sky-blue cravat. Upon Box's entrance, he drew in a deep breath.

"One of the advantages of never venturing outside your home town—for a blind man, at least—is you can always tell where you are by smell alone. Greasepaint and Rheingold's nickel cigars, for instance, tell me I'm nearing the American. You yourself are redolent of bootblack. How they must shine."

Box, who suspected Buckley knew he used bootblack on his hair and handlebars, ignored the last comment. "I been smelling cheap cigars and greasepaint since I was twenty. If I went by that alone I could be in Elko or Baltimore." He sat down in a lumpy horsehair chair and crossed his legs, bouncing his foot. He wanted to be back downstairs when Adabelle took her bows.

"I know you haven't much time. I wanted to set your mind at rest about the *Bulletin* and the *Enterprise*. The reviews will be stellar. I shall certainly return tomorrow evening to catch the rest of Miss Forrest's performance."

Box was on his guard. "You could have sat through the whole thing and let me find out tomorrow."

"You're a direct man, Box. I'm inclined similarly, though public life forbids it in most cases. The reason I'm here is to ask if you were serious about wanting to exhibit Twice Emerson."

"I ain't interested in stuffing him with straw and wheeling him out on a handcart, which is what that sounds like. But I never say anything I don't mean." He returned his snuff to his pocket unsampled. The blind bastard was up to something and Box didn't want to miss anything while he was sneezing or blowing his nose.

"I shall be as frank. You don't like me, nor I you, but we're not so different. I make my living off harlots and hooligans and whatever rubbish washes up on the Pacific shore. You make yours off perverts who happen to look good in the limelight. Don't deny it, now; Leda spent some time talking with Miss Forrest last night, and she has a sense about such things. And now you are contemplating putting a guerrilla bushwhacker on the stage in the middle of a bloodthirsty career."

"The difference being that while he's on stage he ain't out sticking up places and killing."

"A noble by-product, but hardly your purpose. We're the same, no matter what lies we prefer to tell ourselves. What if I were to inform you I know where to find Emerson, or at least where he is sure to stop in the course of his travels?"

"I'd say it was another lie, or you'd be putting in for the reward instead of handing it to me."

"Come, now. I've spent more than twenty-five hundred dollars on Leda in the course of a week, and I daresay you have a similar story to relate about Miss Forrest. Meanwhile there are tens of thousands to be made. Mind you, I'm not suggesting an equal partnership. The theater is a complicated business, and your experience is worth a great deal more than my information. I'm prepared to offer you Twice Emerson in return for a thirty-percent share of the proceeds of a national tour."

"That's a hefty slice, in return for no investment on your part. Meanwhile, I stand a hundred percent of the expenses."

"On the other hand, you can turn me down and reap one hundred percent of nothing. An artistic bill without an artiste is worth precisely that."

"On the other hand, Twice Emerson ain't William Gillette. He may take the offer wrong and shoot me where I stand."

"Temperamental players are your province, not mine. It wouldn't be the first time you'd been shot at."

Box was impressed. Although his dueling past was common gossip on the circuit, the theater was a closed society, and very few details that might damage the profession's rickety reputation filtered through to the outside. He took a pinch to clear his head. Buckley, hearing the squeak of the container's tiny hinges, offered a handkerchief bearing his monogram, but Box declined, snorting into his own.

"I might consider twenty percent," he said, folding the linen precisely along the creases. "I'd need to know the source of the information."

"Thirty percent is the offer. I never haggle."

"Well, it don't cost nothing to listen."

"In your work, perhaps. However, there is no harm in telling some of it, to show good faith. Emerson left a wife behind when he fled Missouri twenty years ago. She obtained a divorce *in absentia* on grounds of desertion, and was obliged to provide the documents when she applied for a business loan in 1881. The bank's headquarters was in San Francisco, and I bought up her debt last year when I acquired controlling interest. Since financial institutions rarely lend money to unmarried women, I naturally included her case when I retained the Pinkerton National Detective Agency to investigate a number of the accounts." He stopped talking abruptly and spun his stick between his smooth white palms. "I cannot continue without some assurance of good faith on your part."

Box dabbed at his nostrils unnecessarily, then returned the handkerchief to his pocket. "Thirty percent, then. If anything comes of it."

"I'll accept your word." Buckley inserted a pause whose significance was not lost: A man's word and his life were of equal value west of Chicago. "The business was described as a melodeon, a concert hall, and since its books were in order and its proprietor was to remain as senior partner, the loan was approved. Unlike the loan officer, however, the gentlemen from Pinkerton visited the establishment in person. Mrs. Purity Peach Duncan Emerson is part owner of the Carillon, one of the most lavishly successful brothels in Denver. If her much-wanted former husband fails to run to her for shelter eventually, I will personally finance your next excursion and never ask for a penny back."

The *whump-whump* of the overture to *Elle Dangereaux* shook the floor. Casper Box rose, clasped Christopher Buckley's hand, and went downstairs, uncharacteristically gripping the banister. He felt woolly-headed, an unaccustomed sensation since he'd given up strong drink. He blamed the snuff.

EIGHTEEN

————

D on't keep thinking about it. Just bust a cap and be done with it.

He sat on an old Arbuckle's crate in the reeking livery stable, his shovel leaning against the filthy adobe wall and the Bulldog revolver suspended between his legs like a limp phizzle, both hands clasped around the handle. His broken-soled shoes were caked with manure, his overalls were streaked with it, and the dust of what seemed like every dump that had ever been taken by a horse and mule in Corpus since the war with Mexico coated his hair and lined his lungs. He'd never known how good he'd had it in the Whordle and Grace Cotton Company warehouse.

The squat earthenware building, windowless and sand-blasted into a dome by the salt winds from the Gulf, contained ten stalls, eight of them occupied at present by docile town horses, all of whom seemed trained not to drop their dung anywhere but inside Honey's jurisdiction. On top of scooping and sweeping it all into a wheelbarrow to be dumped into a huge pile outside, where the owner sold it to farmers for fertilizer—dollar a wagonload, or three for two bucks and a half—he was expected to maintain the carriages in the remaining two stalls, scrubbing mud off the wheels and fenders and polishing the brasswork, all for the munificent wage of a dollar a week and a cot in the lean-to out back. It was all the work there was to be found for a colored stranger in town; he'd applied for a job digging graves in the local potter's field, but had found there was a waiting list. He'd put himself on it, giving his name as Honoré Johnson, borrowing from Johnson Six in Galveston, and had marked an *X* to avoid calling attention to himself through his literacy. The bored city official in charge of the field had misheard him and scribbled *Ollie* next to his mark. So that was the name he was going by now, not that anyone ever called him anything other than boy.

The situation was bad enough on the bald face of it, worse when he dwelled upon the fact that every move he'd made since fleeing New Orleans had taken him another step closer to stony bottom. This was his life, unless something happened to run him out of Corpus and into something worse. Say, wiping a retired Confederate colonel's ass in Fort Smith.

Just go on ahead. One brief taste of metal in your mouth and then a mess for some other nigger to clean up.

"Young man? I'd like the phaeton."

He jerked his head up. He'd lost faith in his senses and hadn't heard the man approaching. His silent entrance, and the strong light streaming through the open door at his back, which appeared to be shining straight through him, came close to convincing Honey that the man was an apparition—summoned, perhaps, by his thoughts of suicide. Well, he'd have to do better than a cheap parlor trick if he intended to talk him out of it.

The man was tall and quite slender, but gave the impression of being heavyset because of the size of his head, which looked bigger yet when he removed his high hat and his hair sprang up, like a clump of weeds when the wind abruptly stopped blowing. It was thick and crinkly and pure white and appeared never to have been cut or combed, and formed a fierce halo with the sunlight showing through it. A short beard, also white, covered his face like a mask from just below his cheekbones to his throat. His skin was a whiskey shade of gold, lighter than that of some white men, but the broad nose and heavy lips were Negroid. In his stiff white collar and old-fashioned stock and tight black coat, he reminded Honey of someone, and it bothered him for some time after that first meeting until he realized the man bore a strong resemblance to a photograph he'd seen of Frederick Douglass.

"The phaeton?" he repeated. His voice was deep and mellow, like the bass note in a cathedral.

Honey realized he'd been staring, and stood. "Yes, sir. You reserved the phaeton?"

"This morning. I'd hoped you'd been informed."

He remembered then that his employer, a nasty little hempen twist who dragged out his "boy!" as if he intended to follow it up with a switch, had said something about the phaeton when he'd reported for work.

"I'm sorry, sir. I'll have it hitched in a moment. You requested the, uh ""

"The mares. They get along as easily as a pair of old maids, don't you agree?"

Honey smiled in spite of himself. In fact, he'd come to think of the sorrel and the blaze-face mares as "the sisters." They started and stopped in a kind of close-order drill, always giving the impression that they'd made up their minds in unison before the command was given. He turned to open their stalls.

"I've always found them cooperative," the customer said. "You shouldn't require the pistol."

He glanced down, saw with a flash of horror that he was still holding the Bulldog, and fumbled it into a pocket of his overalls. "I'm sorry, sir. I was cleaning it."

"You look as if you know your way around it. Has it been so rough a passage, my son?"

Direct questions normally drove him into himself, withdrawing before the assault. He was aware, however, of a deep sympathy in the man's tone, and compassion without bottom. He met the man's gaze. He saw ferocity, iron resolve, and—most familiar, from his own reflection in mirrors—an unutterable sadness. For a flickering instant he felt a nearly violent urge to confide everything to the owner of that gaze. Abruptly he broke contact and unlatched the stall containing the blaze-face mare.

When he'd finished threading the traces, the man thanked him and allowed Honey to help him into the driver's seat with a hand on his elbow, although it was clear from his supple movements that no assistance was necessary. In spite of his wiry strength, Honey judged him to be about seventy, perhaps older. The furrows in his forehead were as deep as raked earth. When he had the lines wound around his wrist, he took off his hat again, removed something from the inner band, and thrust it toward Honey. He reached up, expecting a coin, but his hand closed on a corner of folded paper. The man held on to the other end.

"Can you read?"

"Yes, sir."

The man let go and gave the reins a smart flip. Honey stepped back quickly. The rig rattled off, the driver ducking to clear the top of the open doorway. Honey watched until horses, vehicle, and man vanished into the sun. He unfolded the paper and stared at the coarse black print:

THE FIRST ABYSSINIAN CHURCH OF CORPUS CHRISTI
THE REVEREND D. W. BREEDLOVE, PASTOR
54 TAYLOR ST.
SUNDAY SERVICES 10:00 A.M.–NOON

"And he sent forth a raven, which went forth to and
fro, until the waters were dried up from off the earth."
—Genesis, viii. 7

He read each word aloud, as if it had a significance independent from the rest. Slowly, as in a ritual, he crumpled the heavy-
grained sheet and threw it into a corner.

"Just another Bible-slapper." He picked up his shovel and went
into the stall belonging to the sorrel mare.

At sundown he locked up and threw himself onto his cot, too
bone-weary to take off his clothes. After what seemed only a few
minutes, he awoke to the rattle-rap of his employer kicking his
leather-hinged door. The lean-to's slatted sides cut the morning
light into gray slices. The trade winds had shifted during the night
and Honey's breath smoked in the cold as he pumped water into
the outside basin and dashed the icy liquid into his face.

The phaeton had returned and the mares were back in their
stalls. He rubbed them down, strapped on their nosebags, and fed
and watered the other horses, then pumped more water into a
bucket and washed down the phaeton with a bar of tallow soap
wrapped in a rag, removing a moderate coating of granulated mud.
The bitter little man in charge of the stable, Radget by name, sat on
the Arbuckle's crate, swigging from a glass flask and watching
Honey beneath his drawn brows, as if he suspected him of pilfering
manure and selling it behind his back. Honey was convinced Radget

himself was guilty of this in the absence of the owner, although what he spent it on apart from whiskey he could not say. The man had worn the same leather coat with the elbows out and threadbare dungarees since the day he'd made his acquaintance, and his inattention to such basics as regular bathing did not suggest any sort of high life.

"That nigger preacher takes out the phaeton twice each month, just before sundown, and brings it back before first light," Radget said. "I don't know where he goes, but that same mud always comes back with him. I figure he's got him a woman up in Slaton. White woman, probably, on account of the slanchy way he goes about it. You ever been with a white woman, boy?" He drew it out more than usual; the sun wasn't up yet and he was already drunk, if not still drunk from the day before.

"No, boss, I never." Stooping to scrub the axles, Honey thought of Virginia Ambrose, her fair white belly like a heap of wheat. In New Orleans a man could choose from a wide variety of skin shades.

"That's right and proper. Donkeys oughtn't lay with mares. That's where mule-attoes come from." He laughed, a high thin sound like tearing paper. Honey considered his own calloused hands and now easy it would be to close them around Radget's skinny neck and twist.

He had most of Sunday off. The regulars who could afford them took their own carriages and teams to church, and the rest walked. After he'd fed and watered the horses, he was free. He went to a bath house and laundry that served Negroes and parted with half a week's wages to scrub away the filth of the stable and put on clean clothes. Fresh-smelling and still warm from the iron, the rough work clothes left behind by a former stable hand felt nearly as good as the tailor-mades of distant memory. He was trying to learn to experience the same pleasure from simple comforts that he had taken from imported silks, good cigars, and cognac; but it was a hard climb, nearly vertical, and from where he paused to rest the top looked as gray and bleak as the bottom.

He stopped at the attendant's station, gave him a penny without comment, and watched as the man trickled two inches of fusel oil into a tin cup from a measured bottle. Honey picked up the cup and emptied it in a single draught. He'd learned not to draw it out, try to pretend the harsh, burning stuff was French spirits. It put heat in his stomach and brought a flush to his face.

Outside, the sun was spreading, burning off the fog that had formed on the harbor. He rolled a cigarette, sitting on the bath house steps with his knees together to catch any spill. He was still clumsy at it, and otherwise wasted as much tobacco as he managed to get on the paper. The makings were cheap and went much farther than even the cheapest cigar, but he missed the rich brown leafy taste and still considered the practice of smoking cigarettes effeminate. This was what his life had come down to: Sundays and tobacco and drink and a bath and clean clothing and a stroll along the waterfront where Zachary Taylor had stood to review his troops before invading Mexico. Without it, he would spend more time holding his Bulldog and trying to talk himself into using it than he already did. Or perhaps less. Once would have been enough, without Sundays.

"We missed you Sunday."

Honey looked up at the Reverend D. W. Breedlove, whom he had just helped into the seat of the phaeton. Two weeks had passed since the first time, and the old man looked exactly the same in his black coat and top hat, the latter so finely brushed it glistened like oil. The fierce sad eyes regarded Honey without moving.

"Who's we?"

"The congregation. We missed you Sunday, and the Sunday before that. I gave you one of our leaflets. You said you could read."

"I read it. Sunday's the only day I have that's mine. I don't work like a mule all week to sit on a hard bench and listen to someone telling me I'm going to hell."

"That would hardly be productive, since the main draw is to learn how to avoid it."

"Thank you for your concern. Given my choice I'll go to hell, where my friends are."

"You have no friends, my son. If you had, you would spend more time with them and less trying to talk yourself into committing suicide."

The sorrel mare whickered and tossed her head, as if she agreed. Honey patted her flank. "You're mistaken, Reverend. I've spent too much time staying alive to waste time thinking the opposite."

"May I see your hand?"

"You going to smite me with de power of de Lord, boss?" he grinned his idiot's grin.

"If I could do that, that worm you work for would be ashes." Breedlove held out his hand.

Honey placed his in it, as if to shake hands. The minister turned Honey's over and ran his fingertips over the calluses. He let go.

"You're not accustomed to working with brute strength. Otherwise your palms would be as thick as your heels. The tips of the fingers are spatulated. Are you a musician?"

"I thought so, once. I couldn't get anyone to agree with me." He was sorry he'd given in to the old man's whim. He'd underestimated him, thought him another fool preacher. He wondered if that reward circular had made it this far. Five hundred dollars was more than a colored congregation could put together in a year of Sundays.

"It happens our piano player deserted his post to search for silver in Colorado. Would you consider filling in, until we can find a replacement? I emphasize that the position is temporary. We would prefer it go to someone who is interested in his salvation. However, there is something depressingly Mormon about a service performed without music. Our choir is such that benefits from accompaniment."

"What's it pay?"

"In money? Nothing."

"I'm not your man, Reverend. Salvation's the berries in Paradise, but it's poor coin in Texas."

"I was not preparing to offer it, for playing the piano. I intended to say that there is a home-cooked meal involved, and clothing suitable to the occasion, provided you are not too particular about the fit. You impress me as a man who would feel more at rest in a necktie and coat than plain overalls. Or do I read too much into your sad attempt at plantation speech?"

NINETEEN

Dear Twice,

*I expect youll remember your old Wildwood pal Dick
Yeager that rode with you strait into the Christian Hotel
in Mineral Springs and shot the balls off the cap of the old
lady that run the place on Christmas Day 1863, also the
man that wrote his "Robert E. Lee" on the Know All These
Presents that tied you up with Miss Purity Peach Duncan
of Joplin in the Carroll County courthouse. The knot didnt
hold but I know you wont consider me a jinx or nothing
like that on account of the scrapes we come thru together on
the feild of battle.*

 *Freinds whose names youll recall for certain tell me a
letter addressed to you at the Morgue, San Francisco will
find its way into your hands but I never thought Id write on
account of I been living the strait life since I laid down arms
in 65. Its been a hard row and I come to think the Lord
Jesus dont intend me to be no farmer or He wouldnt send
crows to eat all my seed and hard rain to wash out what the*

crows dont eat and then no rain at all when anything man-
ages to come up. Thats what took me to Denver and to try
for gold. The train fare was stiff and then theres the room-
ing house thats 50¢ a week. I could save by living in a tent
but canvas here is dear and then I need money for picks
pots provisions etc.

Well Im taking the long way around the barn to tell
you Dick Yeager aint your only old aquiantance thats
found a billet here in Denver. Youll be interested to know
or maybe not that your wife owns a place called the Caril-
lon which is very popular with miners and other men if you
take my meaning. Its all decked out in curtains balconys
chandeleirs and that and the girls charge 5 Yankee dollars
for 1 hour in a booth so you know the place aint losing
money.

Im thinking maybe old Twice would care to know how
good his womans doing in case circumstances ever land him
in Denver. If thats the case and for old times sake maybe
youll see your way clear to stake a fello bushwhacker to 50
dollars to set himself up in the prospecting business in
return for the information. You can wire it to me at the
Western Union office in Denver.

your old pal,

Dick Yeager

Emerson, who had never formed the habit of holding on to
things that would complicate a quick withdrawal, had read
through the letter once only, the day it arrived at the Morgue a year
before, and thrown it away. However, reading was a chore, the
words revealing their meanings only after a fight, like oysters pried

open with a butter knife, and he tended to remember them in their original order long after people to whom they came more easily had forgotten the message. He recalled the letter now, burrowed in at the Mission Hotel in Pocatello, as he lay between lumps in the mattress waiting for the ceiling to disappear into shadow. It wasn't the first time he'd thought of the letter since leaving San Francisco. It came into his head every time he got ready to quit someplace, and he poked at the phrase *a place called the Carillon* like the last sweet morsels in a bowl of stew. Had he been another sort of person, he'd have regretted never sending Yeager his fifty dollars or even answering his letter. The information was as precious to him as the Devil's Acre before the chinks had gone and shit in that well.

One of the things Bloody Bill had said that had stuck with him was how many military operations had failed because the planning had stopped with victory, with no thought of what came after. That was how General Lee had lost Gettysburg, a battle he'd won, but that had slipped away because he hadn't the men left to hold on to the field. That made Purity's whorehouse in Denver look better than ever, because come sundown the streets of Pocatello were going to be too hot to tread.

He had thirty-five hundred dollars in gold dust and no way to spend it. If you didn't look like a miner and couldn't answer the questions a miner was expected to, you stood the chance of some merchant hauling down on you and holding you for the law as a claim-jumper or worse. When the dust was tied up in little sacks stenciled U.S. WEST, meaning it belonged to Wells Fargo, you stood an even better chance of being shot for a reward. Before they'd split up, Teddy White had told Emerson of an assayer in Pocatello who traded good coin, somewhat below the market value, for such dust without asking about anything but the weather, and Emerson had gone to him, but the fellow, a pinch-faced Scot, had offered him only a thousand for the lot. Worse, he'd told him he'd have to wait for the bank to open in the morning and in the meantime offered to keep the dust in his safe, because the word was out on the robbery north of Idaho City and strangers in town were being stopped and searched. Emerson believed that part, because he'd spotted a pork belly deputy sheriff with a star pinned to his coat standing on the platform with a shotgun under his arm when Emerson came in on the U.P. from Boise, and had stepped off the other side before the train came to a stop to avoid him. Reluctantly he'd surrendered the dust to the Scot, taking two hundred dollars in good faith, and left, although not before taking a minute to tell him what was in store for him if the remaining eight hundred wasn't forthcoming.

He didn't like it, not by half, and in the hour since he'd left the assay office he'd convinced himself the man had been lying about the amount of cash he had on hand and intended to keep the money and the dust and turn Emerson over to the law for the reward. He could see the thing happening as clearly as if he were living through it. Now he was waiting for dark. He'd hired a good horse from the livery, a chestnut gelding with what looked like plenty of bottom, and he had it tied up behind the hotel, a thirty-second run from the assay office. The place closed up after dark; he'd buffalo the Scot from behind with the heavy Colt's Paterson while he was locking up, force the safe with the short pinch bar he'd purchased at the dry goods store across from the livery, and light out with the dust and the cash, or just the cash if there was enough of it to allow him to leave the extra weight behind.

All of which made him think he'd have had an easier time of it if he'd hit the assay office in the first place, and avoid the wrath of Wells Fargo altogether. But you lived and you learned and you died dumb just the same. Besides, he'd never robbed a stagecoach before, and their time was running out.

When he could no longer make out the rusty stains on the ceiling, he swung his feet off the bed and turned up the lamp on the cracked nightstand. He put on his hat and the corduroy coat, which had begun to soften and conform to his angular figure, the stiff newness working itself out. He'd cleaned and reloaded the Paterson and the Remington, but he inspected the loads again and stuck the one under his belt and the other in the coat's right-hand pocket, working it around a little to stretch the lining so it wouldn't snag when he took it out. The Stevens ten-gauge he'd used on Chester Tibbett and the other shotgun man leaned in a corner and he thought about taking it, but decided it would just draw attention to him on the way to the office, so he left it where it was. He slid the pinch bar into his right boot.

He parted the curtains and looked out the window. The gelding was there, switching its tail at a moth. Ten feet away, someone was standing in the mouth of the little alley, smoking a cigar. He had what looked like a shotgun cradled in one arm.

Emerson watched until the man drew on his cigar, the glowing tip reflecting off a scrap of metal on his breast. He let the curtain fall then and turned out the lamp.

He didn't wait long. A floorboard squeaked outside the door and a key slid into the lock.

It was just a little scratching sound that he might not have noticed if he'd been asleep or sitting up reading a newspaper, but in the dark with all his nerves on end it rang like cannon fire. He lifted the shotgun and braced the stock against his hip.

The knob turned, grating slightly against the socket. He fired one barrel. The door blew apart at waist height, opening a lopsided star of light from the hallway, as large as a man's head. Something fell across the hole, a body against the light. The floor shook beneath a sudden weight and the door drifted open. He thumbed back the other hammer, but there was no one standing in the opening. A man lay across the bottom, blood spilling from a gaping hole in his middle.

Emerson wasn't taking any chances on another man waiting for him in the hallway. He tore open the curtain and flattened against the wall, peering out past the edge of the window frame. His horse was still tied up in the alley, but there was no sign of the man who'd been standing nearby. He threw up the sash and lifted one leg to hook over the sill. It felt heavy. He bent down to remove the pinch bar from his boot.

The window flew apart. Something clipped the crown of his hat and he threw himself to the floor, landing on his shoulder and clawing in his left-hand pocket for his extra shells. He broke open the shotgun, plucked out the smoking empty, and poked a shell into the barrel. He slammed shut the breech, then slid out the pinch bar and transferred his hat from his head to the notched end. He rose into a crouch and pushed the torn crown slowly above the windowsill. The sill exploded and the hat tore away.

He threw aside the bar. The man he'd shot still lay across the base of the open door, a dark patch spreading away from him across the floorboards. A sheriff's star drooped from his striped shirt. The blast from the Stevens had cut his silver watch chain in two, the ends dangling from the watch pocket in his trousers and his breast pocket. Emerson poked his head through the opening, almost on a level with the prone body. Three men, possibly more, were headed his way from the stairs to the ground floor. All held shotguns. He poked the Stevens out into the hall and fired without aiming, then threw himself into a roll away from the door. He kicked it shut, got up, and heaved the marble-topped chest of drawers across it, barricading the entrance and blocking the light coming through the jagged hole.

It was dark in the room now. He waited for his eyes to adjust before peering out the shattered window. The gelding, spooked by the reports from inside the building, tossed its mane and fiddle-footed at the end of its hitch. The loose-bellied deputy still was nowhere in sight.

Emerson's gaze prowled the alley. The building across the way was a billiard hall, with a front porch under construction. A stack of lumber four feet high flanked the alley wall, with just enough room between it and the building for a man to insert himself.

He fished out his last shell, emptied and reloaded the barrel he'd fired, and snapped shut the action. A heavy weight struck the door to his room from outside. He ignored it, drawing a bead on the center of the stack of lumber. He squeezed the trigger, and without waiting to see what he'd hit he swept the barrels around inside the window frame to clear away jagged glass, threw the Stevens out through the opening, grasped the top of the frame with both hands, and swung his legs out into the night air. He hung there for a second, then let go. Simultaneous blasts, from inside the room and from behind the stack of spilled and splin-tered lumber, lit the sky above his head like sheet lightning. For a moment he felt as if he were suspended in mid-air, then he landed on his feet hard, turning an ankle and coming down on his right shoulder. He groped around for the shotgun, couldn't find it, put a hand down to brace himself while he fumbled for the Paterson, and felt the cold steel of the Stevens under his palm. A shadow leapt up from behind the stack of lumber. He swung up the shot-gun and emptied the second barrel into its center. It seemed to fold like a book, but then there was another explosion from the win-dow and a hornet stung his right hip. Emerson dropped the Stevens and ran toward the gelding, drawing the Remington from his pocket.

LOREN D. ESTLEMAN

When he jerked loose the reins, the horse shied from the sulfur stench of spent powder on his clothing, but he got hold of the bit and followed the horse around in a half-circle, putting it between himself and the hotel. He snapped three rapid shots toward the window of his room, swung a leg over the saddle, and held on as the gelding stretched its long legs into a gallop, hanging off the side the way Bloody Bill had taught him. Two men came barreling out the front door of the hotel as he swept past, but he emptied his remaining chambers under the horse's neck before they could raise their shotguns and they ducked for cover.

When he was out of shotgun range, he hauled himself upright and bent low, drawing blood with his spurs. The closed and darkened square of the assay office flashed past in a heartbeat as he ran away from thirty-five hundred dollars in gold. He couldn't catch his luck no matter how fast he ran.

TWENTY

A nd he sent forth a raven, which went forth to and fro, until the waters were dried up from off the earth.' "

The Reverend D. W. Breedlove, Honey had noticed, did not thunder his sermons. He had no need, and in fact were he to lift his great voice above the level of normal conversation he would blow out a windowpane. Instead, his mellow bass wrapped itself around his small collection of parishioners like a velvet cloak. He stood behind the unpainted pine lectern, neither leaning upon it nor resting his great tattered Bible upon its slanted top, but holding it open in his hands and reading the passage in its pointed Gothic characters without benefit of spectacles. The man's eyes and ears existed beyond time; a head bent in distracted conversation in the last row would bring an abrupt halt to his oratory until attention was restored, and Honey had learned the folly of speaking Breedlove's name aloud in a noisy crowd unless one was prepared to respond when the old man questioned him later about the nature of the reference. Some of the children in the congregation were convinced he was God.

Breedlove laid a slip of paper between the pages and closed the book, but still he did not set it down, holding it at the ready like a farmer his spade. Rectangles of paper stuck out between pages top and bottom, straining the spine; which marker belonged to which preserved passage, and what method he used to distinguish one from another, was one of the old man's mysteries, but he never failed to find the verse he required to illustrate the point he was making. He looked like a black candle in his pilgrim coat with his shock of white hair bright in the sunlight streaming through the windows.

"My children, we are all Noah's raven, black and ready to clean up a spill not of our making. This is our lot, and if it should appear less noble than Samson's destruction of the pagan temple, or Jesus evicting the moneychangers from the house of His father, we may take comfort in knowing that someone had to stay behind and clean up."

Laughter crackled through his listeners, although Honey was convinced they had heard these words before. They were like children who could not sleep if one word of their bedtime story varied from the way it had been told a hundred times in the past.

"This is our lot," Breedlove continued, "but it need not be our shame. Many know the story of the white dove, which Noah sent forth, and which returned with an olive branch in its beak to bear witness that the waters had subsided. But the black bird went first, that the dove's white feathers would not be blemished by the mud and offal. His was the first great sacrifice of the new beginning. My children, did not the Lord later give His only son, to spare our damnation? Then was not the raven His favorite?"

Here Honey began to play "This Is Why I Love My Jesus." The congregation sang, some from hymnals, most from memory because the majority could not read. The old upright, seriously out of tune and possessing three broken strings whose keys he'd memorized so he could avoid striking them, clanked out an approximation of Hoffman's notes, providing a close match for Honey's own lack of skill and in effect canceling it out. He wore a black morning coat, long in the sleeves so that his fingers barely stuck out through the cuffs, striped trousers he managed to keep up with braces and a new hole punched in the belt, and shoes that laced all the way up his ankles, themselves an acceptable fit. Garters managed the sleeves of his much-washed linen shirt, and it felt good to wear a clean collar. Sunday mornings it was possible to believe the filthy stable hand didn't exist.

The First Abyssinian Church of Corpus Christi had been built to store grain. The sweet clean smell of it lingered, and golden motes remained to swim in the light slanting through the windows high on the walls. The pews were constructed of unplaned pine and there was a newness to the interior that made Honey think of the House of Rest for Weary Boatmen, by very reason of that place's seeming ancientness; whereas it was as old and dark as sin itself, the church was as fresh as salvation. He himself was unsalvageable. He did not believe in God, or rather did not understand Him, preferring to expect chaos from a universe without order and spare himself disappointment, but he liked the light, bright place and its atmosphere of hope, so different from the reek and murk of the livery. That building had come from the earth, soaked to its iron core with blood, shit, and decay, while the church was made of dawn.

"The First Abyssinian is Baptist in spirit," Breedlove had said while showing Honey around the building. "Where we part is in the concept of a church consisting entirely of those who have personally accepted Christ. We have not all done so, and I confess nothing when I declare there are times when I wonder if His hand does not slip on occasion, emburdened as He is with the cares of worlds beyond our own. We welcome the saved, but we honor those who are still in quest. We are a net built of fine mesh to capture those souls who have fallen through larger holes before they plunge into the pit."

"Reverend, there's no catching me. My faith's ground down fine as dust."

"Well, we shall see if Mr. Deliverance Wisdom Breedlove cannot sweep it into a soul-shaped pile. In the meantime, show me how you play."

"*. . . He has pardoned my transgressions. He has washed me. He has made me white as snow. . . .*"

Honey sounded the three descending notes at the end as the congregation repeated the words "white as snow;" an odd selection, he thought, but then it was an odd church, without a cross in sight and its only decoration a framed steelpoint etching, plainly cut out of an illustrated newspaper and mounted on the wall behind the pulpit, of a group of laborers hoeing rows of crops. There was nothing spiritual in the subject or its execution.

"Georgia, dear, I want you to meet our new pianist. Georgia Breedlove, Ollie Johnson."

She was small-boned, fine of feature, and as light as Honey was dark, but she was colored just the same. She had large eyes with whites as clear as milk and irises as green as uncured tobacco, and in her simple blouse and dark skirt she reminded him of wildflowers wrapped in brown paper.

She bore no family resemblance to the reverend, and Honey considered that she may have been adopted; but then his own mother had been light, though he was as black as black came, and so there was no accounting for what took place between the generations. It was Georgia who swept the church, distributed and collected its meager library of hymnals, and cooked and brought Breedlove's meals when he stayed late, writing his sermons standing up behind his plain pulpit (except for when he drove the phaeton, he never seemed to sit), and led the singing in her thin, clear nineteen-year-old voice. She would tend to the reverend when he was ill, and it would be she who kept the budget, recording the collections in the ledger that was nearly as big as the Bible. She would be the one who stretched them to cover the necessities when she put on her plain but becoming hat and went to the store with a basket on her arm. Breedlove had told him, without irony, that without Georgia the First Abyssinian Church of Corpus Christi would have dried up and blown away like cotton fibers on the wind years ago, its pastor having starved.

The opportunity to play the piano and wear clothing more suited to his sense of himself than the poor inherited rags he wore to work had persuaded Honey Boutrille to visit the church. Georgia Breedlove persuaded him to stay. She did not do so through language—she had neither the old man's gift for oratory nor the kind of presence required to hold her own in even casual conversation—but through herself alone. Not counting Natalie Proudfoot, who was devoted to her Clyde to the exclusion of everyone and everything else, she was the first woman he had known since his aunts had packed him off who did not make her way with her body. He imagined he was in love.

He did not speak to her of his love, nor entertain the fancy that anything would come of it. The sensation itself was a pleasant surprise. Since leaving Galveston, he had sustained his existence with suicide and the comfort he found in its contemplation. Someday, he'd known, he would stop thinking about it and embrace it, and it was only when he realized that what he felt for Georgia was something more than the respite he took from her goodness and simple beauty that it occurred to him he had not thought of suicide since the moment Breedlove had introduced them. He had planned, once the first service had concluded, to obtain his penny draught of fusel oil, smoke a cigarette, and walk along the waterfront, where the stiff salt air would blow away for a time the meanness of his weekday existence; instead he stayed to help her collect the hymnals. On his second Sunday, he found a ladder behind the church, filled a bucket from the pump out back, and climbed up to wash the windows, which had been accumulating dust and city grime since the last time the reverend (who confessed to an uneasiness with heights) had performed that chore; when the panes were clean and the sunlight came through with God's purity intact, Georgia had exclaimed at the number of cobwebs that had thus become visible in the corners of the church. He'd offered to sweep them away, but she'd snatched up the broom before he could get to it, declaring that such work was intended for women, and had smiled at his feeble protests. He'd been more relieved than disappointed. Sweeping was livery duty and would only profane the sanctity of his Sundays.

He awoke to his fourth Sunday in association with the First Abyssinian with a sore throat and a dull ache behind his eyes. By then he had established a routine that required no thought: Dressed in his livery rags, he walked the twelve blocks to the church, where buckets of heated water awaited him atop the tiny laundry stove in a partitioned-off room at the back of the building. There he squatted to bathe himself in a galvanized tub and put on his church clothes. Although Breedlove had told him the clothes were his to keep, he continued to store them at the church to spare them contact with the vile surroundings of his weekday life. On the fourth Sunday, the wind was blowing fierce and cold from the northeast, with bits of sleet that stung his face like barbs as he leaned into it with his filthy straw hat tugged down over his ears and his hands in the pockets of his overalls. His eyes and nose were running when he got to the church. He shivered and sneezed throughout his bath, and after he dried off, his hands were shaking so badly he had to ask Georgia to help him with the studs on his cuffs. As was customary before services, the three sat down to tea in the little three-room house the Breedloves shared next to the church. Honey fainted while Georgia was pouring.

For three days he lay in the reverend's bed, Georgia coming in to bathe his forehead with a cool damp rag and feed him oyster stew. He knew then he'd never completely recovered from the Galveston pneumonia, had been walking around with it resting in a coil waiting to strike again. When the fever broke, the Breedloves pleaded for him to rest, but he feared for his job. Honey won out; the church could not support three adults on the collections it took in. He declined when Breedlove offered to help him dress in his work clothes, but consented to allow Georgia to accompany him back to the stable aboard the trolley. He was unsteady on his feet and the reverend had agreed to lunch with a family in his congregation and could not make the trip.

They spoke little during the ride. Honey hadn't the energy to hold up his end of a conversation, and Georgia seldom spoke unless addressed. They sat at the back of the car and watched a wintry gray Corpus roll past the windows.

They alighted four blocks from the livery. Honey let her take his arm, but he tried not to lean his weight on her. Although he knew from observation that her trim form was reinforced with wire, he was afraid she'd shatter like crystal.

His hope that Radget would be in the back as they approached the livery collapsed when he saw the man leaning with his back against one of the open doors. He was holding his glass flask, and the way his feet were splayed out to keep him from sliding into a heap told Honey the man had started drinking early and hadn't let up.

"Well, sir, here comes Diamond Jim. I thought you'd moved up in the world, got yourself crowned king of Africa or maybe

Grover Cleveland hired you for house nigger. That's why I been the last three days shoveling up horseshit with your name on it."

"Sorry, boss. I been sick."

"Who's that, your nurse? Maybe I ought take sick myself. She's prettier'n a mess of flies."

Georgia, confused, thanked him. Radget made his tearing-paper laugh and swigged, missing his mouth with most of it. His filthy shirt was soaked and so were his dungarees, the latter with something other than whiskey, or so Honey suspected. He'd never seen the man this far gone.

Honey disengaged himself from her arm. "You can go back to the church now. I have to get to work."

She surprised him by raising her voice and addressing Radget. "Mr. Johnson is still recovering. You won't work him too hard, will you?"

"This ain't no gentlemen's club, nursie. Everybody works, 'specially niggers. He ought get down on his knees and thank me for not throwing him out on his ass on account of he ain't showed up all week."

"Watch your language."

"What's that?"

Honey had spoken low. The man really hadn't heard. Honey spoke up. "I said watch what you say around a lady. She's kin to a preacher."

Radget's mouth stayed open, with a string of spittle hanging off one corner. He closed one eye tight—blocking out the double image he was seeing, Honey thought—then straightened with a grunt, stumbling until he found his balance. He corked the flask, slid it into a pocket of his worn leather coat, and went inside the stable, grabbing at one of the timbers framing the door to keep from falling when he turned.

"You get on back to the church," Honey repeated to Georgia. "I'll feel better once I start working."

"What a horrible man. I'll pray for him."

He grinned, but she wasn't looking at him. Her hand grasped his forearm and she took a step away from the livery.

Radget came out the door with a rebel yell. He had the hay fork in his hands with the tines pointed at Honey. Honey stepped in front of Georgia, groping for the Bulldog. It wasn't in his overalls. He'd left it in the pocket of his morning coat back at the church. He swung right, throwing both arms around the woman and hauling her aside just as Radget charged past. The livery man tried to turn in mid-run, lost his balance, and fell, releasing his grip on the fork. Glass shattered. He howled when splinters from the flask in his pocket entered his hip.

Honey was on top of him before he could get his hand on the handle of the fork, gripping Radget's throat in both hands. Radget abandoned the fork to claw at Honey's face. Honey squeezed, intent on making his fingers meet, shouting at the top of his lungs without forming words. Radget's mouth was open, but only air was coming out, hoarse and tortured. His grip on Honey's face weakened. Honey squeezed, lifting Radget's head and pounding it against the hardpack earth. Someone else was screaming, and it was only when he felt hands on his shoulders, pulling at him, that he realized the voice was Georgia's. She was screaming, "Ollie!" over and over. Only the whites of Radget's eyes showed in a face nearly as dark as Honey's. He let go then. Radget's head fell back with a thud and rolled to one side.

The Reverend D. W. Breedlove found Honey sitting on the Arbuckle's crate, still breathing heavily with his hands gripping his knees. He had no idea how long he'd been sitting there, and in fact could not remember returning to the livery after escorting Georgia back to the trolley stop. No word had passed between them from the time he'd stopped strangling Radget. The livery man had been breathing when they'd left him, half senseless and coughing as his lungs worked independently of the rest of him to drag in air. There was no sign of him now and Honey had a dim recollection that he'd not been there when he returned. His most vivid memory was of Georgia's profile on the other side of the trolley window when it pulled away, her eyes looking straight ahead and not at Honey.

"The phaeton, please, Ollie," Breedlove said.

He nodded, understanding the words, and got up to hitch the two sisters to the vehicle. Neither man spoke until the reverend climbed into the driver's seat and placed the bundle he'd brought into the phaeton.

"Would you join me?"

Honey hesitated, then stepped up and sat beside him.

Breedlove was an accomplished driver. Honey lost track of time and distance, and if the reverend had stopped and ordered him out of the vehicle, he would not have been able to find his way back. Twilight was rolling in and Corpus Christi was far behind them when at last Breedlove turned the vehicle around at the top of a low rise and drew rein. The lights of a town—it might have been Corpus, but Honey could only guess at that, as he had not been away from it since he'd been living there—showed to the left and nearly blended with the stars, which seemed to be winking on as if some hand were igniting them one by one. The flat gleam of water showed ahead; the harbor, vanishing into darkness where the failing light fell short of the gulf. The great expanse of black sickened Honey's heart. It put him in mind of his future.

"I come here twice a month," Breedlove said. "No one knows,

not even Georgia. She thinks I like to go out driving, perhaps to pray. She may be right. I never think of it."

Honey said nothing. He could not see as far as the horses now. The reverend's voice was a deep rumble in the shadows at his side.

"They say, people who have never answered the call, that mine is a humbling trade. It's precisely the opposite. All the worst crimes committed in the name of faith, from the slaughter of Christians to the Inquisition to the taking of slaves, were committed because someone whose privilege it was to speak for God forgot that he was only a vessel. You see, Ollie, for most devout people, a man of God is as close as they ever come to the original article in this life. It's natural that some should confuse the two, and it's human that some men of God make the same mistake. It's easy to do, and so very difficult when you stop on a hill like this one, with His earth on one side and His great ocean on the other, and all His universe on display beyond and above. I come here to remind myself that I'm just a man, and a poor one at that. I could not even begin to build a city, like the one whose lights you see. And the men who did were not gods either."

"I think I understand."

"I doubt it. Nor should you, at your age. When you're as old as I am, perhaps you will. I pray you do. So many fail, even on their deathbeds in the fullness of their years. Are you in love with Georgia?"

"I am." The shock of the question had forced him to answer truthfully. When Breedlove said nothing, he continued. "It makes no difference now, because I know she'll never have me after what happened. For a while there I was considering asking you for her hand."

"That's impossible."

"I know."

"You don't. Georgia is my wife."

Honey was silent. He was afraid if he opened his mouth he'd vomit. His naked shame seemed to shine in the dark.

"I thought—" He went no further. His mouth had filled with bile.

"You thought what most people think, that she's my daughter. That's my fault. I never introduce her as Mrs. Breedlove. I dread the horror that I've seen before on people's faces when they find out. It's a terrible weakness, and I know it causes her pain. More evidence that I am not God."

The seat shifted. Honey felt a weight on his lap. He knew it was the bundle the reverend had brought, and he knew what it contained.

"It's a poor gift," Breedlove said. "You're accustomed to better, I suspect. Be careful when you unwrap it; your pistol will fall out."

He knows, Honey thought. Aloud he said, "I don't want anything from you. You've given me too much as it is."

"It's poor enough, as I said. You wanted more." He lifted the reins. "You cannot go back to the stable. Corpus Christi is no longer safe. There's an envelope in the bundle. It should take you far from here. I'm told there's a large Negro population in Denver. It's not as friendly a place as New Orleans to such as we, but it's better than anything you'll find in Texas. After today they'll be looking for you all over the state."

"How long have you known?"

"I told you about your speech weeks ago. Also you've had little practice at being frightened, and in most places that comes with the color. You match the descriptions in the bulletins from Louisiana. However, I wasn't certain until today. Most of us have learned to run away from a weapon in a white man's hands. They call us cowards, but there is no victory in defending oneself against a hay fork only to dangle from the end of a rope for doing it. That's the kind of wisdom you cannot acquire living in a community of black men governed by black men, although I believe you are learning it now. Your life since New Orleans has begun to do for you what this hill does for me." He gave the reins a flip and the mares started forward. "We'll drive the long way to the station, around the livery. They probably think you've stolen the phaeton and horses."

On a side street near the railroad station, the reverend climbed down, shook Honey's hand formally, and returned to the driver's seat. Honey watched him as he drove off, but Breedlove never turned his head.

A train was coming in and the station was crowded. Honey spotted the lawmen easily: Planted at the four corners of the waiting room, they were the only ones not looking toward the platform. Honey mixed with the crowd, waited outside the occupied water closet for an interminable length of time, expecting a tap on the shoulder at any moment, then when the door opened he slid in around the man who was emerging and changed into his church clothes. In morning coat, striped trousers, a fresh shirt and collar, and a soft crowned black hat that he recognized as one of Breedlove's, he felt a little less like a fugitive. He transferred the banknotes from the envelope to an inside breast pocket, inspected the Bulldog's chambers, and thrust it under his belt in the small of his back, where the tails covered it. He left his filthy shirt and overalls in a pile in the corner next to the gravity-flush toilet and went out.

On his way to the ticket window he walked right past one of the lawmen, whose gaze lingered on him a tenth of a second, then continued its journey around the room. He hoped there was a train leaving before any of them felt nature's call. Once they found the clothes he'd left behind, they'd know they weren't looking for a colored man dressed as a laborer.

He bought a ticket on a Southern Pacific sleeper leaving at 8:15 P.M. for San Antonio, where he would change to another S. P. train headed for Dallas, and travel north from there aboard the Missouri, Kansas, and Texas. He turned away from the window, hoping to lose himself in the crowd for the next twenty minutes.

"Honey Boutrille?"

He'd just stepped onto the platform when he heard the voice behind him. Steam from the locomotive champing nearby enveloped him as he turned with the Bulldog in his hand.

The fat man in the rumpled suit lifted his arms, palms forward. There was no star pinned to his swollen vest, but the yellow ivory handle of a belly pistol poked out of his watch pocket.

"I'm not a gun man." The stranger spoke slowly, with a quaver. "I'm a journalist, and I'm prepared to offer you two hundred dollars as an advance sum against royalties for your life story. My name is Torbert."

PART SIX

———

COLORADO PEACH

TWENTY-ONE

—

Y ou say you tangled with some barbed wire?"

"That's right, Doc. The bobwire won."

"I've treated barbed wire injuries. A strand breaks during stringing, takes off an ear or a couple of fingers. This doesn't look like one of those."

"It wasn't like that. My horse threw me. Goddamn jack rabbit spooked it and I fell on the fence. I been hurt plenty worse, so I didn't figure to mess with it, but that was a few days ago and I didn't like the look of the holes. Hurts like hell."

"The wounds are infected. If I didn't know better, I'd say they were caused by buckshot."

"Seems to me I'd of noticed if they was."

"True. Well, strip out of the flannels and get on the table."

Emerson didn't much care if the doctor believed his story. He'd chosen him for his rundown office and the sign out front, which was weathered and flaked so bad you could barely make out the M.D. The neighborhood was as ugly as any in Denver, with its shot-out streetlamps and boarded-over windows, nearly as bad as the Devil's Acre, although less friendly in appearance because

Emerson was a stranger there. A doctor who practiced in such surroundings would be glad of the business and wouldn't waste time
informing the authorities of suspicious wounds. Chances were
he'd treated plenty of those and would just as soon not attract the
sort of attention that might deprive him of his license. He was an
old croaker to boot, and none too clean, with ancient stains on his
apron that might have been whiskey or blood or pus, and smudges
on his spectacles. Wads of horsehair bulged out of splits in his
leather-upholstered examining table.

His patient lay on his back on the lumpy surface and made
pictures out of the pattern of cracks in the plaster ceiling while the
doctor picked with his instruments at the three blue holes in
Emerson's right hip, removing bits of dirt and putrid flesh. They
burned like fire, but he'd felt worse pain prying out the pellets with
his knife in an empty cattle car on the way from Idaho Territory.
He'd let the holes bleed out before pulling up his drawers, but he
hadn't had whiskey to flush them nor clean dressing, and by the
time he got to Denver they were red and puckered and he was running a light fever. It was the way of his luck lately that his busted
ribs had stopped hurting just in time for some county law to open
him up like a tin of sardines, and him minding his own business in
his hotel room planning a small robbery. When they got tired of
looking for him, he'd go back to Pocatello and take out a Missouri
mortgage on the hide of the assayer who'd cheated him of his
hard-stole money and sold him to the sheriff.

"This might sting a bit."

"*Jesus Christ!*"

"If it didn't hurt, it wouldn't cure." The doctor corked the
alcohol bottle, applied cotton to the wounds, and wound a couple
of yards of gauze around Emerson's thigh. He fixed it with a safety
pin. "That's two dollars."

"Hell, I could get a good whore for that."

"Not in Denver."

Emerson got dressed and gave him two cartwheels. The doctor put fresh cotton and a roll of bandages in a sack. "Change the dressing twice a day. You may be down with the fever a day or two. Is there someone who can look after you?"

"My wife."

The doctor squinted through his smeared lenses. "You don't strike me as the marrying sort."

"That's what she told the judge when I lit out on her."

"You must be on good terms."

"That's what I'm fixing to find out."

TWENTY-TWO

The Carillon had had nearly as many lives of its own as had passed through its portals since the first prospector had contracted the territory's first case of clap.

A large tent had stood on the site in 1859, before the clapboard-and-canvas towns of Auraria and St. Charles combined to form the city of Denver. There, miners had drunk and danced with women of easy character on a square of wooden floor laid directly on the earth and retired to Indian blankets spread in the dimly lit corners to fumble with buttons and stays. The floor was moved every Monday to sweep up the gold dust that had spilled through the cracks between the boards, and the customer who came closest to guessing the monetary amount that had thus been recovered received fifty percent of the sum, which he was expected to spend on drinks for those who had assembled to learn the result. For this reason the establishment became known as the Half Chance, and there were old-timers in town who still insisted upon referring to it by that name. It was said that no dollar that had ever wandered into the Half Chance ever came out.

The same could not be said for most of the enterprises that followed.

The first permanent structure built on the lot burned down two weeks after it was finished, when a novice bartender struck a match to peer into a barrel of rye to see if it was empty. The place was rebuilt, only to burn down again during the Great Fire of 1863. The third building, aptly christened The Phoenix, was erected of brick, on the third-little-pig principle, but the contractor skimped on mortar, and when Cherry Creek spilled over its banks in 1864, the torrent took it down as if it were a mud hut. The proprietor, who had stoically outlasted the first three constructions, declared bankruptcy, and the lot was sold at auction to one Stern Flint, an immigrant from Munich who had made his fortune wholesaling leather goods to the Union Army, and whose determination to raise a structure that would prove to be as solid as his name came to pass when the Carillon opened two years later. Three stories of native sandstone, with arched windows all around and staffs flying the flags of four nations, including the Prussian double-eagle of Flint's birthplace, housed a grand ballroom, a mahogany bar advertised as the longest between Chicago and San Francisco (and sworn to in an affidavit signed by an independent arbitrator who had measured its rivals in Virginia City and St. Louis, framed for the inspection of the public in the main room), a stage, and curtained balconies for "private dining" with women employed by the establishment. Two complete kitchens served the formal dining room and a tearoom with a separate ladies' entrance from the street; great pains were taken to protect the patrons of the latter from reminders that it was in any way connected with the Carillon. The upper two floors contained parlors and bedrooms for more discreet assignations than could be arranged in the balconies, Flint's own living quarters, and—since 1881—the private apartments of Mrs. Purity Peach Duncan.

Quarter-page advertisements in the *Post* and *Rocky Mountain News* identified the Carillon as a melodeon, offering musical entertainment of the highest quality. Both Primrose and West's Big Minstrel Festival and Lilly Clay's Company of Ladies Only had stopped there on their tours of the western states and territories. The Half Chance had come a long way from Indian blankets on bare earth.

Inside the enameled white walls of her dressing room, Mrs. Purity Peach Duncan—she had dropped the "Emerson," but retained the "Mrs.," never correcting those who assumed she was widowed—received her business partner, who showed her a telegram that had been delivered to his suite that morning:

STERN FLINT

THE CARILLON

DENVER

I HOPE THIS WILL REMIND YOU OF CASPER BOX WHO

DIVERTED LITTLE BETSY BRASS FROM THE CRITERION

IN 66 STOP IF SO AND FOR OLD TIMES SAKE WOULD

APPRECIATE INTRODUCTION TO MRS PURITY PEACH

DUNCAN EMERSON STOP WILL ARRIVE DENVER ON THE

15TH

BOX

She read the message with the aid of a monocle, favoring her stronger eye on the advice of her physician, who held that weak vision improved itself through effort rather than assistance. The result so far had been an almost constant headache, which she relieved with opium. Large-boned and long-chinned, she was what at age thirty-nine was described as a "handsome woman." In her twenties she had been called horse-faced, and she was under no illusions that the same would not still be true if she were not a woman of property. This morning she wore a plum-colored dressing gown of heavy silk, satin slippers cut low to flatter her pretty feet, of which she was vain, and a turbanlike terry headdress to conceal her thinning hair. In public she affected a variety of elaborate wigs which her hairdresser insisted were imported from Paris. (Mrs. Duncan had found out by accident that they were made in Philadelphia, but she permitted the swindle because the hairdresser was her opium supplier.) For her, "in public" meant the ground floor of the Carillon. She seldom ventured outside its doors, and when she did, she always returned with a nearly orgasmic sensation of relief. The greater world, over which she had no control, was filled with ugliness and pain, and had been since the destruction of the Old Dominion. This had been true in Missouri and Kansas, where she had sold her body out of a succession of board-and-batten shacks and infested soddies, and it was even more so in Denver, where drunken miners unloaded pistols into one another's belly and women too old to support themselves with their bodies froze to death sleeping in doorways. The paintings of placid Greek myths with which she had hung the walls of her suite, and the chamber music she persuaded the orchestra to play between the raucous and bawdy latest selections from New York and St. Louis, were often all that sustained her when she was not actually on the pipe.

"I'm sure there's a story behind how Little Betsy Brass came by her name," she said upon reading the telegram.

"A magnificent creature. She was hardly bigger than my hand, yet when she opened her mouth you would have sworn she'd swallowed sixteen trumpets and a tuba. I believe it was the shared opinion of the medical community that Miss Betsy was born with a diaphragm as big as a pig."

"Charming girl."

"Quite so." Flint was immune to irony. "So petite, yet so *strident*. That scoundrel V. M. Gorham booked her at the Criterion the week the Carillon was to open. We were offering the Chapmans, with banjo selections and dancing, but Little Betsy Brass enjoyed the popularity of novelty, and we were certain to open to a dismal house. It so happened Mr. Box was in town, arranging with the Denver Hall for the appearance of his troupe; we are old acquaintances since New York, where I financed his tribute to the Crusades with music. When he learned of my situation, he wired Gorham, pretending to be Little Betsy's manager, and informed him that their arrival would be delayed twenty-four hours. When their train arrived, quite on schedule, Mr. Box met them with flowers and conveyed them and their luggage to the Carillon, where I had the contracts all ready for Little Betsy's signature. Gorham was apoplectic, but there was of course nothing he could do, except thank me for lending him the Chapman's services so his stage would not be empty that week. Our little enterprise owes its very existence to Mr. Casper Box."

Stern Flint was a Bavarian, whose gentle accent and reserved manner often disguised an excitable temperament. He cropped his fair hair very close to his long skull, and strangers were inclined at first glance to mistake him for a foreign college student. He exercised with dumbbells, ate only raw vegetables and cheese, and lived with a young man whom he introduced as his nephew from Bamberg. He was sixty-eight years old.

Mrs. Duncan said, "I think it would have survived the competition. The Criterion features only entertainment and liquor."

"Perhaps. But Mr. Casper Box is in the way of a good luck charm. I missed him on his last time through and I should very much like to make him welcome." His blue eyes and ageless, fine-boned face implored her. He was never so rude as to ask a person any sort of favor; which was why so many of his "old acquaintances" seemed always to be doing them. Mrs. Duncan believed his story.

"He knows a bit about me. I haven't used the name Emerson since my divorce." This was no secret to Flint, who had seen the documents when they were negotiating their partnership.

"The man has sources. I daresay that if he were ever to publish his memoirs, a number of prominent citizens would be forced to decamp to Europe. It would be a very great favor to me if you would agree to receive him. To yourself, as well; his revues have a way of making money, for himself and everyone connected with him. He has three former wives to support and cannot afford to slow down, however much noise he makes about retiring."

"You needn't have mentioned the last part. If it weren't for you, I'd still be making my living on my back."

"And a very good one it would be. You may take that as an objective observation." There were no secrets on his part either. Their partnership was based on trust as well as profit.

"What is his preference? Lady Jane's appointment book is always filled, but she's cooperative where the good of the house is concerned."

"I doubt he would accept. Tobacco is his only vice, and that only in the form of snuff. He exhausted most of the others before you were born."

"Now I'm intrigued. A man with only one vice is an oddity in Denver."

"I rather think you'll get on." He rose from the horsehair arm-chair, the only overtly masculine piece in her suite, and a gesture toward him. She invited no other gentlemen, and no ladies at all, including her own. The Louis XIV tables and chairs, Venetian mirrors, and Chinese silk wallcoverings—the finest furnishings to be found in private hands within five days' journey of the Rockies—

were seen by none other than the proprietors of the Carillon. "Tomorrow is the fifteenth. Casper always stops at the Windsor, even when he hasn't two nickels to rub together. I'll leave a message with the desk."

"Just Box. The company of jugglers and tightrope artists lost its pleasure a long time ago. If he shows up with so much as an actress—especially an actress—I'll have them both put out, and you can find a new partner."

"You are a conundrum, dear Mrs. Duncan. Not so long ago, a woman stranded in this wilderness would undertake any journey in order to make acquaintance with another woman."

"Not this woman. They're insubstantial and inchoate, prattling on about hemlines and culture, when all they really care about is snagging some male. Then their conversation centers around children and preserves. The only thing one can say in their favor is they're not men."

"And yet you will host a man."

"They at least have the virtue of variety, or in any case the appearance of it. They're all much the same once you get past the bright foil, but until then they're amusing."

She was smiling. He was not. "Was it so very difficult for you on the border?"

"Not as difficult as it was for some. I survived."

He snapped into a bow and took himself out. She twisted the key in the lock, but was so lost in thought she had to go back and check to make sure the door was secure. Yes, it had been difficult on the border between Missouri and Kansas. The Kansas Militia, stopping by the farm on their way to Sedalia, had tied a noose around her father's neck and hauled him up into a beech, just for fun. He'd survived, because they hadn't bothered to bind his hands, but he'd dangled there half an hour hanging onto the rope, and had never been much good for farming or anything else after that. Then her married sister Charity was arrested by the Union on a charge of consorting with rebel sympathizers and locked up in a Kansas City building that had promptly collapsed, crushing her to death along with a dozen other women. And both of them, her father and sister, had supported abolition, the cause embraced by their tormentors. One week later, Charity's husband Enoch, a former Kansas Jay-hawker, had joined Bloody Bill Anderson's Confederate guerrillas. He took a ball through a lung at Baxter Springs and died of pneumonia, but not before introducing Purity to Twice Emerson. Two months later they were married, and the whole country could have gone pro-slave for all she cared. It couldn't have been any worse than life with Emerson.

Being deserted by such as he was the low point. She'd tried to kill herself with rat poison, but took too much and threw it up and what she went through during the next forty-eight hours had determined her not to repeat the attempt. But she'd had no money to live. Missouri was full of men on the move, low on women. She hadn't needed to work out the arithmetic.

No. Stern, she thought as she sat before the mirror on her dressing table, tucking her thinning tendrils beneath today's wig, *it wasn't so very difficult for me on the border. Staying alive is easier than being alive.*

It took all the social skills she had developed as mistress of the Carillon not to laugh at Casper Box as he stepped across the threshold into her parlor the following night. He wore a black broadcloth suit cut to the current fashion, but it was so tight it creaked when he moved, or seemed to. He was a very small man with a large head, and his hair and moustaches were dyed a dead black. He resembled nothing so much as a painted wooden doll of the type used by the professional voice-throwers she sometimes hired to entertain her male customers between liaisons with the ladies of the house.

"Very nice," said he, after a swift circular tour of the parlor, "and all genuine. You'd be surprised, or perhaps not, by the junk some salesmen manage to palm off on people of a certain station. Mrs. Woolworth has a full set of Chippendale chairs in her dining room which can be had at any of her husband's stores."

"Do you know furniture, Mr. Box?"

"I know swindles, Mrs. Duncan. You've a keen eye." He smiled with surprising charm. Evidently, Stern had informed him of the impropriety of addressing her by her married name. She began to question whether she might not enjoy the evening after all.

She was wearing her most becoming wig, auburn arranged in a chignon, and a dress of ivory satin, closed at the throat with an emerald brooch. She bought her own jewelry, declining offers from gentlemen not because she considered them inappropriate but because most men had appalling taste when it came to ornament; their diamond horseshoe stickpins and ruby rings put her in mind of Christmas balls. She felt attractive, and not precisely bound by the laws of nature. Anticipating a dreary two hours, she had smoked two pipes that afternoon. The globes of all her lamps were haloed in white gold and she crossed to the serving tray with a sensation of gliding. "Please sit down. Brandy?" She touched the cut-crystal decanter.

"Tea, if you please, and if that pot ain't just for looks. I'm a man of temperance." He sat on one of the Louis XIV chairs.

She filled two cups. "I thought all you theatrical men imbibed from the cradle."

"And all the way to the grave, if we had our way. I had a heart attack in Baltimore a couple of years back, right in the middle of a tour of Dixie. Doc said it was either drink tea or breathe dirt. I chose tea."

"You have an iron will." She handed him the cup and sat in the matching chair facing his.

"No, ma'am, just scared of dying. I get a little more scared the closer I get. I was too old to fight in the war, but them that did tell me it was the same for them. I don't guess I'm telling you anything new. Missouri, wasn't it?"

She felt suddenly apprehensive. "Yes."

"I hoped you wouldn't mind my mentioning it. It's the reason I'm here."

"In Denver?"

"No, that's business. Well, it's all business, but this one's speculative. You were married for a while to a guerrilla named Emerson."

She said nothing.

"He's in the papers again, but I expect you knew that. Just this morning I read in the *Post* where he's wanted for killing two lawmen in Pocatello, on top of a stagecoach robbery in Idaho City and a California train and sundry other murders. There's three thousand on his head now."

"Mr. Emerson's activities don't concern me, Mr. Box. As you said, he's no longer my husband."

"I think they do. Or at least, your activities concern him. He hasn't a candle's chance in California or the territories. He's bound to show up here, and sooner rather than later."

"There's a flaw in your theory. We haven't seen each other in twenty years. He doesn't even know I'm here."

"The frontier's a small place, Mrs. Emerson. Pardon; Mrs. *Duncan*. The country keeps moving, and there are only so many places to stop and wet your whistle. *I* knew, and two weeks ago I never heard of you. I'm here to ask you that when he shows up, you'll show him the hospitality you're famous for."

"On what authority? Mr. Flint may be in your debt, but I am not. You have the advantage on me, Mr. Box; *I* never heard of *you* before yesterday." She smiled above her cup. What this cost her, she was confident the opium concealed.

Box smiled charmingly. There was no animosity in the expression. He slid a rectangular fold of paper from an inside pocket and passed it across to her.

She opened it. The writing was blurred. She unfastened a button on her bodice and reached inside for her monocle.

"It's a letter signed by Mr. Christopher A. Buckley of San Francisco," he said. "He's the principal investor in the Miners' and Cattlemen's Bank of Sacramento, with branches in Frisco and Denver. The next time you apply for a business loan, you ought to use that glass of yours to study the fine print in the foreclosure clause."

TWENTY-THREE

——

"This is the best we have aboard, sir. Would you care to taste it?"

The porter was a young man with a grave face, nearly as dark as Honey Boutrille's. The long-necked bottle and stemmed glasses remained steady on his tray even as the train heeled into a curve.

"I don't see what the point would be, seeing as how it's the best you have," Torbert said. "You might as well pour for us both."

The two passengers were sharing Torbert's compartment in the hotel car, seated facing each other on plush benches with a hinged table in between. The upper berth was swung up and locked, and south central Texas was rolling past the windows at a steady forty miles per hour.

They'd dined—again, in private—on oyster stew, roast quail stuffed with mushrooms and cranberries, and mashed potatoes, washed down with claret. Boutrille had astonished his host by ordering a second complete bird and eating it entire, albeit at a stately pace and patting the corners of his mouth unself-consciously with his linen napkin; his table manners would pass inspection anywhere on the Boul' Mich'. Torbert wondered when was the last time the man had sat down to a meal.

As the porter filled their glasses, leaving two inches at the top to avoid spillage, Torbert watched Boutrille smoking the cigar he'd given him. It was impossible to tell what the fellow was thinking, but he appeared to be enjoying the smoke. He looked like an apprentice undertaker in his too-large black coat and white collar. The journalist imagined there had not been much opportunity to arrange a proper fitting since New Orleans. He hadn't known what to expect of this killer of men, apart from the fact that he should expect nothing based on the stories he'd heard; but this quiet, guarded young man, swirling and sniffing at his cognac, fell so far outside the brackets that Torbert wondered if he weren't the victim of some bizarre transcontinental hoax dreamed up by Argus Fleet.

Part of his disbelief had to do with his good luck at practically stumbling over his quarry after so many weeks of following his cold trail. If anything, Corpus Christi's black community was even more cloistered than Galveston's, and his inquiries in the shanty saloons and crib joints that served coloreds had met only silence and, upon one occasion, a bartender's urgent request that he leave; the padlock had been off the place only a week, he explained, since the murder of a white drifter had occurred there in August. Since Boutrille had been in Louisiana at the time of this killing, Torbert had obliged without asking further questions. The town's polyglot population did not allow for neighborhoods clearly designated colored or Mexican or French or Russian. Searching for a black button in a black-button box was complicated by the fact that there was no box. The buttons were scattered throughout the city.

He'd fallen back on the journalist's last resort: Haunting the railroad station and docks on the theory that a man who had relocated twice in three months would move again, and a dollar in the hands of a ticket clerk or a bosun's mate might tighten the lead. He would give it a week, then book a compartment on the first train to Chicago. The meatpacking companies could have his services back at a bargain rate. There wasn't a mattress to be found in the Lone Star state that was free of lumps or vermin or lumpy verminous roommates, and the uneven diet had given him a case of bleeding piles.

His first visit to the station had borne no fruit, and the laborers and wharf rats who accepted his coins on the waterfront had seen no one answering Boutrille's description boarding any of the ships. The next day he'd made his weary way back to the station, and had been about to leave when he'd spotted Honey Boutrille coming out of the water closet.

There was no mistaking him, even if Torbert hadn't committed his vital statistics to memory. The sight of a Negro dressed in town clothes was rare enough back home, where the South Side coloreds decked themselves out in loud checks and yellow gaiters, and nearly nonexistent on the frontier. This one, too, did not carry himself as if he were accustomed to living with fear. He was wary, but not broken. He looked people in the eye. Torbert had known of colored men who'd been stripped and beaten for less. It was as if the fellow had dropped down from some dark planet and had not learned how to conduct himself among the ruling class.

Torbert had settled the question by calling Boutrille's name. He had responded with a pistol.

When the porter withdrew, closing the curtains behind him, Torbert asked his guest for his opinion of the cognac. He hadn't tasted his. The flask of whiskey he carried had spoiled him for liquor aged more than three weeks.

"Not as good as New Orleans. When do I get the rest of the two hundred?"

Boutrille's eyes were hooded, but it was clear the money was important. The bones of his face protruded in a way Torbert rec-

ognized from the tramps who congregated near the stockyards. He
had the gaunt look of a hunting creature.

"You saw the wire I sent from Corpus. It should be waiting for
us in San Antonio."

The message—SUCCESS STOP WIRE FOUR HUNDRED FOR EXPENSES
AND HB WHO IS IN HAND—would reach Argus Fleet at his home.
Torbert had no doubt the money would be forthcoming. The old
fox would raid his safe in the Biederman Building in his nightshirt
to comply.

Torbert had given Boutrille seventy-five dollars, leaving himself enough for train fare and incidentals. The money had helped
dispel some of his early suspicion; a man who carried that much
cash probably wouldn't be desperate to collect a reward of five
hundred. Despite that, Torbert was certain the man was just waiting for his opportunity to bolt. He'd been living on his instincts for
a long time and it would take most of whatever reporter's skills
Torbert still possessed to overcome them.

He would have to get as much information out of him as he
could right away, because Boutrille might stick him up for the entire
four hundred and skeedaddle. Torbert had let him see the wire as
much for that reason as to assure him he wasn't alerting the authorities. Fleet was always good for more, and you needed crumbs to
cage a pigeon.

Seated across from him, however, Boutrille looked more like a
black eagle.

"How's the cigar? I don't use them myself. In Chicago, you just
have to breathe the air."

"Not too bad. I usually smoke General Thompsons."

"But not lately."

"Not lately, no." He sounded polite.

Torbert looked at his notes, scribbled in pencil on one of the folded squares of newsprint he carried in all his pockets. Not much there, but then he'd hardly expected a complete biography. The best he hoped for, before the bird flew, or was recognized and apprehended or shot, were some hard facts to tie together a blood-and-thunder narrative like the ones Ned Buntline and Prentiss Ingraham and even Cody himself had invented to dress up the life of Buffalo Bill. Even Pat Garrett, who had known William Bonney before he put a bullet in him, had conspired with his collaborator, Ash Upson, to pen a half-ream of claptrap about Bonney's origins and adventures in order to make *The Authentic Life of Billy the Kid* more salable to a reading public brought up on the tall tales of westerners published by *Harper's Weekly* and the Messrs. Street and Smith. At least a few hours spent in the company of this subject would supply him with the ammunition necessary to answer his critics. He was past considering the irony that the unvarnished truth of his *U.S.S. Minnesota* memoir had been a disaster, and that when he'd traveled to the opposite extreme and tried his hand at pure fiction in his African adventure, he had not been able even to raise the interest of a flummerer like Fleet. These failures had made him a hybrid, neither journalist nor novelist, but a baker of literary souffles, part honest ingredients to support a dish made mostly of air.

"You say your father was murdered by secessionists. Did you witness the atrocity?"

"No, I was asleep in the back of the wagon. My mother told me about it later. She said it was an accident. I didn't find out he was shot in the face until I overheard my aunts talking about it when I was five."

"Did they say what provoked it?"

"He was driving a wagon instead of hitched to a plow."

"You don't sound bitter."

"I barely remember him. I was only three."

Torbert made a check beside the entry, to remind himself to punch it up later. Apathy had no drama. A blood oath, perhaps, sworn to while standing over his father's corpse? Vengeance upon the Confederacy. Winton Saint-Maarten had been described as a Johnny-come-lately guerrilla. He would have to ask Fleet what percentage of his readership resided in the South.

"I'm a little hazy on what you did between the time you left Baton Rouge and when you acquired the House of Rest. What sort of odd jobs?"

"This and that. The distilleries and cotton mills were always hiring. They didn't have to pay a boy as much as a grown man."

There was a story there, but Boutrille wasn't telling it. Torbert had seen enough of New Orleans to guess what it was, and that he couldn't tell it, either. He'd been propositioned by boys no older than twelve or thirteen, painted up like women. Suddenly he felt useless. He refilled the other man's glass. "Tell me about Saint-Maarten."

"There isn't much to tell. He beat up Mademoiselle Josephine and I shot him."

"What passed between you?"

"A bullet." Boutrille drew on his cigar.

"I mean before that."

"What always does? Write that down."

"I didn't come a thousand miles to write something I could have made up back home." He took a drink quickly. He had the uneasy feeling Boutrille had been reading his mind.

"Sorry, boss. You done bought yourself a pig in a poke."

"Stop that."

"Yes, boss." The grin dropped off his face.

Torbert went through his pockets once again, just to be doing something. He knew full well the notes he'd made in New Orleans were in his room in Corpus Christi. He reminded himself again to wire money to hold the room until he could make his way back. His valise was there, along with his toilet and the rest of his shirts and drawers. If nothing else he'd begun to understand the fugitive life.

"Saint-Maarten threatened to cut off the young woman's head, is that correct?"

"Something on that order."

"Exactly on that order. He told you to stand aside or he'd throw it at you."

Boutrille tipped a cylinder of ash into the weighted brass tray. "Who'd you talk to at the House of Rest?"

"A Madame something. She had one eye."

"Madame Pantalon. You can't believe everything she says. She's cokie."

Torbert was surprised—and a little disappointed—that his companion had fallen into so obvious a trap. The man was a confusing combination of shrewdness and naïvete, unpredictable. It may have been part of the reason he'd eluded capture since August.

"I also spoke with Mademoiselle Josephine. She confirmed it."

Boutrille was unruffled. "Don't believe *anything* she says. She'll tell you she's related to Cadillac."

"I questioned them separately. Saint-Maarten was armed with a Bowie knife, a useful tool for chopping down small trees and decapitating young women."

"He might've said it, then. I wasn't much listening to him. He was drunk."

"You were not."

"I was drinking gin. I had cognac earlier."

"You shot him through the eye."

"I was aiming at his chest."

"That's unlikely. He was holding the girl in front of him."

Boutrille blew smoke and said nothing.

Torbert lost patience. "I'm trying to set down your side of the story. Why are you fighting me? You sound like a man determined to hang himself."

Puff, puff.

"Did you fight in the war, Mr. Glidden?"

"Torbert." He'd given him one of the J. P. Glidden cards, explaining it was a *nom de plume*. "It was my privilege to defend the Union at sea."

"A navy man. My grandfather was, too, kind of. He came over in the hold of a ship."

"Then you will appreciate the fact I was opposed to trafficking in human souls."

"I appreciate it, since you say it. It doesn't follow just because you're a Yankee. You saw how things were down here. How they still are. I don't have to work hard to hang myself. Someone's sure to oblige whether I shot Saint-Maarten through the eye to save a whore or in the back fighting over her. I'm asking you why I ought to spend what time I have this side of the rope haggling over the difference."

Torbert wrote that down. He wished he could use it. Fatalistic heroes didn't sell books.

"The Jupiter Press has agreed to pay you two hundred dollars to do just that," he said.

"That's true enough. Start again, and I'll give you seventy-five dollars' worth to start. I'm a whoremonger and a killer, but I'm no cheat." Boutrille drained his glass and pushed it across for another refill.

TWENTY-FOUR

H e shelled out forty dollars for a bearskin coat and remembered one more reason why he missed California.

The pewter sky that had greeted him on the way from the
train station to the doctor's office had sagged and finally split
open, releasing gauzy flakes the size of double eagles that quickly
accumulated on the street and made fuzzy ghosts of the streetlamps and telegraph poles. Emerging from the Rocky Mountain
Miner's Emporium, he turned up his heavy collar against the
whooping wind and followed the smell of whiskey. By the time he
reached a saloon called the Arcade, two blocks north, his boots
were soaked through and his feet felt like flat irons. Two shots of
what the bartender assured him was Monongahela rye were
required before he felt the first needle-pricks of circulation returning to his toes.

He realized then he'd left the sack the doctor had given him at
the emporium, but he decided not to go back for it. When the
dressing he was wearing needed changing, he'd just throw it away,
and if the holes in his hip got to festering, he'd close them with a
cigar tip. It couldn't hurt any more than the alcohol. He'd had the

flat of a red-hot knife blade pressed against a wound during the fighting and he still had all his limbs.

Emerson approved of the Arcade, with its darkened wainscoting and plain bar. There was a friendly spitoon every couple of feet and no one seemed in any hurry to empty it out. Erickson's in Portland had finished him for fancy-trick places. The patrons of the Arcade observed elbow distance and hunkered over their drinks like cavemen protecting their raw meat from theft. If a lawman were to enter demanding for one of them to surrender himself, they would all turn and clobber him full of holes where he stood.

He asked the bartender where he could find a cheap layup. The bartender scratched his unshaven throat. "You can get a cot for a week for fifty cents in the Sons of Heaven, if you can stand the stink. It's the Chinese section."

"No Chinese." Jesus. How far did a man have to travel to get away from the yellow bastards?

"Delaney Street's Eye-talian. You can't follow their jabber, but the rooms are clean. Dollar a week."

"I said cheap."

"Good as it gets. They're charging five a day at the Windsor and turning people away. This here's Denver, mister. You might of noticed the whole town's built of brick. Wood's against the law. After you burn down a few times you learn to pay through the nose."

Emerson ordered another shot and didn't continue the conversation. The little bit he still had from Portland and the two hundred he'd gotten for the gold dust in Pocatello wasn't going to last long at the local rate. He decided to see about a room on Delaney Street. He needed some quiet time to plan out his approach to Purity.

Soft colors and flute music.

Others who smoked told stories of darkened hues—reds turned maroon, blues gone deepest black—and bells gonging at the ends of tunnels, but she had never experienced either. Her world, once the bitter bite of the smoke had passed, became a pastel place, with gusts of warm wind hooting through hollow reeds, occasionally achieving by random averages a recognizable scrap of song. Once, the music had managed to sustain itself without a single errant note for sixteen bars before it trailed off into something unintelligible, although hardly less pleasing. At the time, she remembered, she'd identified the melody and remembered the lyrics, which she'd forborne from singing, fearing to shatter the mood with her tentative voice. Upon awakening, however, she could not recapture the tune. It seemed important that she did, that its choice was somehow significant to the mystery of existence. Each time she smoked, she hoped the incident would repeat itself, but so far it had not, and she could not say if she'd been in pursuit of it for six months or two years. Opium was like that; it distorted time not only when you were under its direct influence, but whenever you tried to recall a specific dream while sober. But she could always count upon the soft colors and flute music, uncontaminated by the touch of a human hand on the brush or fleshly lips on the mouthpiece.

Alone in her dressing room, she opened the mother-of-pearl box her sister had given her before going off to be married and impaled one of the small black pills on the end of a needle. She returned the box to its drawer in her dressing table, lit the spirit lamp on the low table beside the chaise, and lay on her side on the blanket she'd spread over the cushions to protect the satin from stray sparks. She turned the pill slowly above the flame to burn off excess moisture, then transferred it to the tiny metal tube curving up from the side of the bamboo pipe. Laying the needle aside, she inverted the tube above the lamp and watched as the opium softened and changed color, becoming translucent, a glistening pearl. At the moment the first thread of vapor appeared, she righted the pipe and sucked in a deep draught. She held it as long as she could—in the beginning, a minute had seemed inhumanly long, and the acrid taste had nauseated her, but she had built herself up to three, having determined that the longer the smoke remained in her lungs, the longer and more lovely was the dream—then exhaled through her nose, that the hairs and tender membranes might retain what the lungs could not. She placed the pipe on the table and lowered her head to the gently curving arm of the chaise.

The dream this time was different. The white room dissolved into the pinks, aquamarines, and pearlescent hues she sought, but they pulsated in a way she found disturbing, as if she'd been swallowed by some subterranean creature whose pulse beat visibly in the walls of its stomach. The flute played, but there was something vaguely obscene about the sound; the atonal exhalations of a debauched drunk attempting to make music. She felt a nameless dread and a terrible sense of naked shame. Buried deep in her memory—she had not thought of it for years—was the feeling she had experienced at age twelve when her mother had opened the door of the outhouse and caught her seated on the hole with her petticoats rucked up to her belly and her fingers inside her pantaloons. That was what she felt now. Suddenly she wanted to hang off the side of the chaise on her belly and cough the smoke out of her lungs, end the dream before it got worse; and she knew it would get worse, much worse. She could not move. A suffocating weight seemed to be pressing onto her side, pinning her to the cushions. The dream would be dreamt to the end.

Something was beating beneath the unholy strains of the flute, slow and reverberating, with eons of silence between the blows, as if she were hearing it from under water. Then a door sprang open in the throbbing stomach wall and the beating stopped. The rectangular void the door left shifted, became trapezoidal, then parabolic, finally collapsing upon itself and closing, a wound healing over and sealing her inside with the thing that had come in through it. A human shadow, a man. It remained solid while the room squirmed about it. Not a shadow. A face, narrow and clean-shaven. The Devil was not dark. He was fair, with the long sinewy build of a logger.

"Pretty Peaches."

The Devil's speech was the Devil's own: Kansas City twang laid atop the Scandinavian singsong of upper Michigan.

"I don't reckon nobody's called you Peaches in a year of Easter Sundays."

"Twice."

It came out "Twa?" with a question mark. She was aware of that much. Her lips were as thick as hams.

"You used to call me 'Emmie,' remember? Only three people in Missouri knew my first name was the same as my last."

He'd come straight there from the Arcade. He was not a man to plan, and seldom one to stick to a plan once it was made. He'd had two more shots of rye and he hadn't eaten. He'd turned the wrong way after leaving the saloon, forgetting the bartender's directions to Delaney Street and the Italian district, where rooms were to be had for a dollar a week, and by the time he'd realized his mistake, there was the sandstone building at the end of the block with MELODEON painted on all the ground-floor windows and THE CARILLON lettered in an arch over the door. When none of the brightly dressed women in the crowd on the main level proved to resemble his picture of Purity Peach with twenty extra years on her, he'd climbed the curving staircase to the second floor, where a prissy waiter carrying an empty tray had asked him if he'd needed help. Emerson, too drunk and runny-nosed from the cold outside to palaver, had stuck the muzzle of his Remington against the man's forehead and spoken her name. Directions to her suite on the top floor were forthcoming. He'd hit the man a little harder than intended to keep him still, opening a gusher on top of his head with the pistol's butt and dumping him on the floor atop his tray. He'd probably spend the rest of his days pissing on himself if he recovered at all.

The door into her parlor hadn't given him any trouble to speak of. He knew the place was hers by the neat way it was kept, all the fancy furniture arranged in the same pattern as the split-bottom chairs and iron-frame bed in their Clay County shack. The room was deserted and so was the bedroom, hung all over with pictures in frames. The door to the last room was stout, as if she'd been expecting him and had chosen that one to hide behind. But a door was just a door.

He'd thought at first she was drunk, sprawled on a daybed in the middle of the afternoon with all her clothes on. Then he'd smelled the smoke, seen the little lamp and the pipe, fixtures in the Devil's Acre. That had shocked him a little, but no more than when he'd thought she'd been drinking; he'd never been able to get her to touch a drop, even when he was far along himself and tried to force her, for the company. Twenty years was twenty years. Same old horse face, but she painted it now. Waist tiny as ever. When you smoked hop, you didn't wear whalebone.

The look on her face when he called her Pretty Peaches made him mad. He hadn't expected a big welcome, but on the other hand he hadn't been prepared to be looked at as if he were a bucket of piss. When she tried to talk, her lips got in the way and she drooled, a glittering thread hanging out of the corner of her mouth where she lay on her side. That made him madder. He grabbed her by the hair and pulled, to dump her to the floor. The hair came off. He stood there gaping, holding a big wad of yellow curls. Her real hair was cut short and he could see pink scalp.

Now he was enraged. He grasped her wrist and tore her off the bed, tipping over the table and dumping off the pipe and spirit lamp. The oil spread across the carpet like flaming lava. He stamped it out, and while he was busy with that she tried to twist out of his grip. He gave her a backhanded slap across the face. Her head swung around and her body sagged. He hadn't struck her that hard. It was the dope. He grabbed her by the upper arms and shook her. Only the whites of her eyes showed. He gave her a disgusted push. She did a half-pirouette and melted on the daybed, both legs and one arm hanging off the side. Over his own heavy breathing, he heard a tearing sound. She was snoring.

"Hophead bitch."

He pulled out all the drawers in her dressing table, found a box he recognized from when they were married, where she'd kept buttons and hatpins, saw she was using it for something else now and flung it into a corner. It shattered, spraying pea-shaped pellets of opium. At last he found sixty dollars in banknotes tucked inside a gray kid glove and stuffed them into a pocket.

He looked at Purity, wondering how many pipes she'd had and how long it would take her to wake up. He was hungry and wanted to get in his order. He was going to be staying a while and he needed her alert while he discussed the ground rules.

Something moved in the dressing-table mirror. Without turn-ing he slid his hand into the bearskin for his Remington.

"Don't stir a whisker, Twice Emerson. I'll put a ball through your head."

The fellow in the mirror was a little old jasper with black han-dlebars. His suit was so tight that his coat sleeve crept halfway to the elbow of the arm supporting his long-barreled dueling piece.

TWENTY-FIVE

―――――

Y ou're easy to fit, sir. To look at you, no one would believe you
bought it off the shelf."

Standing before the three-way mirror on the second floor of
Cherry Creek Clothiers ("Everything For the Gentleman of Color"),
examining the hang of the three-button Norfolk and the lay of the
collar across the back of his neck, Honey knew there was little truth
in what the clerk said; one of his shoulders was higher than the
other, one arm two centimeters longer than its mate, and no coat
that had not been tailored exclusively for him could mask these
imperfections. The material was good, however, and he was relieved
to leave behind the dour and loose-fitting preacher's suit, and with it
the entire First Abyssinian episode. He supposed he was still in love
with Georgia Breedlove and always would be, but already the memory had begun to take on the silver glimmer of a pleasant recurring
dream. He mourned the sensation more than the loss.

"I'll need shoes, too," he said. "Not boots. Lace-ups, with inch-
and-a-half heels. Two pairs, regular black and black patent leather."
His old brogans looked like the clodbusters they were beneath the
charcoal woolen cuffs.

"I'm sorry, sir. We don't sell shoes. Handelmann's has an excellent selection. You'll find them around the corner on Arapahoe." The clerk, a balding young Negro in waistcoat and shirtsleeves, looked sad; his customer had located an untruth in the slogan "Everything for the Gentleman of Color."

"Do you sell hats?" He unbuttoned the coat. The rise of the trousers was high for his taste, but they draped without pouches. He'd lost three inches off his waist since New Orleans.

"Yes, sir. All kinds. We just got in a shipment of bowlers. Black, with red silk linings. The same kind worn by Mr. Gladstone."

"Do you have any in gray?"

"I'll go look."

"Anyone would take you for a man of property," said Torbert, when the clerk had gone. "If Old Man Saint-Maarten could see you now, he'd double the bounty."

Honey frowned at the journalist's reflection, jammed between the arms of a chair upholstered in brown mohair. "If you raise your voice just a little more, he may do that yet."

"You're safe in Denver. The ones who can use the five hundred haven't the price of the wire, and the rest wipe their backsides with banknotes. They've been reading about you here; I checked with the *Post*. You could order a drink anywhere in town and tell them your name. Color's no barrier for a famous badman."

"I won't test it." They were registered at a hotel across from the railroad station. It had a narrow dusty lobby and mildew in the rooms. Honey, who was using the name Ollie Johnson, had been instructed to enter and exit through a side door opening onto an alley.

"What are you going to do now that you have your money?"

"It won't last long here. The clerk says there's a colored saloon

on Arapahoe, run by a man named Jones. Maybe he needs a bartender."

"Not a piano player?"

"No, I'm done with that."

"Madame Pantalon would approve. She isn't a kind critic.
We're not finished, you know. We've only just touched on your life
as a fugitive."

"You'll have the rest. You paid for it." He took advantage of the
clerk's absence to slip the Bulldog out of the discarded morning
coat and slide it into the Norfolk's breast pocket. The pocket
sagged, spoiling the lines of the coat. He'd left his shoulder rigout
in Galveston. He transferred the pistol to the small of his back. The
barrel nestled into the crease between his buttocks. That was fine
for when he was standing, but an adjustment would have to be
made when he sat. He wondered if he could find out the name of a
good harness maker.

"I believe you. I expected you to stick me up in San Antonio
and light out for the territories."

"I considered it. It wasn't a good fit."

"Alterations are free of charge," said the clerk, returning from
the storeroom. He'd overheard Honey's last remark.

"I might want a little more room under the left arm later."

"Yes, sir. That's not an unusual request here." He was holding a
pearl-gray bowler in both hands, like a covered tray. "I hope it fits.
I made a guess at the size. I'm afraid it's the only gray we have in
stock at six and three-quarters."

"I wear a seven."

"Please try it on. I have a talent in this area."

"I like this young man," Torbert said. "He's found a polite way
of calling a man a liar."

"Certainly not, sir."

The hat was precisely the right size. He would not have believed a man could lose weight in his head. He tilted the hat toward his left eyebrow with a pop to the crown, looked at his reflection, and thought, *Welcome back, Honey. Where you been?*

A green awning with a sawtooth edge flapped in front of the saloon on Upper Arapahoe Street, shedding powder snow as soon as it landed. A yellow legend painted on the canvas read:

LIQUORS

CIGARS

LUNCH

W. JONES, PROP.

Inside, shaking snow off his hat, Torbert was surprised to find a polished, well-swept room, with a walnut bar equipped with a brass footrail, an ornate back bar stocked with a dozen brands of whiskey, gin, and brandy, square flasks of Jamaica Ginger for the sour stomach, and a twinkling assortment of flutes, snifters, and cordial glasses, the last delicately etched by some hand in Baltimore or Boston and shipped at no small expense across a continent bristling with chuckholes, road agents, and renegade savages. A brief counter stood perpendicular to the bar, with rows of panatellas and corona coronas lined up like cartridges in tilted trays behind glass doors. The room smelled of good cigars and whiskey aged in barrels. A Mathew Brady photograph of President Lincoln standing stiffly in his stovepipe hat in front of a tent hung in a giltwood frame behind the bar.

There were as many bowlers and pinch-back suits lined up

along the foot rail as there were floppy hats and overalls. The genial owner, who grasped first Boutrille's hand and then Torbert's, introduced himself as Bill Jones and asked them to name their poison. He was a dusky fifty, with silver in his tightly curled hair and the thinnest moustache Torbert had ever seen. Boutrille ordered a cognac, the journalist a glass of Hermitage. He intended to drink up and return to the hotel, whether his companion went with him or not; Torbert's was the only white face in the establishment, and although no one was staring at him and Jones's smile had been the same for him as for Boutrille, he'd felt a definite change in the atmosphere when he'd entered. The fellow playing the upright—a rather melancholy version of "Cindy," as if the prospects of finding oneself an apple hanging on a tree and marrying Cindy were equally unlikely—had the broad back of a bouncer, and his gimlet eyes were fixed on a mirror mounted on the slant board, giving him a view of the entire room. Honey Boutrille's trail, winding as it did through the shacks and alleys of an America that Torbert had scarcely known existed, had developed in him an outsider's sixth sense. He felt as much a fugitive as his companion.

He still could not convince himself he was standing next to the man he'd been looking for so long. In his heart he'd begun to believe he never would, and the slightly built creature who answered to the name Boutrille, with his careful speech and knowledge of inscams, merely contributed to his incredulity. There were three men dead by his hand, if the accounts could be believed; Boutrille himself had yet to confirm two, and Torbert had learned from experience to divide most eyewitness reports by at least half. This chocolate dandy sipping cognac, resting one pinched foot in its tight new shoe on the rail, seemed less a blacksnake than a rabbit on the dodge.

The frontier was a fabrication, like its false-fronted buildings, and all its legends illusions. He was a rank amateur when it came to making up stories.

Torbert was so quagmired in this realization he ordered a second whiskey without being aware he had done so. Boutrille meanwhile finished his drink and strolled over to inspect the cigar selection. A fellow in overalls, darker even than Boutrille and a head taller than Torbert, swelled up to fill the gap at the bar without seeming to move. He smelled sourly of old sweat and half-digested whiskey; smelled, in fact, like the West. Torbert shrank away involuntarily, and turned to carry his glass away from the bar. A hand the size of a hod closed on his upper arm.

"Didn't I do some work for you oncet?"

The big man had a bottomless voice, roughened at the edges, as if he was accustomed to conversing in shouts. His face was brutal, broad and flat and crisscrossed with old knife scars healed over white. He brought it to within two inches of Torbert's face. The whites of his eyes were swimming in pink and his lower teeth reminded the journalist of the bottom jaw of a steam shovel.

"I don't think we've met." It sounded priggish even to him. He flexed his arm, but the grip tightened.

"I done built you a back porch and you never paid me."

"You're mistaken. I just got into town."

"Liar, is I? I done put in a week's work on that porch. You owe me twelve dollars."

"Reuben, you stop bothering my customers. I told you before." Bill Jones's voice was tense. Torbert was suddenly aware that he and the big man were alone at the bar. The others had retreated to opposite ends.

"My wife gone went and left me on account of that twelve dollars."

Jones raised his voice. "Walter!"

The man who had been playing the piano rose from the stool, but made no move in the direction of the bar.

"Let me go and I'll give you twelve dollars." Torbert's arm was numb below the right elbow.

"I don't want none of your money. I wants my wife. You got her in your pocket?"

Torbert groped for the handle of the Marston with his left hand. Reuben grasped that wrist between thumb and forefinger and he lost all feeling in it as well. Then the big man let go of his arm and Torbert felt the three-barreled pistol sliding out of his watch pocket. Reuben had it in his hand. Something clicked; the hammer rolling back. His sphincter released. The stench filled the room. He felt horrible shame.

"Mr. Jones, I'll take three General Thompsons when you have the chance."

Boutrille's gentle request sounded ludicrous, like something from an English drawing-room farce. Torbert laughed. "Hee-hee." His mouth snapped shut.

Reuben's huge head rotated as if it were mounted on casters. He released Torbert's wrist. Torbert found out his legs worked. He backpedaled along the bar until he bumped into one of the patrons crowded at the end.

Honey Boutrille was standing with his back to the cigar counter. He was holding his ugly pistol at waist level, his elbow tight against his ribs.

The reports were simultaneous. The deep-throated roar of the heavier Bulldog swallowed up the Marston's cough. A dagger-shaped shard of glass tipped out of one of the cases behind Boutrille.

Reuben's breath came out in a little "huh." He looked down at the spreading dark patch on his overalls. His free hand slapped the bar and he sagged against it. Then his elbow bent and he slid into a sitting position on the floor.

The echo of the shots thrummed through the silence. The man standing near the piano came forward then and bent down and scooped the Marston off Reuben's open palm.

Bill Jones said, "Walter, you're fired."

TWENTY-SIX

The Denver Post, Wednesday, November 17, 1886:

A KILLER UNMASKED.

City Marshal R. G. Fitzwilliam reported today that the Negro arrested in the shooting death of Reuben McClellan, Negro, in William Jones's saloon yesterday, and who gave his name as Ollie Johnson, is in actuality Honoré "Honey" Boutrille, the notorious man-killer wanted in New Orleans, La., for the murder of Winton Claude Saint-Maarten, a white man of that city, last August. This intelligence was communicated in a telegram from a police official in New Orleans responding to a description wired by Marshal Fitzwilliam, whose suspicions were aroused by information contained in a fugitive flyer.

Boutrille is suspected in the shooting death of Joseph M. Crank, a Mississippi riverboat pilot, in August, and is believed to have made his way to Denver through Galveston and Corpus Christi, Texas. He is confined in the

United States Jail here pending the outcome of a Coroner's inquest into the fatal incident in Jones's saloon and
announcement of New Orleans's intentions regarding
prosecution in the Louisiana murder.

Emerson's near-illiteracy tested Casper Box's patience, carefully constructed over years of contact with narcissistic actors,
egocentric actresses, dim-witted grips, and indifferent hotel clerks;
all the insufferable marginalia of life on the circuit. Ten minutes
after the theatrical manager had slid the folded front page across
the tiny table in the curtained balcony, the former guerrilla was
still reading the brief item he'd pointed out. Box could actually
read it again off Emerson's lips. Was this the criminal brain that
had outwitted seasoned authorities in Missouri, Kansas, California, Oregon, and Idaho Territory? He wondered whether his retire-
ment would kick in while waiting for the man to sign his name at
the bottom of a contract.

Distractedly, he listened to the musical programme being presented in the Carillon's main room; a burlesque revue by a troupe
he'd first heard in Cincinnati in 1872, with the same pansy tenor
striking the same sour notes in a tune that was old when Francis
Scott Key was learning his scales. Stern Flint's little enterprise was
an institution now. He could pack the house on the promise of a
part-time teamster blowing "Lorna Doone" through a comb. Box
inspected his watch. Adabelle would be in Hamlet's tights now,
berating the slings and arrows of outrageous fortune. When she
found out her dear old Pope Casper the First had deserted her second Denver opening for an audience with a border bushwhacker,
she'd hurl Lizzie's sewing basket at him, or worse. It wouldn't mat-

ter that he'd stood through every rotten aria and overcooked soliloquy that had passed through her lips since Atlantic City. Holding
hands with thespians was just like being married, only without the
occasional sex.

Not that he hadn't had his opportunities, nor that they'd even
slacked off since he'd entered his sixty-first year. When they were
constantly being thrust at you, you lost your taste for even the
sweetest berries. He had no need for such fruits. The theater was his
intoxication, and the longest binge of anyone's life. It was worth its
cost, to his health and his conscience. If it were not, he'd have done
with Twice Emerson in Purity Peach Duncan's dressing room. In
his younger days he'd threatened and beaten the male half of magic
acts, acrobatic teams, and husband-and-wife repertory companies
for abusing their partners, and when he interviewed new ones, he'd
taken pains to determine that their relationships were peaceful,
because firing them meant only fresh torment for the victims. Mrs.
Duncan had suffered nothing worse than a livid bruise on one
cheek, sparing Box the necessity of removing Emerson from society
at the muzzle end of his flintlock pistol. (The indignity of having
had her wig snatched off was something he felt certain, based on his
assessment of her character and experience, that she would place in
perspective.) It had galled him to have to charm the piece of human
offal who sat opposite him into hearing his proposition, but he'd
had the thing on his mind too long, the likelihood of its ever taking
place had been too remote, and his fortune in crossing Emerson's
path despite all the odds in favor of their missing each other
entirely had been too great. To walk away from it then would have
been to tempt all the fickle gods who amused themselves with the
fates of those who answered the call of the stage.

However, because they were an entirely different set of gods from those who controlled events outside the proscenium arch, Box had taken the precaution of laying the pistol on the table within easy reach of his right hand. It was brass-mounted with a smooth walnut stock, one of a matched brace made by O. & E. Evans in Harpers Ferry, and much older than Box himself. The .69 caliber bore, nearly large enough to insert a billiard ball into, was sufficiently impressive to maintain civil discourse.

At last Emerson laid down the newspaper and threw an ounce of raw whiskey down his throat. Watching, Box felt a spasm of phantom pain in his ulcers, long since healed over. "All them niggers ever do is fuck and fight," the guerrilla said. "I never know why they even bother to write it up."

"This fellow Boutrille is different. He's the best thing to happen to newspapers since the Little Big Horn. I'd have admired to sign him on, but as things stand it looks like he's on his way to the gallows."

"I didn't know this was a nigger outfit."

The man's tone made Box grateful for the flintlock's presence. "The theater's not like any place you ever worked. Jews and Catholics work the same stage and often room together. I had Robert E. Lee just about talked into a lecture circuit with Frederick Douglass when the general died. They would have debated emancipation versus states' rights."

"I don't know nothing about them things. All I know is niggers stink worse than chinks."

Emerson had an aroma all his own, quite noticeable in the confinement of the balcony. But Box didn't press the point.

"I showed you the article so you could see how high the interest is in gun men such as yourself. A great many people would pay to see an exhibition of your shooting skill—with tins and bottles as your targets, of course. Especially in the East. The interest in things Western has never been greater. Buffalo Bill could charge a dollar a head and fill every seat."

"Fella in California told me Cody loads his pistols with sand. Any little shit kid could drop one on the ground and hit what he was aiming at."

"We'll rig up a piece of canvas for you to fire at by way of demonstration. A good clean hole will settle any questions on that score. Er, I assume you *are* a skilled marksman?" He remembered most of Emerson's shooting scrapes had taken place at close range.

"Cap'n Anderson made sure of that. We fired more rounds at tree branches and Lydia Pinkham's than we did at Yankees. I can light up your cigar at fifty paces."

"Unfortunately, I no longer smoke. We'll arrange something quite as noteworthy."

"Hunnert a week, you say?"

"To start. Once the costumes and sets and the initial booking and traveling expenses are paid, we'll discuss a rise based on profits. I've never operated in the open air, so there will be logistical problems to consider that I cannot yet go into. I have an acquaintance with Sells Brothers who can enlighten me. In the meantime you can make a great deal more on the side, selling your autographed picture. Peripheral commercial interests are not something I care to concern myself with. I'm in semi-retirement."

"I ain't had my picture took in twenty years."

"If you don't care to pose, you can always offer to sign programs for a fee." He wondered if Emerson could even write his name.

"I ain't decking myself out in pink sleeve garters and face paint."

"I'm thinking more along the lines of a frock coat or buckskins, but the choice is yours. Weapons, too. A handsome pair of silver-chased Colts with pearl handles would look well."

"I'm partial to my Remington."

"What about that cap-and-ball in your belt?"

"That's for show. I might could get it engraved, only no pearl grips. That's for gents that sit down to piss."

"I know just the engraver. He outfitted Doc Carver and Captain Bogardus. He'll make fine jewelry out of your Remington."

"Nobody touches the Remington but me."

Box sighed, but he didn't pursue the argument. Scratch an outlaw and he was just another temperamental performer. "You'll sleep in featherbeds and drink the best whiskey. It's a better offer than Anderson ever made."

"I wouldn't lay a cartwheel on that. Bloody Bill only stole the best of everything and divvied it up fair. Women, too. I put the spurs to a Jayhawker senator's daughter in Kansas City. I'd of stood her up alongside Lotta Crabtree any old day. What about women?"

"There you can take your pick." Box put on his best leer and leaned across the table; not that his conversation would shock anyone on the balcony level of the Carillon. "I had the *real* Lotta Crabtree."

"Horseshit."

He leaned back. "I had a knife-throwing act then. There's nothing like limelight and a little business with a shiny weapon. Better than hard candy and flowers. You'll have more beautiful women than you can shake your stick at."

"Horseshit," Emerson repeated. But his narrow face was dark with thought.

"You've been wasting time, risking your neck robbing trains

and banks and freezing your ass off in dry washes waiting for posses to give up looking for you, when you could've been sucking champagne out of Sylvia Starr's bellybutton. There ought to be a law against it; which there is in seventeen states, but they won't hang you for it." He was enjoying himself immensely. When making his pitch, he usually felt a little ashamed, thinking of Lucifer trotting out his visions of treasures and kingdoms. But Emerson was no Jesus.

"What's to stop some law dog in the crowd from arresting me?"

"The excursion schedule will exclude those states and territories where you're wanted. It's been my observation that local authorities are in no particular hurry to step in on behalf of their far-flung colleagues. As for bounty hunters, you'll have to take your chances with them, just as you have from the beginning of your, er, enterprise. It wouldn't look well to provide you with an armed escort. The theater is a business, don't forget. My competitors ain't bashful about pointing out my performers' shortcomings to friendly journalists."

Emerson waved a black-nailed hand. "Bounty men are yellow as wheat. What's to stop *you* from wiring Sacramento or Boise? Western Union's a sight cheaper'n all them things you was talking about, costumes and such."

"I could have done that any time since I threw down on you upstairs. In any case, you and I both know those rewards are seldom paid to the deserving parties. Some fat desk man with a star pinned to his shirt always steps in to claim it for himself."

"You talk like a man who's tried."

"Actually, I heard it in prison." He smiled at Emerson's expression. "The circuit ain't for ladies of good family. It's been going on a lot longer than your border wars, and run up a good many more casualties. But I ain't telling you anything you didn't guess when we met. I'm a long way from the first man who ever pointed a pistol in your direction, but I'm betting not many of the others walked away to bray about it."

Emerson was silent for the space of three bars from the orchestra below. Then he fisted the bottle and poured himself another shot. The whiskey smelled as harsh as spent powder, but it might have been mineral water for all the effect it appeared to have on him. "When do we start this shindig?"

Box removed a fold of stiff paper from his inside breast pocket. It was a boilerplate letter of agreement, one of a bale he traveled with, with blanks to be filled in with names and specific performance expectations. He tugged at a bell rope, and when one of Mrs. Duncan's girls poked her head through the curtains to take their order, he asked her for a pen and a bottle of ink.

TWENTY-SEVEN

———

The Coroner's Court judge had a gourd-shaped head with a ginger-colored thatch on top and a blunt nose that looked as if someone had knocked off the end with a hatchet. His robes needed brushing and pressing and he smelled like moldy newspapers. His name was Huneker. The moment he entered the oak-paneled humidor of a courtroom in Denver's domed and colonnaded county building and eased himself into the horsehair chair behind the bench, Torbert rolled him up and poked him into a pigeonhole labeled PROVINCIAL HACK. Nothing Huneker had done or said since had caused the journalist to reconsider the designation.

"You never saw this man McClellan before?" he asked Torbert for the third time. The second time, the witness had been on his guard, suspecting an attempt to trap him into giving a different answer. Now he was confident the man was just a bad listener. Civilization—and the political spoils system—had come to the frontier at last.

Torbert raised and resettled himself in the witness chair. The hard embossed leather seat aggravated his piles. "He was a complete stranger, although he didn't seem to think so. He mistook me for a man who owed him money."

"And he pulled a gun on you."

"He pulled my gun." Once again he described the events. He was able to do so now without re-experiencing his paralyzing fear. Sheer repetition had made the details remote, as if he were recounting something he'd read in a newspaper. His old journalist's instinct was coming back. For two days he'd thought it never would. He'd succeeded, for instance, in editing out all memory of how he'd disgraced himself when Reuben had pointed his own pistol at his belly and cocked the hammer.

"But you were not in actual danger at the time Boutrille shot McClellan."

"I wouldn't say that."

"You said McClellan was no longer aiming at you."

"No, he was aiming at Boutrille. He forgot about me when Boutrille called out."

Huneker consulted the sheet of foolscap upon which he'd been scribbling. His hand was faster than the court recorder's, but his script was dilapidated; blots and spatters showed clear through the paper whenever he turned a page. "Boutrille asked the proprietor for a cigar?"

"Yes. It was a ploy to divert McClellan's attention from me to him."

"That's speculation. He might just have wanted a cigar. You said that's what he went to the counter for."

"He isn't blind and deaf. He knew what was happening. If he'd cried out McClellan's name or shouted a threat, McClellan would have fired, either at me or at him. Asking for cigars confused him long enough for Boutrille to claim the upper hand."

"Speculation. You and Boutrille are friends?"

"We're partners in a literary venture. I'm writing his biography."

"You're writing a book about a Negro?"

"About a Negro—adventurer." He'd almost said *mankiller.* "His case is unusual."

"Negroes don't kill one another in Chicago?"

"Boutrille has never killed except to defend himself and others." He kept his voice level. He hated this stale little official.

"Once again, you're speculating. Please confine your testimony to the facts as you know them. Who fired first, McClellan or Boutrille?"

"They fired at the same time."

"Are you sure? Another witness said Boutrille's gun went off first."

"The shots were simultaneous."

"You seem very certain about that for a man whose life was so recently in danger."

"I'm a professional journalist. Close observation is my stock-in-trade."

"In that case I suppose you can tell me where McClellan's bullet went."

"It broke a window in a cigar case behind Boutrille."

The judge paged back through his notes. "A foot above his head, according to Marshal Fitzwilliam. One might make the case that McClellan missed him deliberately. Perhaps he lacked Boutrille's killer instinct."

"Or perhaps he was a bad shot."

"Thank you for your testimony, Mr. Torbert. You're dismissed."

As Torbert stood, Huneker raised his voice. "The court will now hear from Mr. Boutrille."

The journalist had planned to repair to the nearest saloon—
never a long walk in Denver—but instead he found a seat in the
gallery. There weren't many vacant; Boutrille's adventures had evidently been reported by the local press and more than the usual
number of loafers and curiosity-hunters had turned out that day.
The smell of chicken fat, onions, and mustard from a dozen paper-
wrapped luncheons was making headway against the institutional
odors of brass polish and furniture oil. There was, too, a pungent
aroma of cedar and graphite from the restless pencils of the press,
whose dirty bowlers never came off except for hearses and ladies.
Not so long ago, Torbert had considered himself one of them, but
the incident in Bill Jones's saloon had separated him from the tribe
in a way that made him look upon them as interlopers. He
observed with distaste their rumpled clothes, the pockets bulging
with folds of newsprint, like his own, the permanent notches in
the corners of their mouths where they stuck their cigars, always
half-smoked and cold. They were always scribbling, never looking
up from their notes lest they miss a word or an inflection, and yet
they always managed to get things wrong.

Honoré Boutrille entered the courtroom through a side door,
between Marshal Fitzwilliam and a deputy. His wrists were mana-
cled, but he had his hands folded in front of him and had gathered
up some of the chain so that they weren't immediately noticeable.
His suit looked freshly pressed and brushed. Since the United
States Penitentiary in Denver was no more likely to offer a valet
service than any other, Torbert assumed the prisoner had taken
pains to remove and arrange the coat and trousers beneath his
mattress so that his own weight would preserve the proper creases
and prevent lint and dust from collecting on the material. His
shirt, collarless, was nonetheless buttoned neatly to the top. His
shoes flapped slightly without their laces, but he had managed

somehow to maintain their shine. In fact, he looked better kept than either the marshal with his soup-stained vest or the deputy, whose knobby wrists had outgrown the cuffs of his homespun shirt. His face was absolutely without expression. When he laid his hands on the Bible provided by the bald-headed bailiff and took his seat on the hard chair, he might have traded places with the untidy drone behind the bench and been accepted for the judge in charge of the proceedings. Except, of course, for his color.

Huneker went at him hard, and Torbert saw that he was a keen cross-examiner when assured his subject belonged to a stratum lower than his own. Boutrille, however, kept his temper, answering politely but firmly, refusing to follow the path down which the other was determined to drive him: "Nosir, boss, I sure never intended no harm to Mister McClellan. I only drawed my pistol so's he wouldn't hurt Mister Torbert."

"Mr. Torbert is your friend?"

"I wouldn't never claim the liberty. He's been mighty Christian to me and I seen it as my duty to help him out."

"You're aware that Denver has an ordinance against carrying firearms within the city limits?"

"Yes, boss, I am now. I was new in town then, though, and didn't know the particulars of the place just yet."

There were notices posted on every telegraph pole and in the front window of every establishment, but Huneker didn't point that out; he evidently assumed Boutrille could not read. Nor had he brought up the point when questioning Torbert. He himself had seen at least two pistol butts sticking up from the belts of spectators present, and had no reason to believe there weren't at least a half-dozen more in concealment. Such ordinances seemed little more than an excuse to place suspect characters in confinement.

"Ignorance is not a defense," said the judge. "Boutrille, you've killed three men that this court is aware of, and I have no doubt there are other victims in your past. Can you think of any reason why Marshal Fitzwilliam should not charge you with willful murder in the case of Reuben McClellan and hold you in custody until such time as you can answer the charge?"

"Yessir, boss. I never done it."

Torbert thought Boutrille was applying the field-Negro act with a ladle, but it appeared to be succeeding with the people in the gallery. He'd sat in on many a trial and could tell when the atmosphere was lifting or lowering; brief nods and a quiet chuckle at Boutrille's remark about not knowing the particulars of the place told the journalist this was not a lynch mob. Juries, however, were a different case. The men seated in the paneled box in their clean town overalls and Sunday suits were blank-faced and attentive, exchanging not so much as a glance in response to Boutrille's answers. If they found the man in the witness chair criminally responsible for McClellan's death, it would not be the first time a panel of Good Men and True decided against public opinion.

Huneker was easier to read. After dismissing Boutrille, he asked the marshal to return for further questioning upon reincarcerating his prisoner. Fitzwilliam did so, and proceeded to repeat his own earlier testimony, which because of his absence from the scene of the killing until after the fact added nothing in Boutrille's favor and much against him, underscoring as it did the grisly details. The judge was either opposed to Negroes in general or determined to set an example for other out-of-town gun men to consider before they set out to breach the peace of Denver, and came just short of saying as much when he delivered his charge to the jury following Fitzwilliam's departure. His performance was unabashedly transparent and likely to succeed. He smacked down his gavel, calling for a recess while the jurors deliberated.

"A word, Mr. Torbert?"

In the crowd drifting toward the exit, he turned and had to look down to make eye contact with a very small man in a very tight suit, whose lacquered black hair and moustaches with the tips ruthlessly waxed and curled put him in mind of a sideshow barker. He wanted to smile, but the man's fierce eyes warned against it. "Yes?"

"Casper Box, Box Company Players. I have a proposition which you and your friend Boutrille may find of interest."

"I've been reading about your man Emerson," Torbert said. "He's an ape."

Box's expression was humorless. "You do apes no kindness. I've worked with them onstage. They're peaceful creatures unless threatened. Emerson's a savage. However, he's *my* savage."

The menu in the gilded and papered main dining room of the Windsor Hotel offered frogs' legs, mock turtle soup, sweetbreads, and Yorkshire pudding. The linen was as white as paper and nearly as stiff, and one could read a newspaper through the china. Torbert felt out of place in his travel-worn suit, but the liveried waiters appeared to be attending a number of rough-hewn miners and cattlemen with borrowed cravats poking out from under their twill collars in the same obsequious manner as their better-tailored customers. Box had bribed the maitre d' to post a busboy at the courthouse with instructions to come running when the jury was in.

Torbert cut into his sliced leg of mutton, only to lay down his utensils when a stream of red juice ran out. The incident in Bill Jones's saloon had ruined him for anything less than well done.

"It's premature for me to discuss a shooting contest," he said. "Mr. Boutrille may not be available for years, if he isn't sentenced to hang."

"Bosh. Denver ain't Tombstone. There is an appeals process, even if he is found guilty. I'm not persuaded he will be. He made a better show of himself today than that tramp Huneker."

"That may work against him. Huneker is white."

"Then the point's moot, and you and I will have had a pleasant repast, which no one can take from us. I'll be blunt, Torbert. I can get a better deal with a noose hanging over your nigger's head."

"He isn't my nigger."

"Yes, well, Miss Stowe ain't present. I'm an admirer of yours, you know. I read your book about the Hampton Roads battle, with a thought toward buying the rights for an open-air spectacle along the lines of Henry Pain's 'Siege of Vera Cruz.' I couldn't get the backing, so you never heard from me. That hasn't stopped me from following your career."

"You must have used a strong glass."

"Entertainment's a small world. I get around in it." Box buttered a roll. "When I read in the paper you're with Boutrille, a lot of things fell into place. I can get a season out of a wanted Confederate guerrilla potting tins and bottles and recounting the details of his misspent life for the edification of youth. If I put a black gunsharp in the same arena, I can get a European tour. Fight the Civil War all over again, only this time soak the suckers two bits a head to watch."

"It's barbaric."

"I ain't suggesting they shoot at each *other*. What would I do for the second show? Look, there's no use getting muckety. You didn't hitch your wagon to Boutrille to save his immortal soul. You just got finished telling God and everyone there's a book deal in it."

"I'm his biographer, not his business manager. You'll have to discuss your proposition with him."

"He don't know me from Adam. He trusts you. I had a hard enough time signing Emerson, and he's white. I used a pistol."

"What makes you think Boutrille trusts me?"

"He saved your hide."

"That's why I trust *him*. You heard him say it was his Christian duty. That's a long way from a partnership."

"He couldn't even sell that one to Huneker, and Huneker's a jackass. I'm offering fifty-fifty, with no investment on your part. Slice up your half any way you like. Honest Abe wouldn't give you a better bargain." He watched Torbert sip his sherry. "You can sell copies of your biography at the concession stand. I won't even take a cut."

"I'd have to discuss that part with Argus Fleet. He's my publisher."

"That's your headache. I've got an investor of my own to answer to. Talk it over with your boy."

"He isn't—"

"We had that conversation." Box's sharp gaze flicked past Torbert's shoulder. "Here comes your kid from the courthouse. These frontier juries don't take long when they ain't deliberating in a saloon."

"We have, your honor."

The foreman was a tall Finn with cold blue eyes and a tobacco-stained moustache, a gunsmith by trade. Black-powder burns showed on his lapels when he rose from the box.

Judge Huneker rubbed his blunt nose. He'd buttoned his robes crookedly and he had the groggy, disgruntled look of a man whose afternoon nap had been interrupted. "How do you find?"

"We find that the deceased, Reuben McClellan, met his death at the hand of Honoré Boutrille in the course of defending his life."

"Whose life, McClellan's or Boutrille's?"

The foreman looked startled. "Boutrille's, your honor."

"The hell you say." Raising his voice above a murmur, Huneker polled each of the jurors. All agreed with the foreman. "Very well. However, Boutrille will remain in custody until such time as the State of Louisiana sends a delegation to escort him back to Baton Rouge to face charges in the murder of Winton Claude Saint-Maarten."

Marshal Fitzwilliam stood up from the gallery and cleared his throat.

"What is it, Pat?"

"Your honor, I received a reply this morning to the wire I sent the attorney general in Louisiana. He said the state will accept custody of Boutrille if Denver will undertake the expense of delivering him."

Someone hooted. Huneker smacked his gavel. "Repeat that, please, Marshal."

Fitzwilliam did, appearing uncomfortable. "I reckon they don't consider Saint-Maarten important enough to fetch the nigger back through a Colorado winter."

A hand slapped Torbert's back where he stood among the crowd gathered at the rear of the courtroom. He knew without turning that the hand belonged to Casper Box. This time the judge gave up trying to gavel down the reaction from the gallery. "Release the prisoner," he shouted. "Coroner's Court is adjourned."

TWENTY-EIGHT

A dabelle Forrest despaired of ever hammering her Lizzie into anything remotely resembling a maid to a lady of quality.

They had been traveling in the luxury of Pullman parlor cars for months, and yet the creature in charge of her wardrobe insisted upon reporting to train stations in a shapeless duster and floppy bonnet designed to ward off sparks and cinders of the type shed by greasy yard engines pulling rickety day-coaches in Albany. She looked like a shrunken gnome with the dirty linen hem dragging the platform and her fingers barely poking out of the turned-back cuffs; something out of a provincial touring company doing the Brothers Grimm. Heading for the steps to the car she'd reserved, the Quick-Change Queen of Atlantic City picked up her skirts and her pace, distancing herself from the woman waddling in her wake. All her many trunks were safe on board, and the first warning whistle was blowing.

"Adabelle."

Her own dignity prevented her from breaking into a sprint to avoid the tiny figure hurrying her way from the opposite end of the platform. Casper's sail-brimmed hat cast a shadow that all but swallowed up his body. He had something cradled in the crook of one arm that she thought at first was a baby, although in all the world there was no one (except she) who was less likely to be found in that situation. She slowed, signaling defeat, and as he drew near she saw that the object was a green bottle nearly as large as he, with its neck wrapped in gold foil.

"I've been saving this for the trip east," he said, panting. "I'd hoped we'd share it, but under the circumstances I'd be grateful if you'd accept it as a gift in honor of a successful relationship."

"Thank you, Casper. Lizzie?"

The maid caught up with her and took the bottle from him in both arms. She woofed beneath its sudden weight.

Casper took off his hat. "I wish you'd reconsider. I managed six acts in four theaters in '79."

"I daresay none of them involved thieves and killers." She shook her head with a distracted smile at the porter standing by the steps, who had leaned forward to offer her a hand up.

"I wouldn't risk a wager they didn't," Casper said. "What are your plans?"

"Colonel Mapleson is planning a new production of *Lucrezia Borgia* at the Academy of Music. He's been after me for a year to play the lead."

"Lucrezia's a soprano."

"As am I." She hurried on. "I'll place all the quick-change costumes in storage and send you the bill. I'm sure you'll find a repertory company to take them off your hands."

"It should just about cover what you owe me on our contract."

"We've been over that, Casper. The agreement was that you would manage me exclusively. Now I ask you, which one of us is more likely to come off well in court?"

"It all depends on how many costume changes you have planned."

The whistle blew again. The conductor bawled. Adabelle smiled tightly. "Good-bye, Casper. I hope your new act doesn't kill you and strip your corpse." She offered her gloved hand.

He took it. "Good luck, Adabelle. Mind your next conquest don't land you in the women's workhouse."

The little man was still standing on the platform when she took her seat and looked out the window. He lifted his hat, but she looked away as the train began moving.

Nearing Cheyenne Wells, she left Lizzie snoring in their compartment and went to the dining car, which was nearly filled at that hour of the afternoon. A table opened up while she was speaking with the steward, and he seated her. The tablelands rolling past the window held no interest, but then she had never been one to occupy herself with the sights, unless they involved the Tuileries or the canals of Venice, lovely things fashioned by cultured hands; the raw mountains and roaring cataracts that had challenged the hearts of the pioneers who had preceded her served only as reminders of how many uninspired miles separated her from civilization. She drew the shade.

She was sufficiently unimpressed with her fellow passengers to indulge herself in one of the small cigars she smoked when she was alone. She blew an azure jet toward the paneled ceiling and searched the menu for the rare bland dish that would not upset her stomach while traveling. She had her mother's delicate digestion and her father's capacity for alcohol, and she looked forward to settling the one and serving the other with Casper's champagne when she returned to the compartment. He had excellent taste in food and wine, incapable as he was of selecting a theatrical bill that did not smack of the circus. If only . . . But she had promised herself she wouldn't dwell on disappointment. The arts promised so much, and those in charge were determined to serve the bear-baiting tastes of the unwashed millions.

"Pardon me, madam. Would you mind sharing your table with this young lady?"

She glanced up, annoyed, at the steward. The woman standing beside him was a strawberry blonde in her twenties, wearing a sturdy but becoming traveling dress with a short velour cape clasped at the neck by a gold pin in the shape of an arrow. Her hat was last year's but handsome, wedge-shaped, with decorative plums bordering the low crown. Her eyes were a startling shade of green, and good teeth showed in a nervous smile. Adabelle considered her tiny waist and rounded, almost heavy hips with frank hunger.

"Certainly not." She pressed out her cigar in a heavy glass tray. "Please join me."

The young woman slid into the plush seat opposite and unbuttoned and removed her kid gloves, revealing white, rather plump hands without rings. She had some baby fat still, and Adabelle decided she was younger than she had appeared at first. She had not been pinning up her hair for long; it would tumble to her shoulders in thick waves threaded with unassisted red. Her uncertain smile remained.

"Thank you so much. I hope you won't think me rude, but aren't you Adabelle Forrest?" Encouraged by Adabelle's nod, she plunged ahead. "I saw you once entering the stage door at the Alcazar Theater. I couldn't go in, of course, but I read about you in the *Post*. You're my first actress. The first one I've met, I mean. Are you on your way to another engagement?"

"I hope so. I've left the company I was with, but I have a new production waiting for me in New York, if they haven't cast my part. Where are you traveling?"

"Only as far as Wichita. That's my home. I was caring for my aunt in Denver. She had pneumonia, and for weeks it didn't appear as if she were going to recover. She's quite well, now. My father sells dry goods in Wichita. He needs me there to help him with the books." She flushed suddenly. "Gracious, here I've told you everything about me but my name. I'm Christine Lessup." She offered her hand.

Adabelle took it. It was soft apart from the calluses on thumb and forefinger. "I shall call you Christine, since it appears we're to be friends for the next four hundred miles. I have a very old friend named Christine; Christine Nilsson. Were you by any chance named after her? She's sung simply everywhere for many years." She knew quite well Nilsson wasn't old enough to have inspired a full-grown namesake; but then the closest they'd ever come to meeting was when Adabelle auditioned for a part Nilsson had originated, and failed to get it.

"I was named for my grandmother, I'm afraid. She never sang anywhere."

"I shall pretend you didn't say that, and behave as if we were intimates." She looked up at the waiter who had paused beside their table. "Please put my friend's meal on my bill."

"Oh, I couldn't let you do that, Miss Forrest."

"Adabelle, if you please. The thing is settled. It's an occasion, you see." She patted the young woman's hand, and left it there. "You're my first bookkeeper."

TWENTY-NINE

—

"I t's a shooting contest?" The *Post*.

"Not exactly," said Box. "It's more of a demonstration of the skills that made these two men notorious."

"Who are they going to rob and murder?" The *Rocky Mountain News*.

"Their past indiscretions are past. The programme will include an uplifting monologue by each man, apologizing for his transgressions and pledging to follow the straight path from now on."

"What, no temperance lecture?" The *Times*.

Box ignored the question. He smiled at the grave young woman from the *Queen Bee*, Caroline Churchill's weekly, aimed at the wives and daughters of Denver. "The lady has yet to ask a question."

She did not return the smile. "Are you not guilty of harboring two fugitives from justice?"

"Neither Mr. Emerson nor Mr. Boutrille is wanted in the state of Colorado."

"But are you not in some way complicit in their depredations, indirectly if not directly? I mean to ask, how do you justify parading a pair of murderers before the public as entertainment?"

"Murderers by whose lights? These men have been convicted of nothing. Mr. Boutrille, in fact, was acquitted of murder on the grounds of self-defense in this city only the day before yesterday."

"You're referring to the verdict of a Coroner's Court jury, which hasn't the authority to convict or acquit. He could still be tried in criminal court."

"That's unlikely. The late Mr. McClellan had no friends." Box sought out the comparatively friendly face of the gentleman from the *Post*. "Nate, you look fit to bust."

"My readers will want to know how an ex-bushwhacker and a former slave get along."

"You can see for yourself next week, when they meet for the first time."

A battery of questions followed, during which Box helped himself to a pinch of snuff. The gaslit suite at the Windsor Hotel he had rented for the press conference, normally reserved for presidents and visiting grand dukes, was hazy with smoke from the case of cigars he'd provided, along with a sampling of every whiskey label carried by Denver's six-hundred-plus saloons, various French wines, and a magnum of champagne wallowing in untouchable majesty in a tub full of ice. Sliced bread, salmon, herrings, pickles the size of potatoes, and a roast loin of beef covered a platter as large as a barrel hoop on a table relocated from the main dining room. Most of the budget he had set aside for the remainder of the Adabelle Forrest tour had gone into the spread, much of which would go to waste; but thirty years of theatrical promotion had taught him that a room full of well-fed and -lubricated reporters meant a dozen columns in the afternoon editions.

"Gentlemen—and lady—a moment." He raised a palm and

held it there until the voices subsided. "This is a competition, not an acrobatic act. Mr. Boutrille's manager and I have chosen to sequester our clients from each other until the day of the event, lest the cameraderie of the pistoleering breed destroy the competitive edge."

The man from the *Commonwealth* spoke around a mouthful of roast beef. "You don't represent Boutrille?"

"This is a collaborative project. The gentleman in question has requested anonymity, and I've given my word of honor he shall have it."

"A secret financier?" asked the *Rocky Mountain News*. "My information is you're in partnership with Christopher Buckley of San Francisco."

This was no surprise, as Box had stopped at the Western Union office to wire Buckley that he'd secured Emerson's cooperation, and read the telegram aloud to the clerk within the hearing of customers waiting in line behind him. Samuel B. Morse had nothing on casual eavesdroppers when it came to spreading intelligence. "Mr. Buckley is a silent partner in the enterprise," Box said. "His role is not active."

The *Queen Bee* woman raised her voice above the masculine barrage. "Has the anonymous gentleman's reticence anything to do with the scheme's immoral nature?"

The *Post* said "Haw-haw!" and choked on his Old Gideon. No one moved until the *Rocky Mountain News* sighed and smacked him on the back.

Box waited for peace, then: "We're presenting a lesson for today's youth, from the mouths of two men who strayed off the straight-and-narrow and lived to regret it. We ought to pass the hat and raise a new roof for the Presbyterian church."

The *Commonwealth* swallowed. "Speaking of roofs, where's

this sermon fixing to take place? We could be up to our arses in snow by next week. Your pardon, miss." He touched his bowler to the *Queen Bee*, who made an unladylike snort in response.

"A gent by the name of Lawson's been kind enough to offer us the use of his stock barn on Sixteenth Street. It seats a hundred, and we can get in two shows before dark. I'm thinking you've most of you covered your fair share of auctions on the premises."

"How much is Clem soaking you for that pile of bricks?" The *Post*, having exchanged his whiskey for a tumbler of ice water, had recovered from his attack.

Box said, "Let's just say his mare don't need to foal next spring."

Several reporters asked in unison for the date of the event. Told it would take place a week from Sunday at 3:00 P.M., the *Rocky Mountain News* pointed out that most of the local clergy was opposed to entertainment programmes on the Lord's Day, but nodded along with his colleagues when Box explained that morality-themed recitations were exempt from complaint; tent and medicine shows had been getting around that unwritten ordinance for years by bracketing fire-eaters and snake-charmers with lectures against idolatry and other un-Christian practices, like fire-eating and snake-charming. They wished Box good luck, accepted free passes, filled their pockets with sandwiches, and trotted out to file their stories. Even the female from the *Queen Bee* left munching a pickle.

The theatrical manager remained to supervise the removal of the libations and comestibles (he'd made a deal with the local Masonic Lodge for the leftovers), then put on his hat and a fur-lined coat and boarded a trolley a few blocks from the hotel, having determined that no enterprising journalists were following him. After alighting, he walked an additional four blocks and knocked at the door of a simple but well-kept house in a colored neighborhood with a ROOMS TO LET sign in a ground-floor window. The landlady, a small woman with medium-gray skin in widow's weeds, recognized him and told him to go on up.

Ernest Valerian Torbert, in shirtsleeves with his vest unbuttoned and his belly spilling over his belt, answered the door at the end of the second-floor hallway with one of Box's Evans flintlock pistols in his right hand. The city marshal had confiscated his Marston for the duration of his residency in Denver and Box had broken up the set. Torbert and Boutrille had checked out of the railroad hotel to avoid contact with former Confederates and southern sympathizers disgruntled over the decision by Louisiana not to bring Boutrille back for prosecution in the Saint-Maarten case. It had turned out to be a wise precaution: One hour after they checked out, deputies had investigated a complaint that a bullet had been fired through the window of Boutrille's former room from ground level. Fortunately, no one else had checked in and the only casualty had been a painted glass lampshade.

"The press is with us," Box greeted Torbert. "And you wanted to fill them up with beef jerky and a couple of bottles of Old Tub."

"You didn't tell them about me."

"You're as much a secret as Custer's teeny phizzle. I thought all you journalists liked to make yourselves out the hero of the story."

"I'm not writing it. J. P. Glidden is." He glanced out at the hallway. "You're alone?"

"I had a brass band, but they turned yellow when the street turned black. Ain't you going to invite me in?"

"We've got trouble." Torbert stepped aside.

The room looked tiny even to Box, who didn't mind close walls and sloping ceilings. There were explosions of cabbage roses on the paper, two narrow beds, a single splitbottom chair, and a chimney lamp on a cracked nightstand. Honey Boutrille sat atop one of the counterpanes with his back against the iron bedstead. He had his shirttail out over his drawers and his smooth black hairless legs ended in fine-spun cotton socks without garters. The coat and trousers of his suit hung from a wooden hanger on the back of the door Torbert had just closed. The man appeared to fear wrinkles more than lynch mobs. He was smoking a cigar.

"This ain't so bad. I've crawled out of smaller holes than this." Box unwrapped the stolen Windsor towel from the bottle of cognac he'd hidden from the reporters. "Couple of hits from this and you'll think you're in the Palmer House in Chicago."

"I sure do thank you, Mr. Box." The man on the bed made no move to take it.

Torbert laid the pistol on the other bed. "Did you hear me? I said we've got trouble."

Box uncorked the bottle, found a china cup in the drawer of the nightstand, filled it, and held it out. This time Boutrille accepted. "You boys will have to take turns if you don't like drinking from the bottle. Mrs. Washington runs a fine house, but she's close with the crockery. Trouble and theater's like gin and bitters. Let's hear it."

Boutrille sipped from the cup. His expressionless face said nothing about the quality of the cognac. "I'm not such a fine shot as you and Mr. Torbert like to think. The truth is, I couldn't hit the ground with my hat."

"Hogwash. You killed four men. Torbert told me about the one in Galveston."

"That man in Galveston was pure luck. I had all the time in God's world, and he wasn't shooting back. The others were as close as me and you. A blind man could have done it."

"Hogwash."

"I'm not lying." He said it without changing tone, but the "Mr. Box" was absent.

"You ain't a liar, just ignorant. Do you think it was good marksmanship carried a hell-raiser like Hickok to the ripe old age of thirty-nine? I hope to kiss a skunk's arse it wasn't. Killing a man who's out to kill you is instinct. You're born with it or you ain't, and if you ain't, you're just as dead with a gun in your hand as a teat. Any runt kid with a good eye and cowshit for brains can knock bottles off a fence."

"But that's what you're asking me to do."

"There's tricks in this business you can't guess at," Box said. "Cody charges his pistols with sand, and you can make a big fat target look small and hard to hit. Then there's practice. I can paint a nailhead on an end wall and you can hit it a hundred times out of a hundred if you know the drop and what to aim at."

Torbert said, "It sounds like fraud."

"Truth's what they pay two bits a head to get away from. You didn't sell meat by telling the suckers it'd give them the runs or worse if they didn't cook it inside a week. They want to see a couple of notorious gunmen in person before a slug or some cracker with a rope takes them off the circuit. In ten years or less they'll all be gone, jailed or dead or in county politics. We're giving the rubes what they asked for. The rest is show business." He paused to take out his snuff box. "Look at Honey; he knows what I'm talking about. That's why he didn't say a thing about his shooting skill when he signed his name to the contract."

"I shoveled out horse stalls seven days for a dollar in Corpus," Boutrille said. "After that, a hundred a week was so big I couldn't see around it."

"This ain't confession and I ain't a horsecollar preacher. You did what you had to do to get along, same as the rest of us. I'm a fair shot, as the evidence of my standing here bears out; that pistol I lent Torbert is one of two, and they don't travel with me just to impress the ladies. By the end of the week I'll fob you off on the good folk of Denver as the second cousin Annie Oakley don't talk about."

Torbert produced a flask from his hip pocket and twisted the cork, playing with it. "Don't tell your boy Emerson what Boutrille told you. From what I read I wouldn't trust him to stop at bottles and painted nailheads."

"You can't believe everything you read. You ought to know that better than anyone. *The Blacksnake of New Orleans.*" Box sneezed and blew his nose. "Emerson and Boutrille are going to be using half-loads, to protect the tender ears of the audience and to avoid a stray shot killing a paying customer. There won't be any fatalities." He put away the snuff box. "I'm headed back to town. You boys need anything?"

Boutrille smiled for the first time since they'd met. "Another bottle of this good cognac would suit me down to the ground. And a box of General Thompsons. This is my last one."

"I need more writing paper," Torbert said, "and a bottle of ink."

"How's that flask? I hung onto some Hermitage."

"I'm considering abstaining. Rye never wrote a good book, no matter what you've heard."

"That's the ticket. I threw it over myself when my belly blew out in '77. You could learn from a couple of old dogs, Honey. That stuff don't mix with gunpowder."

The smile evaporated. "I'll give it up when Emerson does."

"I want him out of here."

Purity Peach Duncan had appeared on the second-floor landing in the Carillon as Box was climbing up on his way to the third. She wore a champagne-colored dress that set off her pale-gold wig and her monocle dangled from a ribbon pinned to her collar. It could not have been comfortable for her to screw it into her eye socket, which was swollen beneath the coat of powder that covered the bruise.

He paused three steps from the top, a position of disadvantage that soured his mood. "What's he been up to, then?"

"Nothing that I know of. Plenty that I suspect. I don't want him under my roof."

"Strictly speaking, the roof ain't yours."

"You and Buckley can tear up my mortgage and throw me out in the street. My worst day there was better than my best day with Twice. I have to sleep with the bouncer seated outside my door."

"If he's behaved this far, he'll keep it up through next week. After that we'll head east. I've got St. Louis waiting to hear how we do in Denver."

"Put him up with you at the Windsor. I can't sleep knowing he's one floor above me."

He doubted that, having smelled and seen the evidence of opium in her dressing room; but he made no mention of it. "Well, there's a legal question there. If I register him in a hotel, a case can be made against me for harboring. I'll make it worth your while after next Sunday. If Buckley's happy, I might be in a position to persuade him to forgive the balance due on the joint."

She was silent just long enough to encourage him. "I want that in writing."

"You'll have it next Sunday."

"Today. Put it in the form of a promissory note, pledging to assume my obligation to the bank in San Francisco in the event an application to forgive the debt is rejected."

"That's—"

"Highway robbery? You can consult with Twice as to whether

the term is appropriate. If the paperwork isn't here by nightfall, I'll notify Marshal Fitzwilliam that I intend to bring a charge of battery against your star performer. That should hold him until the authorities in the states and territories where he's wanted can send someone with a warrant."

"You're a tough businesswoman, Mrs. Emerson."

"Duncan. I learned the finer points from you."

He found Emerson sprawled in his aromatic flannels in the Morris chair in Stern Flint's sitting room. Flint had taken a suite in the Windsor—at Box's expense—until his quarters were vacant. Emerson's hat was on the back of his head and the bottle Box had left him with the night before lay empty on the Brussels carpet. "Bring whiskey?"

Box had made a stop at the hotel. He set the bottle of Hermitage he'd brought on a cherrywood table. "How a man can drink so much and shoot so straight's a mystery," he said.

"Let's find out." Emerson raised his Remington and closed one eye. Box waited, motionless, until he lowered it. A baggy grin lengthened the guerrilla's narrow face. "No challenge. I shot sparrows smaller'n you."

"At fifty paces. I heard the speech. Anyway, I'm the sparrow that hatches double eagles. We're all set up for next Sunday. Did you read that script I wrote?" The sheets, printed in block capitals to assist Emerson's scholarly shortcomings, lay fanned out at the foot of the chair.

"It's horseshit. I got to say all that about defending Southern womanhood?"

"They'll sop it up like gravy. It don't matter if they believe it. They'll feel better about bringing their kids."

"That what the nigger's fixing to say?"

"His friend's in charge of that. It won't be the same, but it will amount to the same thing." He didn't add that in Boutrille's case it would be closer to the truth.

"What's his end?"

"Same as yours."

"Pay me more. I don't work for coon's wages."

"The entire colored population of Denver doesn't make that much. You've got nothing to beef about. You didn't make a penny sticking up the Southern Pacific."

"Pay him less, then. I didn't fight a war to keep his kind in five-dollar whores."

Box changed the subject. "Lawson says he'll have his stock cleared out by tomorrow. We'll go over there tomorrow night. Maybe you can get in some practice."

"I want a woman."

"What's your preference? There's a whole line downstairs."

"I want Purity."

"If you go near her again, I'll shoot you myself."

Emerson's foggy blue gaze slid over him, stopping at the right pocket of his fur-lined coat. The twin of the flintlock pistol Box had left with Torbert pulled it out of line.

The guerrilla moved a shoulder. "She's bald. She weren't high on looks when she had her own hair. Send me up a fat little red-head. Hand me that whiskey first."

"Get it yourself. I've pimped before, but I ain't nobody's bartender."

"O.K., little man. The sun don't shine on the same dog's ass all day long."

Box stopped on the second-floor landing. The Carillon's bouncer, a short man but built as wide as he was high, sat on a narrow chair beside the door to Purity Peach Duncan's apartments. No part of the chair showed. His short-cropped head came up as the theatrical manager approached.

"You know me," Box said.

"Yes, sir, I do." His tone waited.

"You armed?"

"No, sir, I ain't."

The pistol came out. Muscles bunched in the bouncer's thighs. Box made a juggling motion—he was rusty—and thrust the curved handle toward the other man. "I'll be back for this. It only fires once, so pick your shot."

"Yes, sir." Very little of the Evans showed when the bouncer's hand wrapped itself around it.

PART SEVEN

WHITE ALWAYS MAKES THE FIRST MOVE

THIRTY

———

C. E. Lawson's stock barn, built originally of frame and wooden siding, then razed and rebuilt of brick to comply with Denver's strict new ordinance designed to end the cycle of devastating floods and fires, looked more like a school than a building where horses and breed bulls were bid on by cattlemen from as far away as Omaha. Double-hung windows engineered for light and ventilation pierced the walls at stately intervals and brick stencils had been used to impress Lawson's initials into the lintel above the door.

Inside, visitors were welcomed by the sweetish warm moist odors of fresh manure and green straw and bleachers erected against the two long walls, with a corral in the center where the stock was paraded before the spectators for inspection and bidding. In the ten days since the Box Company Players had received permission to use the barn, the number of lanterns suspended from the rafters had tripled, casting light into corners unseen since the roof had gone on, patriotic red-white-and-blue bunting had been strung between each pair of windows, and colorfully painted bull's-eyes and silhouettes (of savage Indians, uniformed Mexican troops, and road agents in bandanna masks) had been nailed and

staked about in what appeared to be random locations, with playing cards and bright foil tobacco pouches attached to the end
walls. (Less obtrusive, except to the two men who would stand in
the center of the corral, were the homely grease canisters and
bread tins perched atop stepladders; marks to aim at and assure
oneself of piercing a nearby Jack of Diamonds through its single
eye. Box himself had brushed tar over the numerous fresh bullet-
pocks in the bricks where practice shots had missed, disguising
them from casual scrutiny.)

Outside, a twenty-foot banner commissioned from the Queen
City Publishing Company stretched across the front of the building,
proclaiming, in vermilion on yellow, that the DUEL OF THE DESPERA-
DOES would take place inside on Sunday, with crude likenesses of the
participants—one as black as soot, the other as white as chalk, facing
off from the ends. Those same grim visages plastered every telegraph
pole and cooperative farmer's barn within five miles of Denver, identified as "Honoré 'Honey' Boutrille, the Dark Angel of New Orleans,"
and "Emerson 'Twice' Emerson, the Scourge of the Border."

On the morning of the day of the exhibition, tarnished-silver
clouds unfurled themselves from Pikes Peak to the eastern horizon, threatening snow. Casper Box paced a ditch between the door
of his room at the Windsor and the window, inhaling snuff in a
steady stream and calculating the cost of mobilizing crews of volunteers to clear Sixteenth Street of drifts from Brown's Bluff to
Cherry Creek.

"You son of a bitch, I lit a candle last Sunday," he told the sky.
"Today it's your turn."

Shortly after noon, a wedge of blue split the overcast, and when
it came time to leave for Lawson's barn, the threat had shifted south
toward Colorado Springs.

"There's the fellow. Go out and treat yourself to a plague of boils." He clapped on his hat and coat and went out, sliding his arm into a sleeve of his coat.

He retrieved his flintlock pistol from the Carillon's bouncer, who reported that no incidents had taken place, and collected Emerson, who he was pleased to see had put on the outfit Box had bought for him at Vawter's: Fringed buckskins, a blue flannel shirt, glistening stovepipe boots made to his measure, and black Stetson, the last chosen to accentuate his whiteness; a pale color would have called attention to his deep tan, confusing the issue. Not that it mattered, Boutrille was blacker than that hat, but Box couldn't resist the embellishment. He wondered what Torbert had engineered for his man. Box bridled at this division of responsibility. He hoped to buy Torbert out once the show caught fire back East.

"Where's the holster?"

"I never use 'em." Emerson stretched and peered at himself in Flint's cheval glass. His rangy build and fair hair, its ends curling over his collar, were made to order for the costume.

"Strap it on. Pistols spoil pockets."

The holster was attached to a shiny brown leather belt with loops for cartridges. The guerrilla buckled it on and transferred his New Model Remington from the pocket of the buckskin coat to the holster. "I feel like a goddamn bank guard."

"You look like Deadwood Dick."

"I don't know who that is, but if he looks like this and likes it, I bet he can suck the paint off a barn."

The theatrical manager slid a pasteboard box out of his coat pocket and held it out. "Put these half-loads in those loops. I had the gunsmith run off a fresh batch. I didn't know if you were low."

"Take me a month getting used to full loads again. I don't like the weak recoil." Emerson slid open the box and thumbed the shells into his belt.

"You can say good-bye to full loads. Your outlawing days are past."

"I reckon." Emerson handed back the box, tugged the Remington out of its holster, freed the cylinder, and spun it with his palm. It buzzed like a rattlesnake.

"You're hitting a quarter-inch high," Torbert said. "Aim for the center of the eagle."

Boutrille said, "I was."

"You're shooting at the head again. Aim for the chest."

Torbert removed the ventilated Jack of Diamonds from the spring clip Casper Box had nailed to the mortar between bricks, stuck it in his left coat pocket with the others, and clamped a substitute in its place, adjusting the card so that it hung straight up and down and flush to the wall. Then he went over and made sure the rectangular bread tin hadn't shifted from its position nailed to the top of its stepladder. The spread wings of a bright yellow eagle decorated the tin from end to end, with several ragged bullet holes punched through it. Allowing for gravity and the air currents he and Box had spent most of one day arranging the larger target so that a shot fired directly at it would perforate the eye of the face card; Box had explained that it was an old trick, well known to knife-throwers. "The rubes never catch on that it's all stage direction. They're only visiting. We live here."

On their first session, Boutrille had winged the eagle a number of times, then begun a serious run on Denver's stock of pasteboards. Torbert, who had won sharpshooting medals during his navy hitch, would never have attempted it. He decided that Box, who had gone on so much about instinct, wasn't quite the blowhard he had thought him at first.

"Try it now." Torbert backed away from both targets. "Take

your time and concentrate. A hundred people will be looking at you and you'll have to shut them out."

"That part's easy. Folks have been doing that to me my whole life."

Boutrille removed his Bulldog from the shoulder rigout Torbert had had a harness maker build to the Negro's specifications and lowered his arm, letting the weight of the pistol pull it straight while he drew a deep breath and released it. When a weapon similar to the one he was familiar with could not be found in Denver, Casper Box had bribed a deputy marshal to release Boutrille's own from custody; his investment in the production he'd planned for so long bordered on reckless. Boutrille breathed in again, then raised his arm to shoulder level, closed one eye, and fired. The reduced charge made a report like a shallow cough. Torbert, who'd counseled more delay, was startled, but choked off his protest when brick dust spurted from high on the playing card. He strode over, tore it free, and stared at the circle of light showing directly through the Jack's eye.

"How'd I do, Mr. Torbert?"

"Better."

Boutrille showed one of his rare grins. "Better than better, Mr. Torbert."

"Before you take any bows, let's see how you do against Sitting Bull."

"Sitting Bull" was the name they'd given the silhouette target of a feathered Indian staked out at the far end of the corral. Box had had the Queen City Printing Company run off one hundred copies of the garish caricature to paste to the tin cutout, which was riddled with holes from practice rounds. Right on the end of Torbert's suggestion, three rapid shots rang out, obliterating the paper warrior's leering face. Torbert leapt back, an involuntary movement and half a second too late to save himself if any of the bullets had gone wide. He'd been standing within five feet of the target.

He whirled on Boutrille, infuriated and terrified.

Boutrille's face had gone gray. He shook his head. The Bulldog dangled at his side. They both turned toward an icy draft stirring from the direction of the door to the street.

Casper Box pulled the door shut behind a fourth man, who stood in front of it with his feet spread, holding a smoking Remington revolver at hip level. He was got up like a prairie scout in buckskins with knee-high boots and a broad-brimmed black hat. Torbert, who had never before laid eyes on the tall rawboned figure, knew at once who it was. The man's teeth were bared in a self-satisfied snarl.

"I reckon Custer could of used a man like me." He plucked out the spent smoking cartridges and replaced them with three from his belt.

"Box, your man needs a leash. Or did you put him up to it?" Torbert was shaking.

The little man's eyes were white around the irises, and Torbert knew he was as surprised as any of them. He recovered himself in a heartbeat, however.

"Emerson don't hit what he don't aim at. I ain't lost an act before curtain time in thirty years and I ain't about to start now. Tell your boy to get dressed. The show opens in less than an hour. People are lining up outside." Boutrille had on his town clothes, complete with Norfolk coat and bowler cocked to one side.

"I told him to wear what he's comfortable in." Torbert unshipped his flask and swigged. His period of abstention had lasted three days, ending after his second night of insomnia, a malady from which he had not suffered previously. He'd been under the impression that stage jitters confined themselves to performers.

"We'll talk about that before the next stop. The yokels don't pay to see a gunsharp rigged up like a nigger banker." Box made introductions all around. No one stepped forward to shake hands. Emerson swept his gaze over Boutrille without stopping, then slung first one leg and then the other over the corral fence. He picked up the playing card Torbert had dropped when Emerson fired at the silhouette target. He glanced at the hole, then crumpled the card and let it fall.

"Hang up another'n."

Torbert didn't move. He could see his breath. The heat of two barrel stoves placed at opposite ends of the barn didn't reach to the middle.

Emerson's teeth still showed. He slid the Remington into its holster and hooked his thumb inside the cartridge belt.

Torbert produced a fresh card from his pocket and went over to the wall. It took three tries to hang it up. He never took his eyes off the guerrilla.

Emerson waited, still grinning, until the journalist joined Box, who had entered the corral through the swinging gate. Then he scooped out the Remington, made a swift adjustment in his stance, and knocked the bread tin off the stepladder. In the next instant he shifted his aim and plugged the face card through the eye.

"We didn't buy our bread in no stores when we rode with Bloody Bill." He reloaded.

Torbert and Box both looked at Boutrille, whose eyes were hooded. He took a box of half-loads off the fence and replaced the one he'd fired. "Let's warm up some," he said.

THIRTY-ONE

Emerson forgot his script twice, forcing Box to prompt him from outside the corral, and several times his voice fell to a murmur. When someone in the audience shouted for him to speak up, his head jerked in that direction, he flushed, and his hand went to his holster; Box and Torbert both started for the fence to restrain him. Then Boutrille strode in from the tack room, and the swell of interest from the bleachers distracted the guerrilla from his purpose. Box employed his back-row voice: "Ladies and gentlemen, children of Denver; he was born a slave, wasted his youth on dissolution, low women, and strong drink; but discovered his true purpose when called upon to defend the life and honor of a young lady in his charge. May I present, from the Louisiana bayous, by way of the plains of Texas: Honoré 'Honey' Boutrille, the Dark Angel of New Orleans!"

There was cheering and some catcalling. Boutrille, as rehearsed, found his mark, swept the Bulldog from beneath his left arm, and plugged the toothy, painted image of a Mexican soldier in imperial uniform squarely between the eyes. The silhouette spun on its axis in a red-and-white blur. A whoop arose from both bleachers; the Alamo was more deeply ingrained in the hearts of Westerners than the Civil War and Reconstruction. Boutrille was an *American* nigger, and take that, Santa Anna.

Box's head ached, from a combination of too much snuff in the morning and too much shooting in close quarters throughout the afternoon. Half-loads or not, the noise made by two pistols firing in turns inside a brick enclosure caromed around inside his skull. The smoke stung his eyes and scorched his nostrils and his throat scratched from the sulphur. Finally he'd been forced to beg his featured performers to refrain from any more practice while the gray-blue fog dissipated, lest the ticket-holders give up trying to find their seats and demand their money back. Actually, he was more concerned for his voice. It was his chief theatrical asset, and if his smoke-cured throat gave out in the middle of an announcement, the effect would be as devastating as a clear miss on the part of either gunman. Box made a note to apply himself to the problem of ventilation beginning with St. Louis.

The inventory would also need to be increased. There had been the danger during the impromptu rehearsal of using up all the targets needed for both shows, not to mention the ammunition he and Torbert had brought. Emerson had emptied and refilled the loops on his belt a dozen times, and the discarded brass shells from Boutrille's Bulldog alone made a glittering carpet on the hardpack floor. Such things made one nostalgic for Adabelle Forrest and her endless costume catastrophes. Box was in new territory here for all his years of entertaining Mr. and Mrs. Two Bits a Head and the little thin dimes.

One glance at Torbert and he felt less callow. The journalist's pinched features indicated that he was suffering as well, and he at least had had the experience of combat. Meanwhile the Scourge and the Dark Angel kept him busy replacing riddled playing cards, tobacco pouches, and paper dastards.

The script Box had prepared for Emerson had gone out the window, although he remembered to paraphrase parts of it while reloading. When he mixed up his verbs and pledged to "*get* restitution for some things I done in the heat of war," there was grumbling among the Yankees in attendance and some sniggering, and the guerrilla's face went dark once again. During other pauses, Boutrille delivered pretty speeches in simple words about making one's way in a hostile world, avoiding comments on slavery and race, so that they seemed to apply to everyone in attendance. This was a frontier crowd, who understood hardship and the little victories, and they hung on every phrase. Torbert was a plain writer, but he knew his audience. Box welcomed the challenge of persuading him to write something as appropriate for Emerson.

The spectators applauded thunderously when Dennis Sheedy, a silver-bearded former Denver store clerk who had returned from Montana with bales of money from a cattle empire covering eight states, stepped forward to inspect the first Jack of Diamonds and attest to the fact that it was intact. When, after Emerson had fired at it, he examined the card again and held it aloft to show the hole through the eye, they rose to their feet, shouting and pounding the bleachers. Whether they were celebrating the shot or the cattle baron was unclear, but from that moment, Box began to relax. His gamble had paid off—provided he could prevent western law enforcement from arresting his troupers.

Then Twice Emerson missed.

His target was a tin-and-paper road agent with a figured bandanna pulled up over his nose, mouth, and chin and a horse pistol in each hand, and during practice he had plugged it two dozen times out of twenty-four. Box figured he was overconfident, or his finger had spasmed on the trigger before he was ready. In any case his slug sailed past the silhouette and spanged off the brick wall behind it; had he been using a full load, the ricochet might have endangered someone in the audience, but as it was the bullet lost momentum and dropped to the ground somewhere inside the corral. Someone—probably a Yankee—hooted.

Box looked at Emerson, who grinned incredulously, rolled his shoulders, and shook the shells out of the Remington's cylinder. Box let out his breath.

Then Boutrille fired—at the same target.

The half-powered slug struck the tin with a clunk and spun it. There was a brief silence while the audience took in its breath, then it exploded. They'd been wanting to root for the nigger all along.

Box and Torbert exchanged a glance across the corral. The journalist's face was unreadable. His gaze shifted, and Box followed it to Emerson, who was busy reloading.

Box looked at Boutrille, who was doing the same. Then the theatrical manager shifted his attention back to Emerson, just as the guerrilla poked in the last cartridge and spun the cylinder. Automatically, Box glanced down at the loops on Emerson's belt. He'd been replenishing the man's supply from boxes of half-loads, watching him poke the cartridges into the loops so that he always had several ahead. It didn't do to let him stand waiting with an empty pistol and no replacements on his person. Torbert had been doing the same for Boutrille, who dumped the extras without ceremony into a pocket.

Pocket.

The loops on Emerson's belt were filled. He'd reloaded the Remington with cartridges from a pocket in his buckskin coat.

Torbert made the discovery simultaneously with Box. Shouting, both men lunged toward the two performers standing a few yards apart in the center of the corral.

Boutrille finished reloading and looked up just as Emerson

fired from his hip. The full report walloped the air inside the barn. A spray of what looked like red powder erupted from Boutrille's coat, to the left of the buttons and just above the waist. He stepped back as if he'd been pushed, straightened his gun arm, and fired the Bulldog; fired a second time just behind the first, as if to double the effect of a weak load. Emerson's Remington went off again, but this time he struck high on the wall behind Boutrille and the slug whistled away at a right angle and buried itself in a rafter with a noise like crackling firewood. Emerson was falling.

Someone shrieked, a woman or a child. The bleachers on both sides rumbled, spectators scrambling over one another to get to the exit. Torbert, who like Box had stopped short when the shooting started, hesitated, then heaved himself up and over the fence as Boutrille's legs folded.

The Negro was lying on his left hip when Torbert reached him, propped on his elbow with his pistol still in his right hand, aimed at Emerson. A shadow was spreading along his right side. The guerrilla's pistol lay in the dirt where it had fallen from his hand. Torbert reached across Boutrille's body and closed his fingers over the Bulldog. The metal was hot, but he maintained his grip. "He's through," he said.

"That makes us equal." Boutrille chuckled and spat blood.

The Denver Post, Tuesday, November 30, 1886:

GUN MEN LINGER.

Word has reached these offices that "Twice" Emerson, the Missouri bush-whacker, and "Honey" Boutrille, the Negro man-killer from Louisiana, remain aware and breathing, although they are not expected to live through the night.

Boutrille, suffering from a mortal stomach wound, and Emerson, expiring of loss of blood from two bullets received in the upper chest, linger on, respectively, in Mrs. Rosie Washington's rooming house on Upper Arapahoe Street and a parlor in Fred Shepheard's home on Sixteenth Street near the site of the bizarre shooting that took place Sunday afternoon in C. E. Lawson's stock barn, in which the two bad men fired upon each other in what is believed to be a settling of old scores connected with the War of the Southern Rebellion. One hundred of Denver's citizens, including the *Post*'s own Nathan Hingle and the Honorable Dennis Sheedy, witnessed the battle during a public shooting exhibition sponsored by Mr. Casper Box of Atlantic City, N.J.

Not since the wild days of the early prospectors has the Queen City witnessed an event to compare with this past Sunday's. . . .

The doctor was taller and fatter than Torbert, wrapped in yards of black broadcloth with the empty left sleeve folded and secured to the shoulder with a Masonic pin. He and the journalist had created a swift bond when they discovered that they had both served with the U.S. Navy at the time of the Hampton Roads battle, although the doctor had been at the reins of an ammunition wagon onshore when a stray four-pounder had snatched off his arm above the elbow. Panting from his climb up and down the stairs, he placed his cylindrical black bag atop the newel post to fish his glove out of his coat pocket.

"I can't do anything about the internal bleeding," he told Torbert. "You might as well give him what he wants."

"He's been asking for cognac."

"Let him have it. It can't hurt him now, and it can only help with the pain."

Torbert blew air. "What do I owe you?"

"Not a red cent. Most of the fools around here think the war began and ended with Gettysburg. You might send me a copy of your book."

After the doctor left, Torbert went upstairs. Mrs. Washington was a decent woman, but she wouldn't let boarders bleed in her parlor.

Boutrille lay on the iron-framed bed with one dark bare arm stretched out on the white sheet. The whites of his eyes showed when he looked at his visitor. "That doctor's a good man." His voice rose barely above a whisper. "Doesn't fill your head with promises."

"He says you can have some cognac."

"In a bit. You could open the curtains."

The curtains were open, spilling in late-afternoon light. Torbert looked out at a band of black cloud on the horizon, then turned up the lamp on the nightstand. "Looks like snow."

"I never saw snow in my life till I came here."

"Quite a thing."

"I don't care for it much. What about Emerson?"

"Still hanging on. Those were two fine shots you made. You didn't even need the bread tin."

"That's that instinct Mr. Box was talking about." His voice trailed off.

After a little silence, Torbert bent low to see if he was breathing. Boutrille's eyes opened. Their faces were inches apart.

"Still here," he said. "Did you get enough for that book?"

"Enough so I can fill in the rest. It won't be called *The Black-snake of New Orleans*."

"That's too bad. I'd buy a book called that. You think I should've missed that target?"

"No."

"Why not? It sure got that man's skin up."

"I think he'd have found some excuse. I wouldn't have agreed to Box's scheme if I'd known anything about the man. I read the papers, but they said the same things about you. I'm sorry, Boutrille." It tasted like bitter metal on his tongue. In the end, even the language had turned its back on him.

"It would've been some pack of drunks with a rope if not Emerson. I like it this way better. I believe I will have a sip of that good cognac, Mr. Torbert."

The bottle was on the nightstand. He found the china cup, filled it, and lifted Boutrille's head to tilt a few drops between his lips. The effort of swallowing exhausted the patient and Torbert lowered his head.

Boutrille rolled his tongue around inside his mouth. "That Mr. Box knows his labels. I wouldn't be too hard on him. He's trying to make his way, just like the rest of us."

Torbert said nothing. Boutrille arched his back, sucking air between his teeth. Torbert put down the cup and gripped Boutrille's hand. The hand gripped back, cutting off his circulation. When the spasm passed, a trickle of sweat found its way into Boutrille's right eye. He blinked, fixed Torbert with his gaze.

"Don't tell him I went first."

"Who, Box?"

"Not Box. Emerson."

Fred Shepheard, a former prospector who had quit when he had enough to build a house in town and live in it for the rest of his life, was a little brown bald man with white handlebars, sunburned forever. He'd gotten used to the comings and goings of doctors and reporters. He grunted and got out of Torbert's way and Torbert followed the sound of Emerson's cursing to the front parlor. A stack of quilts covered the guerrilla almost to the top of the back of the settee upon which he was lying. "Jesus, I'm burning up!"

"Croaker said to keep you warm." This was Casper Box. The little man stood with his back to the fire in the hearth, both hands in the pockets of his tight suit. He nodded a greeting at Torbert. "Marshal outside?"

"I didn't see him."

"He's there, depend on it. Or one of his deputies. He's waiting till one or the other dies so he can arrest me for conspiracy to commit murder. He ain't satisfied with harboring."

"I guess I'm in it, too," Torbert said.

"He don't know about your part. I told him I hired you to help out."

"Don't do me any favors."

"I ain't. If you don't get that book written, I'll miss out on some good press. In this business if they ain't talking about you, you might as well throw it over and breed hogs."

"A lot of good the press will do you in prison."

"I've been to prison, and I've been married. In prison they let you out in the yard. Anyway, I'm sixty. They'll give me five years and consider it life. All I have to do is wash the black out of my hair when I go to court. If I reserve the Metropolitan now, it'll be ready for me in '92. I'll fill it up with something."

"Who the hell's that?" Emerson's voice was shrill.

"Torbert."

"Nigger dead yet?"

Box read the answer in Torbert's eyes. "Ask him yourself."

Torbert approached the settee. The guerrilla's face was stubbled and pale beneath a slime of sweat. His eyes were swollen and fevered. He had trouble fixing them on the journalist's face. "They tell me I'll be back in camp with Bloody Bill soon."

"I heard that."

"It don't matter if I outlast the nigger."

"He's still hanging on."

"Horseshit."

"He's improving, the doctor said. He might make it."

"Horseshit." He looked away. His white teeth clamped his lower lip. "I shouldn't of aimed for the gut."

"That's the second time you missed."

Emerson was breathing heavily, in pain. Torbert couldn't tell if he'd heard him. He bent over the guerrilla and repeated what he'd said. Their faces were inches apart.

"Horse—" Emerson drew a sharp breath. It came out in a long whoosh and he lay as still as Boutrille.

THIRTY-TWO

O ne hundred citizens of Denver were present in C. E. Law-son's stock barn the day Honoré Boutrille and Emerson Emerson shot each other fatally, although by the turn of the twen-tieth century, more than a thousand claimed to have witnessed the incident. Asked about these claims at the time of his second trial, Casper Box responded, "If I'd sold that many tickets, I could afford a better lawyer." He was convicted of a reduced charge of reckless endangerment and released from the Colorado U.S. Penitentiary after serving fifteen months.

The following letter surfaced during an estate sale in Holly-wood, California, in 1948. The envelope was stamped ADDRESSEE DECEASED—RETURN TO SENDER.

> *E. V. Torbert*
> *Dearborn Hotel*
> *Chicago, Ill.*

> *January 16, 1912*

Dear Mr. Torbert:

*I regret to report that I cannot at this time carry out my
intention to produce a photoplay based upon your book,*
The True and Authentic Life of "Honey" Boutrille, the
Dark Angel of New Orleans, As Told to His Biographer.
*My financial partners inform me that the prospect of a col-
ored hero would make nickelodeon audiences uncomfortable, and since I admire the book far too much to "make
him white," as has been suggested (I am quite serious
about this; it is the cross one bears when dealing with Yankee investors), I must turn to other projects.*

*It is my fond hope that I will be in a position to discuss an
arrangement later, perhaps after the Civil War photoplay I
am planning has been released and my stock is a bit higher.
In the meantime, I look forward to visiting with you one
day and comparing our experiences with the late Casper
Box, whose counsel was so enlightening during my brief
career on the New York stage. Until then, I am*

Yours very truly,

D. W. Griffith